PROTECTION RACKET

A gripping thriller with a great twist

JAMES WARREN

Published by The Book Folks

London, 2025

This book is a work of fiction. Names, characters, businesses, organizations, places and events are either the product of the author's imagination or are used fictitiously. Any resemblance to actual persons, living or dead, events or locales is entirely coincidental. The spelling is US English.

ISBN 978-1-80462-273-5

www.thebookfolks.com

Prologue

Late evening, Thursday, June 18, 2009

J. Robert Simpson stood in front of the waist-high, mahogany liquor cabinet in his corner office. He sipped eighteen-year-old single malt Scotch while gazing at the lights of Manhattan through floor-to-ceiling windows. The past two weeks had been miserable with one rainy day after another, but a fortunate break in the weather had occurred hours earlier, and that evening, the city seemed more alive.

Simpson examined his reflection in the window and confirmed no strand of his gray-streaked medium-brown hair was out of place. He turned his head to examine the right side of his large, square jaw and noticed a shaving nick had almost healed. He placed his Scotch tumbler on top of the liquor cabinet and adjusted his striped silk tie. He then chuckled to himself for completing an unnecessary task, as he would soon remove the tie along with other articles of clothing.

Simpson again grasped the tumbler, took another sip, and grew impatient. He lowered his glass and glanced at his Cartier watch. His date had said she needed to make a brief phone call before coming upstairs, and too much time had passed. About one minute later, Simpson heard his office door swing open, and he smiled. He again placed his drink on top of the liquor cabinet and turned to his left. Instead of his statuesque date, he saw a much shorter person, wearing a gray wig. His smile turned into a scowl, and his short temper flared.

"What the hell? Get out of my office!"

"No," the intruder coldly replied.

Simpson was about to engage in an expletive-filled tirade when he noticed the intruder point a .38-caliber revolver at his chest. His left hand trembled, and fear overwhelmed him.

"Over there," the intruder said, waving the gun towards a black leather couch, then back to his chest.

Simpson remained frozen in place except for the trembling in his hand.

"Sit down on the couch, now!"

Simpson started to perspire and was unable to obey the order. "What do you want?" he said.

"Just do as I say, and no one gets hurt. Sit down!"

He took three tentative steps forward and sat in the middle of the couch.

The intruder pointed the revolver toward one of two navy-blue throw pillows lying on the couch. "Pick it up."

Simpson turned his head and saw the pillow. He nervously nodded several times. "Okay, okay," he said in a hushed voice. He grabbed the pillow and held it with both hands in his lap.

"Hold it higher."

"Huh?"

"I *said* higher! I don't want to see your face."

Simpson raised the pillow until he saw nothing but deep blue. His hands shook, and he could feel sweat trickle down the back of his neck.

The intruder moved toward him. "By the way, when I said no one would get hurt, I lied."

Chapter 1

Wednesday, September 16, 2009

The phone rang, and David Lee was asleep in his comfortable queen-size bed. Following the second ring, he rolled to his right and glanced at the alarm clock on his dresser: 6:50 a.m. He let the call go to his answering machine and rolled back onto his stomach. After two more rings, the machine activated.

"This is David. I'm sorry I can't answer the phone right now. Please leave a message."

"David, are you in? It's Irene," he heard after the beep. "I've been trying to reach you since yesterday afternoon. You have a hearing in court this morning!"

David groaned and rolled over again. With his right hand, he reached for the landline phone on the end table.

"Are you there? Did you hear what I just said?"

David brought himself to a sitting position while his feet dangled inches above the hardwood floor. He picked up the phone. "What are you talking about?"

"We've got a new client, and it's a murder case. She has an initial appearance at ten."

He snapped from groggy to fully alert, and his eyes popped wide. "We have a what! Why didn't you tell me beforehand?"

"Her parents came to the office late yesterday afternoon. I tried calling you."

"Well, I had a date and turned off my cell phone. I wanted to give her my undivided attention." David ran his left hand through his hair. He guessed he had never turned his cell phone back on and had not checked his answering machine last night.

"So, you were with her all night?" Irene asked in a judgmental tone.

David clenched his jaw and wanted to reply, "None of your business and you're fired." Instead, he controlled his anger and responded in a more matter-of-fact tone. "No, we got together early because she had a flight before dawn out of JFK. Afterwards, I worked in the office until 11:30 or so. Did you send something to my work and home emails?"

He waited for the apology he knew he would not receive.

"Uh… No," she said with less attitude.

"You said it's a murder case?"

"Yeah. The hearing's at ten. Can you make it? I know Marc can't, and I haven't called Bev, at least not yet."

David closed his eyes and groaned again. "Don't call Bev. I'll make the hearing."

"Okay. I'll send the intake sheet to your home email right now. The client's name is Amanda Morelli, and her parents are Paul and Lorraine. I told them to meet you at the usual place inside the courthouse at 9:30."

"Fine. What do they look like?"

"The Odd Couple."

"What? You mean Felix and Oscar from the TV show?"

"Uh-uh," Irene said. "Two different sizes. Paul's big with broad shoulders and a barrel chest. He has thick, kinda wavy, salt-and-pepper hair and an apple-pie face."

"An apple pie what?" David asked as he shook his head.

"An apple-pie face. You'll see. Lorraine's much shorter, you know, petite. She looks much younger than she is, like Dick Clark. Just a few faint wrinkles. She also has short, dark hair, which looks natural but isn't."

"Whatever. I'll get over to the courthouse after I get ready and eat breakfast."

"Fruit Loops again?"

"Goodbye, Irene."

David stood and shuffled towards his large bedroom window. He opened the thick burgundy curtains, revealing gloomy skies casting a pall over the city. "That's just perfect!"

Most mornings, David had breakfast straight after getting out of bed, but this time he first needed a hot shower to relax and collect himself. While showering and shaving, he grumbled about Irene and asked himself why she was the receptionist/office manager at the Law Offices of D'Angelo & Lee. Of course, he knew the answer. Irene's full name was Irene Popova D'Angelo, and everyone related to his law partner, Marc, was part of one big, happy family, even if she married into it. He acknowledged Irene performed her job well most of the time and treated the clients with respect. However, sometimes she had been a royal pain to him.

While he remained annoyed at Irene, thoughts about the case intrigued him. Although he had handled other murder cases, it was his first since he and Marc opened their own law firm. The gravity of the case would present a challenge, but David knew he could manage it. He also considered the massive number of hours that would likely be required to defend the case and possibly take it to trial. While David and Marc's hourly rates were not excessive, they needed to make a living. He hoped Amanda Morelli and her family had the financial resources to cover his bills. Irene should have made at least a cursory review of his new client's assets and income before signing her up. He also wondered what would happen if Amanda could no longer pay them. Perhaps a judge would declare her indigent, and the court would cover their bills, just as when he had represented poor defendants.

After David finished in the bathroom, he put on a terry cloth robe and plodded toward his laptop, which was sitting on his small dining-room table. He turned it on and shuffled to his tiny kitchen. He studied three cereal boxes on the counter and grabbed one.

"Fruit Loops? I think not, Irene. Lucky Charms today."

Irene was hardly in a position to criticize anyone's eating habits given the awful snacks she brought to the office. While he didn't have the best diet, he was slim and healthy. He also ran and worked out at the gym whenever he had the time.

David set the cereal bowl on the dining-room table, accessed his email, and opened Irene's attachment. While he ate, he read the intake sheet, which said Amanda Morelli was thirty-five, divorced, and had no children. She lived in an apartment in Murray Hill. She was currently unemployed and had been an attorney with Thorton, Saxer & Caldwell. Amanda's parents were retired and lived in Bensonhurst. Paul had been a union representative, and Lorraine had owned a travel agency.

The victim was J. Robert Simpson, a partner at Thorton, who had been shot to death in his own office. Irene had provided news articles and press releases about Simpson. David skimmed through them and discovered the deceased had been a high-powered civil litigator. However, he had never heard of Simpson as he paid little attention to the news.

Upon reading the next item, David almost choked on his breakfast. The Morellis had paid $30,000 in cash! At least this revelation gave some indication they could afford him. He also pondered whether Paul and Lorraine had ever heard of muggers.

David opened a link about the Thorton firm, which told him it was in Midtown East, about three blocks from his law office. Thorton handled mergers and acquisitions, business litigation, and appellate law. He checked the courthouse website and discovered Judge Conrad Graber had been assigned to the case. David knew his reputation, which was both favorable and unfavorable for him and his new client. The judge was lenient on bail but unfortunately possessed an inflated ego and a tendency to be a pain in the behind.

After finishing breakfast and changing into a business suit, David left his East Village apartment and hailed a taxi. During the drive through rush-hour traffic, he blocked out the surrounding noise and ignored a mild stench of body odor inside the cab. He read the intake sheet again and smiled. He was a born litigator and always got a buzz before the first hearing of a challenging case.

* * *

When David walked through the main entrance to the courthouse in Lower Manhattan, he checked his watch: 9:15. Near the end of a long hallway, Paul and Lorraine Morelli sat on a bench, holding hands. Irene's description of the couple was mostly accurate, including their different sizes, but David did not believe Paul's face resembled an apple pie. All he could see was an older man with a round face and a scattering of wrinkles around the eyes.

As David approached them, Paul twice tugged the collar of his white dress shirt in quick succession. David also noticed that his blue tie was crooked, indicating he normally wore casual clothes. Lorraine donned a light-blue sweater and had a serene appearance. Both Paul and Lorraine stood and greeted him with warm smiles.

"Good morning. I'm David Lee," he said pleasantly. "You must be Paul and Lorraine."

Paul nodded. "That's right." He gave David a firm handshake.

Lorraine then shook his outstretched hand, and he noticed the scent of lavender perfume.

"Hey, I don't mean to rush you, but Amanda's hearing will start soon," Paul said. "So, if you don't mind, let's get down to business, okay?"

"Fine, fine," David replied.

The big man retrieved a white folder that was laying on the bench. "Your assistant told us to bring this stuff." He opened the folder. "Here's the paperwork for our home, where we've lived over forty years. We paid off the mortgage a long time ago." Paul flipped to another document. "Here's what we have in the bank." He pointed to a line in the middle of the page. "See, right here: $163,000 and change." He turned to another page. "We co-own a ten-unit apartment building in Flatbush with a good buddy of mine and his wife."

"What about the other stuff?" Lorraine asked.

Paul smiled. "Yes, dear. It's in here. It says the mortgage on the building was paid off. Here you go." He handed over the folder.

"Thanks," David said.

Paul looked over David's shoulder. "Hopefully Daniel can make it."

"Daniel?"

"He's our son. He lives in Westchester County." The big man refocused on David. "By the way, and no offense, we figured your law partner would help our daughter. He's a nephew of another good buddy of mine. Your assistant said he wasn't available, but she didn't tell us why."

Paul's comment struck David as odd because they supposedly knew Marc but were unaware of his health. "Sorry, Irene should've said something. Marc contracted leukemia, and he's been off work for some time. He's improving and will be back in the office by the end of the year."

Paul nodded.

"I'm sorry to hear that," Lorraine said. "So, you're a defense attorney too?"

"Yes. Our firm handles mostly criminal defense and some civil rights cases."

"Civil rights, huh," Paul said. "Anything we might know about?"

"Possibly. Just before Marc got sick, we settled an excessive force case against the NYPD. We also sued a school district in Nassau County on behalf of the parents.

Campus security for the high school did some really stupid things. We settled that one too."

Paul and Lorraine looked at each other, and their facial expressions indicated they were impressed.

Paul waggled his right index finger in the air. "Yeah, yeah, that's right. I think I heard about the school district thing on the news." He turned back to David. "Have you had many criminal cases? What about a murder case? You know, my Amanda didn't do it."

David held up his right hand momentarily. "One thing at a time. I've been an attorney for eight years, and I've had many criminal cases, including murder."

Lorraine tilted her head. "How old are you?"

"Thirty-three. I know I'm younger than some lawyers, but I know what I'm doing. If you'd like, I'll put you in touch with some of my past clients. Perhaps they'd give you some peace of mind."

Lorraine seemed oblivious to his last comment. "Are you Chinese?"

"Yes, I am."

"How tall are you? Six feet?"

"Almost five eleven." David wondered what was happening inside Lorraine's head.

With a wide-eyed expression, she turned toward her husband. "Oh, honey, that's why he reminds me of that neighbor who lived down the street. What was his name?"

Paul patted her on the shoulder and grinned. "You're thinking of Tony Wilkins, and he wasn't Chinese."

"I still see the resemblance, just look at his–"

"Look, we need to focus on your daughter's case," David said politely. "This morning, Amanda will enter a plea of not guilty, and we'll get to bail. I'll see if CJA finished their write-up and we'll–"

"What's CJA?" Paul asked.

"It's the Criminal Justice Agency. They interview defendants before arraignment and make recommendations whether they should be released on bail. Now as I was saying–"

David stopped talking as he noticed Paul's attention being diverted elsewhere. Both parents' lack of focus amazed him.

"Hang on for a second, Counselor," Paul said. "Our good friends Pete and Debra are here."

David glanced over his shoulder and saw another Italian couple in their sixties approaching. He paid little attention while Paul, Lorraine, and their friends chatted about an inconsequential dinner party. While most parents would have been anxious before an initial hearing, Paul and Lorraine behaved as if it were a sunny day with no worries.

After chatting with the newcomers for about a minute, Paul asked, "You were about to say something about bail? How much will it be?"

David raised an eyebrow. "That might be a tough one. Let's go inside the courtroom, and I'll see what I can do."

David waited while the two couples discussed another trivial matter. He shook his head in disbelief and entered the courtroom alone, where the usual gaggle of attorneys, clients, and family members milled around among the rows of benches in the gallery.

David spotted Jacqueline Marshall, one of the district attorney's most experienced prosecutors. Her reputation preceded her and could be summed up in one word: formidable. Marshall appeared deep in thought as she leaned over her podium and reviewed paperwork. David noticed she had changed her hairstyle from a short Afro to a slicked-back look.

"Hey," he said. "So, we're finally crossing swords again. It's been a while."

She remained stone-faced and did not take her eyes off her paperwork. "That's right. The CJA report is over there." She pointed her thumb toward the small table at the far end of the courtroom.

David ignored Marshall's attitude, strolled to the table, and took a copy. He skimmed through it and found no surprises. The report listed the usual biographical information for a criminal defendant and revealed Amanda had no prior arrests or convictions. It also contained a list of available financial resources and sources of collateral for bail, including her brother's house.

David peered toward the back of the courtroom, where Paul, Lorraine, and their friends were taking their seats along with another couple in their late thirties. He had brown hair, and she was a blonde.

Paul mouthed, "That's Daniel, Amanda's brother," and something else David could not make out, probably the name of Daniel's wife.

David ambled toward Marshall. "Can we talk about bail?"

She stepped away from the podium, faced David, and stared upward into his eyes. "Bail?" she said without a hint of levity. "You're kidding, right? We indicted your client for murder."

David forced a smile. "I know, but she has no priors and many ties to the community. How strong is the evidence against her? Do you have a confession?"

Marshall did not verbally respond or gesture in any way, leading David to assume Amanda had not confessed. "What about the murder weapon? Do you have it? How about any eyewitnesses?"

Marshall put her right hand on her hip and continued to stare at him. "We've got plenty of evidence, such as your client sending a fascinating email to her little friend in the office. It said, 'Let's kill him.' Three days later, Simpson was shot twice in the head. I highly doubt it was just an interesting coincidence."

David was startled but tried not to show it. "Well, let's talk about discovery. I'll send a demand letter to you by Friday."

She gave a dismissive wave. "Don't bother. I'll send it by Tuesday next week, Wednesday at the latest. I hope you have plenty of storage space."

"Sure. Now, getting back to bail. You know we have Judge Graber today. He's about to retire and he's in a giving mood." He tilted his head and bent at the waist. "If I make a reasonable bail request and you stand firm, what happens? Another thing, is my client young and attractive? How will that factor in?"

Marshall exhaled through her nose, and David guessed she was swearing in her thoughts.

"Do you have anything else besides what's in the CJA report?" she asked.

David gave her the folder Paul had provided. He could hear Marshall flip through the pages while he scanned the courtroom.

"They're not here," she said without taking her eyes off the documents. "You're looking for reporters, right?"

The answer was yes, but he didn't reply.

Once Marshall had finished reading, she returned Paul's folder and glared at David. "What do you have in mind?"

"Well, half a million sounds like a decent number, because my client doesn't have significant financial resources."

Marshall scoffed. "I know, and I can guess why. I was at her apartment when the search warrant was executed. She really knows how to spend money on clothes and shoes. You should like that." She pointed to his jacket. "You're wearing Brooks Brothers, right? As for half a million… no. Her family can assist and pay a bail bondsman. One million cash or bond, no less."

"Give me a moment, please."

David spun around and walked confidently towards Paul. Once he reached the rail between the attorney's tables and the gallery, he leaned forward. "One million, all cash or bond," he whispered. "Think you can handle it?"

Paul pouted his lower lip and gave a thumbs-up sign.

David gave a brief wave of his right hand in acknowledgement and then looked over his left shoulder. He didn't have to relay the message to Marshall as she was watching from a distance.

* * *

Close to ten o'clock, David took a seat in the gallery's front row. He hoped Judge Graber would not arrive late, but his reputation indicated he was never on time. By 10:15, David was tired of waiting. He reflected on the many stories he had heard about Graber, such as his constant talking about himself and his alleged connections to celebrities. No one had time for that, especially in court. He imagined the judge was on the phone, bragging about himself without paying attention to the time.

Finally, David heard, "All rise!" as Judge Graber entered the courtroom. His black robe somehow covered his enormous girth. He had a short and well-groomed beard, and his thinning, gray hair touched his collar.

David glanced again at his watch, which told him it was 10:40. He wanted to blurt out, "Thanks for showing up," but knew better.

Graber fell into his chair. "Good morning, everyone," he said in a booming voice. "Please call the first case."

"Calling case number 09-36472," the court clerk bellowed. "People versus Amanda Morelli."

David moved forward and took his proper place. From his left, Amanda shuffled into the courtroom with hunched shoulders and a hung head. David guessed she was a petite five four, about an inch taller than her mother, and her thick auburn hair flowed about three inches past her shoulders. Once Amanda lifted her head, David noted her high cheekbones and large brown eyes, which were bloodshot and surrounded by dark circles. He imagined she had almost no sleep during her night in jail. Even in her less-than-ideal condition, Amanda appeared twenty-five, not thirty-five, which meant the Dick Clark genes had to run in the family. David also noticed the judge taking a long, leering look at Amanda, and he thought, one way or another, this pervert would grant bail.

"Jacqueline Marshall for the People, Your Honor."

"David Lee for the defendant. One moment, please?"

"Of course," Graber said as he waved his right hand.

David leaned toward Amanda and whispered, "Your parents just hired me. It'll be all right. You'll get released from custody in no time."

She showed a wan expression and remained silent.

David turned his attention to the judge. "Thank you, Your Honor."

"Ms. Morelli," Judge Graber boomed. "The People have charged you with one count of murder in the first degree. How do you plead?"

"Not guilty," she said in a low and cracking voice.

Graber's eyes narrowed, and he leaned forward. "I'm sorry. I didn't hear you."

"Not guilty, Your Honor," she said, louder.

"Parties on bail?" Graber leaned into his chair and shifted his eyes toward Marshall.

She stood with an air of confidence. "Your Honor, the parties have agreed to one million dollars, cash or bond."

"Standard terms and conditions?"

"Yes, Your Honor."

"Excellent!" Graber flashed a smile. "So ordered, and the Court thanks both of you. Let's call the next case."

David whispered to his client, "We'll talk really soon, okay?"

Amanda stared at him for a moment, and then a court officer whisked her away.

David peered into the gallery and saw Paul giving another thumbs-up. David left the courtroom, and all six members of Amanda's party followed him like lemmings. Paul provided a brief introduction to his son and daughter-in-law, but David didn't catch her name – perhaps Trudy.

Daniel, Trudy, Pete, and Debra said a few words to Paul and Lorraine before leaving the courthouse.

David then addressed Amanda's parents. "So, here's what you need to do to get your daughter released–"

"Don't worry about it," Paul said as he held up his hand with the palm facing out. "We brought a bail bondsman and can take care of it." He scanned the hallway. "Now, where is he?" His expression changed to knowing recognition. "He's right over there, talking to that guy who looks like another attorney. The bail bondsman's a friend of a good buddy of mine."

David had difficulty understanding Paul and Lorraine's behavior. They had brought plenty of paperwork and a bail bondsman to court but had not hired a defense attorney until after the police took their daughter into custody. They should have known she had been under investigation.

"I guess you'll take care of it," David said. "On another note, I'd like to talk to someone at Amanda's old firm. Any ideas?"

Paul looked in the air. "Try Valerie, Valerie Fernandez." His eyes refocused on David. "She was Amanda's paralegal, and they're friends. I think she's still working at Amanda's old firm. Nice girl. Right, honey?"

Lorraine smiled. "Oh yes. She and her kids came over for dinner a couple of times. We also saw her at the office Christmas party two years ago. It's too bad they didn't have one last year. Right, Paul?"

"Okay," David said. He didn't need them spinning off onto another tangent. "Could you tell Amanda to come to my office on Friday at 11:30? Beverly should have returned from court by then, and I'd like Amanda to meet her."

"Who's Beverly?" Paul asked.

"Beverly Cohen. She's of counsel to the firm."

Paul and Lorraine gave puzzled looks.

David released a faint smile. "Beverly was a partner with my old law firm, and she retired a couple of years ago. She heard about Marc contracting leukemia and offered to help out for a while. She's an excellent criminal defense attorney."

"Okay," Paul said. "We'd love to meet her, and thanks for getting my daughter released on bail. We'll be seeing you." He shook David's hand.

Lorraine did the same. "It was nice to meet you," she said. "I hope you can come to the house for dinner sometime."

"That'd be nice," David replied.

Paul and Lorraine walked down the corridor, hand in hand, and engaged in idle banter.

David again noted their carefree mood sharply contrasted with their daughter's indictment for first-degree murder, which carried a sentence of twenty-five years to life imprisonment. He went outside and found a spot on the courthouse steps where he believed no one could overhear him and made a call on his cell phone.

"Irene, it's me."

"Oh, the hearing's already over?"

David rolled his eyes because the hearing should have concluded much earlier. "Yeah, that's right. We're done, and Amanda got bail. Please send a copy of the intake sheet to Marc."

"Right now?"

"Yes, now. Thanks."

"Okay."

"Bye."

David ended the call and said aloud to no one, "Gee, Irene. When would it be a good time to send the information, maybe sometime next year?"

He made another call and heard a groggy, "Hello."

"Hey Marc, can you talk for a few minutes?"

There was a brief pause. "Yeah… sure. Why don't you come on over and give me a great, big hug?"

David chuckled. "That's what your wife is for."

"I know but Steph's not home right now, and you're *the* best hugger."

"You wish. Look, I need to discuss a couple of things, and the first one's Irene."

Marc let out a heavy sigh. "What did she do now?"

"She got mad at me because she couldn't reach me while I was on a date."

"That undivided attention thing, right? By the way, who was the date?"

"Beth."

"Oh yeah," Marc said, as if he had made an important scientific discovery. "She's a flight attendant with Air Canada."

"Yeah, that's her. Anyway, I need you to talk to Irene about her attitude *again*. Also, she signed up a client without speaking to me. Bev wouldn't sign anyone up, and she didn't speak to you about it, right?"

"Ah, crap. She did that? Who's the new client, another bozo arrested for a DUI who'll refuse to pay his bills?"

David gave a wry smile. "Not exactly. Her name's Amanda Morelli. She's been indicted for murder. She's accused of shooting another attorney in her own law firm."

"What? Wow! When's her first appearance?"

"Already happened this morning, and she was ordered released on bail."

Marc chuckled. "She got bail after being slapped with a Class A felony? You're good but not *that* good. You had help."

"Well, yeah," David sheepishly said. "Judge Graber. Anyway, Irene's sending you the intake sheet on Amanda. On another note, there's something odd about her parents." He flicked his left arm in the air. "Well, a couple of odd things. Paul, that's her father, asked for you and said you're the nephew of one of his friends, but he didn't know you had leukemia. I think he handed me a line of bull. Can you check to see if anyone in your family knows him?"

"Sure. No problem."

"Thanks. Talk to you later."

Chapter 2

Early afternoon, David arrived at the drab, off-white building containing the Law Offices of Thorton, Saxer & Caldwell with his black leather briefcase in hand. He observed no interesting architectural features; it was only a large box with windows. A plaque to the right of the entrance stated, "The O'Connell Building."

David entered the harshly lit lobby with a tiled floor and a marble countertop for the security desk. The directory on a wall told him to proceed to the tenth floor. Before leaving the lobby, he decided to check for any security measures on the ground and tenth floors, which were obviously inadequate during the evening of the murder.

Two turnstiles stood in front of four elevators. Two bored security guards stood behind them and watched individuals swipe key cards as they passed through the turnstiles. Since David did not have a card, he reported to a third guard at the front desk, where he showed his identification, signed his name in the register, and listed his intended destination. Without a word, the third guard waved him away. David noticed two black half-globes with security cameras affixed to the ceiling, one on each side of the lobby.

David passed through a turnstile, then he entered the first elevator on the right where he detected a musty smell rising from below. Perhaps the stain on the floor caused the smell, but he had no desire to get down on his hands and knees to conduct a closer examination. He also saw a camera in a back corner, just below the ceiling. The elevator had two columns of buttons for floors numbered B2 to 14 and a slot above the buttons. He had seen a similar slot in the elevators for the building containing his law office, where an individual needed to insert a key card to operate the elevators at night and on the weekends.

When David arrived at the tenth floor, the Thorton firm's entrance was across the hallway. Before going any further, he stopped himself. He suspected the killer would not have used the main elevators in order to avoid the security guards, and so there should be another way to access the floor.

David turned right and traversed a long hallway, which had the same awful overhead lighting but no security cameras. At the north end, he made another right turn and walked to the end of a shorter hallway. He opened a heavy metal door, which revealed access to a freight elevator. The door could not be opened from the other side without a key card, so he placed his briefcase on the floor and wedged it against the door to prevent it from fully closing. He summoned the elevator, and seconds later, its doors opened.

Upon entering the freight elevator, David pushed a button for another floor, and nothing happened. He pushed two other buttons with the same result. He then spotted another key card slot above the buttons and concluded the freight elevator would not work without a card no matter the time of day. He glanced higher and saw another security camera in a back corner next to the ceiling.

David left the freight elevator and stood next to a door to a stairwell, which probably led to an emergency exit on the ground floor. He retraced his steps and found doors leading to two interior staircases, one on each side of the elevator banks. From the hallway, anyone could open these doors, but the other side had no handles or knobs.

David returned to the Thorton law firm's entrance and approached a middle-aged receptionist, who sat behind a sizeable dark-colored desk. Her lethargic movements and sad eyes surprised him as he expected a receptionist to project a more inviting and enthusiastic image. A seven-foot, clear plexiglass wall stood behind her with the law firm's name etched near the top.

"May I help you?" she said with a flat affect.

"Yes, please. I'm David Lee, and I'm here to see Valerie Fernandez."

The receptionist's eyes drifted toward her phone. She grabbed it and put her right hand over her mouth, which prohibited David from understanding her brief message. Shortly thereafter, a woman in her early forties glided towards him with long, wavy coal-black hair flowing behind her.

"I'm Valerie," she said with a serious expression. "You're David?"

"Yes. Nice to meet you." Given her lack of warmth, David didn't bother to extend his hand.

"Uh-huh. Let's talk inside."

Valerie escorted David toward a large conference room boasting floor-to-ceiling glass walls and a glass door. He counted sixteen chairs around an oblong table and noted the lack of curtains or blinds to prohibit more private meetings. Almost the entire floor had an open concept filled with bright but soft lighting. The cubicles for the support staff filled much of the middle space. The attorneys' offices surrounded the cubicles and had glass walls and doors.

There was one obvious exception to the floor's layout. An office in the northwest corner had solid walls and no apparent door. David speculated he could not observe the door from his vantage point. It was in a prime location, which meant it probably belonged to one of the firm's partners, and perhaps someone placed a premium on privacy. There were also several empty cubicles and offices, and the firm's atmosphere seemed depressing. No one was in a good mood.

Once the conference room door closed, David sat and retrieved a notepad and a pen from his briefcase.

Valerie took a seat next to him and crossed her arms.

"As I explained on the phone," David said, "I'm a defense attorney, and I'm sorry to tell you Amanda's been indicted for murder. She made her first appearance in court this morning, and she's being released on bail."

Valerie frowned, and her eyes dropped toward the beige carpet. "Oh, that's too bad."

"You don't seem shocked by the news."

She looked at him with resignation. "No, not really. I knew the cops searched her place. An arrest wasn't a surprise, but I know she didn't kill anyone."

David inched forward in his chair. "Why do you say that?"

"Earlier that day, Amanda went home sick, and she was asleep all night."

"Okay, how do you know that?" he asked as he scribbled on the notepad.

"She told me. Besides, I think I know her pretty good. She's not a violent person."

"All right. If you don't mind, I'd like to ask you a few questions about yourself and the law firm."

"Go ahead," Valerie said with her arms still crossed.

"So, how long have you worked here?"

"About twelve years. Since I started, I've been a paralegal, and this was a great place to work until recently."

"How so?"

"As opposed to some other places, the senior partners cared about their employees. I found out the hard way. I'd only been with the firm about seven months when my husband, Henry, passed away one night. We were told he had an aortic aneurysm, and it ruptured."

David felt a punch to the stomach. "I'm really sorry."

Valerie briefly smiled. "Thanks. The people here provided me with lots of emotional support, and the Old Man insisted the firm would pay all the funeral costs. I never expected that."

"The Old Man?"

"Old Man Thorton," Valerie said as she relaxed her arms. "I mean Charles W. Thorton. He started this firm, and everyone loved him. Still do, I guess. He always asked how we were doing, and he was interested in our families. He couldn't have been a greater boss or a greater person. The Old Man had a big personality and a great laugh."

David nodded and scribbled a few notes. "What about the others at the firm? How was the workload?"

"The other senior partners knew we had our own lives, and they tried not to overwork us most of the time. My job was kind of boring, but we all got along. The pay was good but not great."

"Uh-huh. What about Amanda?"

"I enjoyed working with her. After we met, we quickly became friends, and we went to lunch together, sometimes once a week, sometimes a little more."

David suspected Valerie was the "little friend" who received the "Let's kill him" email, but he did not mention it. Instead, he asked, "No one around here seems to be in a good mood. Why did things change?"

Valerie scoffed and crossed her arms again. "Because Big Bastard arrived."

"Who?"

"Robert Simpson, the guy who was shot. He sometimes called himself Big Bobby, and he referred to a body part by that name. Guess which one?" Valerie's frown returned. "Some of us called him Big Bastard because it was more fitting. He was an a–hole and made lots of sexual comments and innuendos. Sometimes comments were followed by touching. He never touched me, which was fortunate… for him. You know what I mean?"

Valerie's colorful language and candid responses surprised David, and Simpson's behavior appalled him, but he tried not to show it.

"What do you mean by 'touching'?"

"You know, touching a woman on the arm, shoulder, sometimes the back."

"Anything else?"

Valerie groaned. "What he did wasn't bad enough for you?"

"Sorry, I just need to ask," David said with his left hand raised, hoping to convey he had asked an innocent question.

"Yeah, okay. I never heard about Big Bastard touching anyone in more important parts or sexually assaulting anyone, but it wouldn't surprise me if he'd done something like that," Valerie said angrily. "I mean, he was bad enough in the office. He was a total pig and didn't care who he offended. I know I'm not supposed to speak ill of the dead, but there's nothing good to say about him."

David grimaced and scribbled again. "Did he treat all the women the same way?"

"Of course! He treated Walter really badly too."

"Walter?"

"Walter, Walter Bennett. He was a paralegal who worked on the ninth floor. Nice guy, really quiet. He tried very hard to keep his private life, you know, private. Somehow, Big Bastard found out Walter was gay, and after that" – Valerie briefly raised her hands – "whenever he saw Walter, the taunting was out of control. Most of the time, Walter avoided him by staying downstairs. The rest of us weren't so lucky."

David stopped scribbling and focused on Valerie. "Where was Simpson killed?"

"Back there." She pointed over her left shoulder toward the back corner with the solid walls.

"Did Simpson want an office where he could work in private?"

Valerie's head lurched back, and her eyes widened. "You're kidding, right? It was the exact opposite. His office looked like all the others. That a–hole loved it because he always wanted to be seen. How'd he put it? Something like we'd 'see him work his magic.'"

"Why does it look different now?" David asked.

"After Big Bastard was killed, some crew arrived. They cleaned up the blood, replaced the couch, stuff like that. Still, no one wanted to look over there. The firm hired another crew, and they put up the walls, which helped some, I guess."

"Valerie, can you let me see the inside of that office?"

"Not possible. Now it's solid walls and no door. Come back with a sledgehammer."

David tried to process what he had just heard. He did not understand why a law firm that cared about its people welcomed aboard such an obnoxious jerk and why the office was so depressing. If everyone had hated Simpson, they couldn't be mourning him months after his death. David would need to speak with a partner to obtain another perspective. He was about to ask another question when a slim, white male with an oval-shaped face and deep frown lines opened the conference room door.

"Who the hell are you and what are you doing here?"

"I'm David Lee, Amanda Morelli's defense attorney, and you are?" David stood and offered his hand.

The other man did not reciprocate. "Richard Caldwell," he said. Turning to Valerie, he barked, "Get back to work and speak to this guy on your own time." He turned again and stormed away.

Setting aside his poor first impression, David went after Caldwell and had to speed-walk to catch him. "Can I speak with you for a few moments?"

Caldwell stopped and spun around. "You can't be serious," he said with a sneer. "I have more important matters on my plate, such as trying to save what's left of this damn firm."

"But I just need a–"

"I spoke with the police enough times, and you can read about it in their reports. I'm sure you'll get copies of them soon enough."

Caldwell's attitude did not discourage David, and he pressed on. "If you don't have the time, can I speak with another partner?"

"I suppose that'll be the only way to get rid of you. Try Saxer. You can waste his time. After you speak with him, let me know what the hell that idiot is doing! He's practically abandoned the firm, and I *really* need to rip him a new one. Follow me."

David trailed Caldwell at a brisk pace towards the southwest corner of the building until they reached the cubicle of a female paralegal, who appeared as worn out and depressed as everyone else.

"Remember Morelli? This is her defense attorney," Caldwell barked. "Give him Saxer's phone numbers." He abruptly left before receiving any acknowledgement of his order.

Without saying a word, the paralegal typed on her keyboard, examined her computer screen, and wrote three phone numbers on a sheet of paper. She tore the sheet from the notepad and handed it to David.

"Thanks," he said. "Could I speak with you for a few minutes?"

The paralegal sighed. "No, I don't have any time to spare."

"Well, I only need a list of those employed by the firm. I'm not asking for anything else, just the names."

The paralegal frowned.

"Please," David said. "That's all I need."

"For what month and year?"

David paused in thought for a moment. "How about January 1, 2009?"

The paralegal typed again, printed a list, and gave it to him.

"Thanks."

With a frown still on her face, the paralegal rose from her chair and motioned for David to proceed toward the receptionist.

"Hold on a minute," he said as he raised his right index finger. "I left my briefcase in the conference room."

While he strode toward it, he scanned the floor, searching for Valerie. He wanted to say goodbye to her but failed to spot her. David packed up his briefcase and glanced toward the reception area. The same paralegal stood next to it with her arms folded. While her attitude bothered him, he nonetheless made a quick exit from the floor.

Once he arrived in the lobby, David approached the nearest security guard, who stood next to a turnstile.

"Excuse me," David said.

"Yes?" the guard replied while focusing ahead.

"Do you know there's a musty smell in one of the elevators?"

"We're aware. Someone will take care of it."

"Could I ask you some questions about building security?"

"No."

David felt discouraged but didn't need to badger the guard. He hoped Frederick Ferguson, his favorite private detective, would be available. Freddie could investigate the building's security and take care of other matters.

Chapter 3

Thursday, September 17

David glanced at his watch and realized William Saxer was late for their two o'clock meeting. Irene, a stocky, middle-aged woman with shoulder-length gray hair, sat at the reception desk. She wore her awful pale-pink sweater with a small stain at the waist. David had asked her to take it to the dry cleaners at least three times. She had apparently ignored him and did not care enough about her personal appearance. He found her attitude disappointing, especially as, to a large extent, she was the law firm's public face.

David decided to pass the time by talking to someone else. He declined to call Marc and possibly interrupt his well-needed rest. So, he instead went to Beverly Cohen's office. While David, Marc, and Irene affectionately called her "Bev" amongst themselves, they never used the nickname in front of her because she was too serious and formal.

Bev was reading legal documents through her stylish glasses and was dressed professionally, as always. David and Marc had established that proper attire for the firm included business casual, which Bev ignored. David was uncertain about her age and believed it would be impolite to inquire. There were a few clues, including her marriage to Stanley for nearly forty years, her short white hair, and some wrinkles, the most prominent hidden underneath bangs. David could not find any faults with her, except that her smile almost never revealed itself.

"Hi, Beverly," he said. "Got a couple of minutes? Saxer said he'd be here at two, and he's late."

Bev looked at David without revealing her current mood. "You have many good traits, but patience isn't one of them."

"Only good traits, not great?" He flashed a devious grin.

"Cute," she replied with a slight frown. "I heard about your new client, Amanda Morelli. Who's the ADA?"

"Jacqueline Marshall."

"Interesting." Bev removed her glasses and stared into the distance. "I know her but never litigated against her. She's a heavy hitter, which means the DA's office isn't fooling around." She returned her focus to David. "Did you know our old firm tried to hire her?"

"No kidding?"

"We brought her to the office and gave her the nickel tour. We offered her a partnership and a generous signing bonus, but she declined."

David pretended to be hurt. "No one offered me a partnership."

"You weren't with the firm long enough to be considered." She returned her glasses to their proper place.

"Yeah, I know. Did you hear about Amanda's parents showing up with thirty grand in cash?"

"Yes. Irene told me about it. Any thoughts?"

David shook his head. "Besides believing they're naive about muggers and crime, not really. I haven't asked where it came from. They have money in the bank, but perhaps they don't fully trust them. If so, I can't blame them after the mortgage meltdown and the stock market coming close to a complete panic not too long ago. Maybe they stashed some of their life savings in their mattress."

"Could be, but remember, don't jump to conclusions."

David held up his hands with the palms out. "I know, I know. Gather the facts first. You've told me that quite a few times." He glanced again at his watch and wondered where in the world Saxer was.

"Anything else?"

"Yeah. Marshall mentioned Amanda sent out an email to her so-called 'little friend' in the office with the message, 'Let's kill him.'"

"That's certainly not good," Bev said stoically.

"Yeah, I know. She didn't say if Amanda sent the email from work or from home. I can't imagine any law firm allowing the police to rummage through their emails and violate attorney-client privilege. No way Marc and I'd allow it."

"Agreed. Our old firm would've vigorously litigated any attempt to seize emails. Most likely, Morelli sent it from her home computer." Bev pursed her lips. "However, there's another possibility. If she sent the email from a work computer, the police might've arranged for an attorney to review them and not reveal sensitive communications. Then again, we shouldn't speculate. It'll become clear once you review the discovery."

"Sure," David said even though he was unconvinced.

He knew Jacqueline Marshall was a straight shooter but had doubts about the NYPD. During his civil rights case against the police, their attorneys had failed to turn over copies of two personnel files, which had forced David to file a motion to compel with the court. The attorneys claimed someone had misfiled the documents, and it had taken time to locate them. Such a mistake could have happened, but David suspected they tried to hide what turned out to be damaging information.

"This murder case will chew up a lot of my time," David said. "Could you take care of some extra matters for me?"

Bev leaned back in her chair. "That's why I'm here. What'd you have in mind? Another rich kid with a drug problem?"

David gave a wry smile. "Yeah. Another rich kid, but it's not exactly routine. Remember the college kid who came to the office with her parents last Friday afternoon?"

"Vaguely."

"Well, it doesn't matter. Susan has a nasty little cocaine habit. A few weeks ago, she and two sorority sisters went to visit the Statue of Liberty, you know, after it reopened last Fourth of July."

"Yes, I remember. Go on."

David could not contain his enthusiasm. "Before climbing the stairs to the crown, Susan wanted to snort a line of coke in the bathroom, and her friends tried to talk her out of it. They made too much noise and attracted an older woman's attention. First, she saw the argument, and then the cocaine. The woman got a park ranger, who arrested Susan for possession."

Bev remained stone-faced.

"Susan gave the park ranger a fistful of attitude and refused to go with him. Apparently, she didn't realize park rangers are law enforcement officers, and she almost got charged with resisting arrest. The National Park Service wanted to make an example of her, and since the Statue of Liberty is a national monument, that means federal jurisdiction. I guess the US Attorney's Office agreed to prosecute for the press release and some deterrent effect. They even charged Susan with a felony."

She raised her left eyebrow. "A felony for first-time possession? That's not consistent with federal law. What am I missing?"

"It's her third arrest. The first time she was a juvie, and the second occurred three weeks after she turned eighteen. Susan's parents want to get her into rehab, but I got the impression she has other plans, such as continuing to be a spoiled brat and a recreational drug user. Maybe she'll listen to you, and you can help her get her life on the right track."

"I'll see what I can do. Anything else you have for me?"

"Maybe, I was thinking about–"

David heard an unfamiliar male voice. He turned around and saw a slender man in his late fifties, about his height, with light-brown wavy hair. He was talking to Irene, and his drab brown suit matched his boring yellow tie.

"Sorry, Beverly. I'll get back to you."

David strolled to the stranger at the front desk.

"William Saxer, but you can call me Bill," the man said as he put out his hand.

David shook it.

"Sorry I'm late."

David kept his thoughts about tardiness to himself. "Okay. Would you like some coffee?"

"No, thanks. Never drink the stuff."

"Okay. Let's talk in my office."

Once they sat, David grabbed a fresh notepad from a desk drawer. "Mind if we start with some background information about your law firm?"

"Sure," Saxer said with a weak smile. "Let see… Charles Thorton founded the firm in 1974. Caldwell and I joined several years later. For many years, our firm was prosperous and stable. The Old Man was proud that we never laid off anyone, at least no one before this year." Saxer's cheerful expression momentarily disappeared. "Anyway, our firm's organization was a little different from other law firms. Just before Simpson came on board, there were thirty-one attorneys in total, five senior partners, nine junior partners, and seventeen associate attorneys. Only the senior attorneys voted on strategic decisions. The junior partners were well paid and usually remained with the firm for years. Many associate attorneys departed after they did not make partner, which was fairly typical."

"Yes, of course," David said while taking notes. "Please, continue."

Saxer nodded. "Right. We had the usual number of paralegals and support staff. The other senior partners and I tried to create a positive work environment, and the turnover rate for the staff was significantly lower than other firms." He smacked his lips. "My mouth's a little dry. Do you have any water?"

"Sure. Not a problem." David reached into another desk drawer and retrieved a bottle of water. "I hope you don't mind it's not cold."

Saxer smiled. "No, that's fine."

David held out the bottle.

Saxer tried to grasp it, and it slipped from his hand.

"Sorry. I'm a bit of a klutz," he said.

He picked up the bottle and took a large sip of water, then continued with his story.

"Once the economy went south, the firm's financial situation dramatically changed for the worse. Our biggest client went bankrupt almost overnight and left a mountain of unpaid legal bills. Unfortunately, new clients weren't coming through the door. Due to the economic downturn, many clients wanted quick settlements to limit their legal fees and the damage to their bottom lines."

David kept taking notes without lifting his head. "What happened next?"

Saxer sighed. "Nothing good. The firm rapidly ran through most of its cash reserves, and we faced the prospect of laying off a sizeable portion of our attorneys and staff. The Old Man injected a considerable part of his personal fortune to right the financial ship, but it provided only a short-term fix. Meanwhile, everyone tried to work with a business-as-usual attitude, but we were fooling ourselves."

"So, that's when Simpson came on board?" David asked.

"Right. We needed a miracle and thought we'd found it in J. Robert Simpson. To convince him to join us, we offered to make him our newest senior partner. We knew he had a falling out with his prior firm, but we didn't investigate what happened and didn't care."

Saxer paused, which caused David to look up from his notes.

"That wasn't very smart, was it?" Saxer asked. "We only knew Simpson had a reputation as a ferocious litigator and brought with him a client with deep pockets. He had a long-term relationship with Bennington, a pharmaceutical company fighting off a massive class action suit. Joining the firm made sense for him. He needed litigation support, both lawyers and paralegals, to properly mount a defense, and payments from Bennington made a significant difference. We became more stable, although things were still precarious. I thought the firm's financial situation would improve once the economy did." He took another sip of water.

"How would you describe Simpson's personality?"

Saxer's mood darkened. "His presence was incredibly toxic, and he had a massive ego," he said as he held out his arms. "He berated everyone around him. It didn't take too long to notice he treated the women horribly and constantly bragged about his sexual conquests. He sometimes called himself Big Bobby, but among themselves, the women called him Big Bastard. While I wanted everyone to maintain a level of professionalism, I ignored the negative comments about him."

"It was really that awful?"

Saxer scoffed. "Absolutely. About two weeks before the murder, Simpson, a few others, and I were having a meeting about the Bennington case in the tenth-floor conference room. Big Bobby noticed a tall blonde messenger talking to our receptionist and skipped out to meet her. He spent so much time with this woman that the rest of us gave up waiting and returned to our offices. Can you believe it? Needless to say, it was really frustrating and exasperating." He took another swig of water.

"Did you or anyone else talk to Simpson about his behavior?"

"Of course. The senior partners tried to convince him to stop it, and he couldn't have cared less. He knew what we knew: without him and his deep-pocket client, the firm wouldn't survive. Old Man Thorton wanted to part ways with Simpson anyway, but the other senior partners and I prevailed. I really didn't want to oppose the Old Man, but I thought I had no choice. I stupidly believed we could tolerate Simpson until the economy got back on track, but I also knew we risked a lawsuit from the women at the firm."

Saxer hung his head, looking sadder than a hound dog who had received a scolding after destroying his owner's flower bed.

"We really screwed up, didn't we?" he said.

While David agreed, he did not want to make Saxer feel any worse. Instead, he asked, "What happened after Simpson's murder?"

Saxer sighed and lifted his head. "Even though I couldn't stand him, I was in shock. The police asked if he had any enemies, and I told them, 'Take your pick.' After being exposed to him for a few months, I thought anyone who had ever encountered Big Bobby would've hated him."

David stopped taking notes. "Yesterday, I saw empty cubicles and offices, and I met Caldwell. He was in a rotten mood."

Saxer swallowed and appeared as if he needed a moment to compose himself. "Yeah… Richard wasn't always like that. I can't blame him… The firm's dying." He became teary-eyed and took another sip of water.

"What happened?"

"After Simpson's murder, the firm tried to hang onto Bennington. Upper management liked us on a personal level but believed we didn't have the necessary experience to handle the class action suit. So, the firm lost Bennington in mid-July. The Old Man wanted to inject more capital into the firm. He put two of his three houses on the market, but they never sold, and no new clients came through the door. Thanks to the murder, the firm was famous for the wrong reason."

Saxer shook his head, and his lower lip trembled.

"Immediately after losing Bennington, we told the staff about the firm's financial situation. It was a difficult meeting, and… many tears were shed." His lower lip quivered again.

David said nothing and thought it was best to wait until Saxer was ready to continue.

"The senior partners offered to write letters of recommendation, and anyone could look for another job during normal working hours. About a third of the attorneys and staff found other jobs or have been let go.

The latter received the equivalent of four weeks' salary, and I don't know where the Old Man found the funds for the severance checks. The firm will need to release another third very soon. Caldwell has been talking to a couple of law firms about absorbing the last third."

Saxer hung his head for about thirty seconds and then raised it long enough to gulp the remaining water in his bottle.

"I'm really sorry about what happened," David said. "I'm not trying to give you a tough time, but I need to ask you about something else. Caldwell said you had abandoned the firm."

With his head still hung, Saxer rubbed the light-gray carpet with his right foot. "That's not true. I tried to think of solutions to our financial problems, and I didn't come up with any decent ideas. No one else did either. I was constantly talking to Bennington's executives. They didn't leave us due to a lack of effort on my part."

"Are you leaving the firm?"

Saxer looked at David and gave a weak smile. "As a matter of fact, yes. For the past few years, I've been an adjunct law professor at CUNY in Long Island City. I really enjoy teaching, and one professor is retiring. I'll be taking her place and will be on the faculty full time starting in the spring semester. I would've left even if the firm was financially sound. I liked being a lawyer, but I was getting burned out. It's time for a new chapter in my life."

"What about the other senior partners? What's going on with them?"

Saxer sighed again. "The Old Man was devastated. He was already semi-retired, and lately, he hardly ever comes to the office. Tim Zhang is also getting up in years and quit." He snapped his fingers. "Just like that, without any notice. Michaelson's still there, and I think he'll follow Caldwell to another firm."

"So that's why Caldwell feels he's left holding the bag?"

"I guess so."

"What about Amanda Morelli? Was she a capable attorney?"

"Amanda…" Saxer stared into space. "I suppose I need to be honest about her. She was competent but never seemed too happy. Before the economic downturn, she applied to be a junior partner, and the vote was five to zero against. We didn't believe as a partner Amanda would actively solicit or attract new clients. I know she hated Simpson just as much as the rest of us, but I never imagined she'd shoot him."

"Who said she did? Maybe the police and the DA's office made a mistake."

Saxer shrugged. "Yeah, maybe. I hope so."

"Well, Bill, that's it for now. I really appreciate you coming to the office."

"Sure. Call me if you need anything else."

Chapter 4

Friday, September 18

Although David had asked to meet only with Amanda, she arrived with her parents. He first heard and then saw Paul and Lorraine having a pleasant chat with Irene. Amanda appeared sullen and did not take part in the conversation. Her hair was pulled into a ponytail, and she didn't wear any makeup. Nevertheless, David thought she was attractive.

David greeted the Morellis and brought them to the conference room, which was much smaller than the one at Amanda's old firm. It only had eight chairs and a rectangular table with a glass top. A television and a combination VHS/DVD player rested on a stand along the back wall. While Paul and Lorraine appeared ready to engage in conversation, Amanda slumped in her chair.

"How's your partner doing?" Lorraine asked.

David appreciated her interest. "He's slowly getting better. Thanks for asking."

"Is he hurting for money?" Paul asked. "We brought another twenty thousand."

Without hesitation, Lorraine opened her purse and retrieved a bundle of cash.

David was alarmed and tried not to visibly react. "Please, put it away. Both Marc and our firm are doing fine. Marc was wise enough to buy long-term disability insurance shortly after he got married. So, he's been collecting from the insurance company. On top of that, once Marc started improving, his wife Stephanie returned to work."

"That's nice," Lorraine said as she closed her purse. "What does she do?"

"Steph was a flight attendant. After they got married, she transferred to another job with the airline so she could be home more often. She now works on the ground at JFK. Getting back to the money, I'm not trying to lecture anyone, but it's not a good idea to walk around this city with a large wad of cash."

Paul waved his right hand. "Don't worry about it. I have a question. How long is it going to take before this case is over? Amanda needs to get past this and get on with her life."

Lorraine nodded in agreement, while Amanda had an expression David interpreted as "You've got to be kidding me."

David nodded and tried to be diplomatic. "Well, I understand where you're coming from, but there are certain realities to consider. The first one is the Speedy Trial Act, which gives the DA's office six months to prepare for any felony trial, and this case started with the indictment earlier this week. So, the DA doesn't have to be ready until mid-March next year."

Paul raised both hands and eyebrows. "That's nuts! The Speedy Trial Act doesn't sound speedy at all."

David's eyes tilted upward momentarily. "I know. Many times, the law doesn't make sense, but we're stuck with it. Besides, I'm going to need time to prepare a proper defense if this case goes to trial. The DA's office is sending over discovery next week, and Jacqueline Marshall told me there'll be a lot. We'll also need to conduct our own investigation and see if we can punch any holes in their case." Given Marshall's past performances, David doubted he would find a flaw in her armor. "There's one other thing to remember. While this is my biggest case, I have a few others, and I have to give my other clients the proper amount of attention."

Paul exhaled and flicked his right hand across the conference room table. "Do you think there's a chance the case won't go to trial?"

David considered how to phrase his answer as he wanted to be honest yet subtle. "There's always the possibility we'll find an issue with the prosecution's case. After all, nobody's perfect. If we find a flaw, perhaps the judge will grant a motion to dismiss. Unfortunately… this scenario seems unlikely. The district attorney's office tries to get all its ducks in a row before charging someone with murder."

With a despondent expression, Amanda dropped her right elbow on the table and pressed her forehead into her palm.

Paul appeared unfazed. "But Amanda didn't do it, and that's the big flaw. One day, they'll figure it out. If there's anything you need from us, please let me know."

"I'm sure we'll be in touch quite often."

David knew he would be in constant communication with Amanda but was uncertain whether any interaction with her parents would be productive or worthwhile.

Paul and Lorraine asked David questions about his family. He politely answered them while giving as few details as possible, because he avoided telling his clients, or their parents, about his personal life. After a few more minutes of innocuous conversation, David told Paul and Lorraine he needed to speak to Amanda alone. They were about to leave when Lorraine excused herself to use the restroom. Paul and David made small talk until she returned, while Amanda slumped in her chair and said nothing.

After Lorraine returned and sat down, she said, "I think you said Marc's married. Does his wife work?"

Paul patted her hand. "Honey, David told us already. She works for an airline at JFK."

Lorraine laughed a little. "Oh yeah. Just old age creeping up on me."

"Don't worry about it," Paul said. "It happens to all of us sooner or later. David, we'll be seeing you."

* * *

Once Paul and Lorraine had departed, David attempted to boost Amanda's spirits, even though he figured it would be a futile gesture.

"Since it's a nice day outside, why don't we walk to a restaurant for lunch?" he asked. "One of my favorites isn't too far away, and you might love the food and the atmosphere. Okay?"

Amanda shrugged, which was close enough to an agreement.

* * *

While walking two blocks to reach the restaurant, David and Amanda didn't engage in conversation due to the noise from the traffic. When they arrived at their destination, the sign outside included the word "Café", but the interior was consistent with a diner. It was furnished with red leather booths and chairs, neon lighting, and images from the 1950s on the walls. Other customers had taken most tables and the seats at the counter. Between the clanking of silverware on the plates and the various ongoing conversations, the noise level was almost uncomfortable for any person with normal hearing.

A young host with short red hair, a big smile, and slightly crooked teeth, approached David and Amanda. "Back again, huh?" she said to him. "Give me a few, and I'll be right back." She hustled to a far corner of the restaurant.

"How are you feeling?" David asked Amanda after a few moments of silence. "You look better today, not as tired."

"I'm fine. You looked a bit tired too."

David gave a little grin. "Yes, well, not a big deal. We got through the hearing, didn't we?"

The host returned and led them to a small booth in another corner. Once they sat, she supplied their menus and left to attend to other customers.

David was grateful the booth somehow dampened the noise level. He leaned toward his client. "You know, the food here is really good. I've never had a bad meal."

Amanda scanned the menu with little interest. She had not yet finished when a young African American woman with chin-length braids came to their table.

"Are we ready to order?" she asked with a smile.

"Not quite," Amanda said. "Start with him."

"I'll have a burger and fries, please."

Amanda skimmed the menu one more time and twisted her mouth, then she closed her menu and handed it to their server. "I don't know. The same for me."

After the server departed, she finally engaged with David. "My parents told me you've been doing criminal defense for seven years."

"Eight years, actually. At my old firm, I mostly represented white-collar defendants. Marc's a former prosecutor, and we met in law school. About four years ago, we formed our own firm. We've had some white-collar defendants, and we're assigned to federal and state defendants who are indigent. In multi-defendant cases, the public defender can't represent everyone. We've also represented many rich kids with drug problems."

"You also told my parents you've handled other murder cases."

David gave a half-smile and nodded. "That's right. This is my fourth one, and Marc was second chair for a murder trial when he was with the DA's office. They're not so different from other criminal cases, except the stakes are much higher, obviously."

Amanda grimaced. "Geez, you didn't have to remind me. I know what I'm facing."

David felt a little embarrassed. "Sorry. Do you want to hear about the other murder cases?"

She slumped on her side of the booth. "Sure, whatever."

"Okay. While at my old firm, I handled the first two pro bono, and other attorneys pitched in, especially Beverly Cohen. The first one concerned an adult son who committed a mercy killing. His mother was dying of cancer and really suffering from an incredible amount of pain. We pled it down to second-degree manslaughter, and the judge was rather lenient in sentencing."

Amanda was listening but did not react.

"The second murder case was quite different. We represented the second of two defendants, and both stupidly insisted on going to trial. Big mistake. The evidence against them was overwhelming, and they got hammered at sentencing. I filed an extensive appellate brief for both defendants, but it doesn't look good."

Amanda frowned and looked at the table. "That's not too comforting."

"Well, sometimes people are guilty."

The gloom on her face became even more apparent.

David leaned forward. "Look, I didn't mean to imply anything about you, okay? That's just what happened."

"Yeah, I get it. It's probably not a good idea to hear about the third murder case, but fire away."

"Are you sure?"

"Yeah, whatever."

"All right. It was a three-defendant case, and I represented the third one, Benny Chang. Benny and his two friends were accused of robbing a liquor store at gunpoint, and things went sour. Thus, the murder charge. The DA alleged his friends were inside the store, while Benny was the lookout. The case went to trial, which resulted in a hung jury: eight to four to convict for the others, and nine to three to acquit for Benny. Nine to three was surprising because the evidence against him was very weak. Anyway, the DA's office is retrying the case against the other two and dismissed the charges against Benny."

Amanda appeared perplexed. "Why'd that happen?"

"Best guess… The DA believes they have a better chance the second time by focusing on the other two. Good for my client, I guess, but he'll get himself arrested again. He's pretty young and already has a long rap sheet. Before the end of the year, he'll be back in jail."

"Are you going to represent him again?"

David scoffed. "Fat chance. The public defender can deal with him." At that moment, his cell phone rang. He checked the caller ID and let it go to voicemail. "Mind if I ask some questions about you and your family?"

Amanda shrugged.

"Your parents told Irene you're not working. When did you leave Thorton and why?"

She made a sour face. "Terrific. More great table conversation. I thought Valerie told you about it. I was fired after they discovered the police searched my apartment and my parents' place. I didn't tell anyone at the firm except Valerie, and I know she didn't say anything. Somehow the senior partners still found out. The firm was already in rotten shape and letting people go. Others got a severance package but not me." She leaned forward, and her eyebrows drew closer together. "Just to be clear, I *didn't* kill Simpson."

David smiled in an effort to dissipate the tension. "I never said you did. I'm only asking questions to get to know you and to better understand the case. Okay?"

Amanda's face relaxed. "Yeah, okay."

"Getting back to the search warrant, did the police seize anything?"

"No, nothing from either place."

"What were they looking for?"

Amanda looked to her right and stared at a wall. "Let's see… a .38-caliber handgun, some clothes… a purse, a gray wig, a cane, and something else…" She tapped her right index finger on the table several times. "Two cell phones."

David suspected the killer wore a disguise but was uncertain why the police searched for two cell phones. At first blush, searching for only one made more sense.

"Did you ever talk to the police?"

"Yeah, a few times. They wanted to interview everyone at the firm. Saxer and Caldwell said it was each person's choice, and they encouraged cooperation."

Good grief, David said to himself. The partners told potential suspects to cooperate with law enforcement. Any competent defense attorney would have encouraged them to take a more cautious approach.

"I'm fairly certain your partners didn't give good advice."

"Maybe, but I didn't see the harm. I had nothing to hide."

David received a text message from Marc.

> Remember when you told me Paul Morelli said I was a nephew of one of his friends? He lied. None of my uncles knows him.

David read the message and tried to keep his best poker face. He glanced in Amanda's direction and noticed she was staring at her lap, which meant he avoided an awkward conversation. On the other hand, Paul's misstatement raised a concern. David could not imagine a reasonable explanation as to why he'd fabricated an indirect association with Marc. It was a trivial matter, and David did not care why Amanda's parents had chosen his firm, but it meant he couldn't trust Paul. He just hoped his daughter wasn't also dishonest.

"So," David asked, "do your parents always walk around town with a stack of hundreds?"

Amanda rolled her eyes. "Stupid, right? I don't know much about their finances except they never worry about money… or practically anything else. After I lost my job, Dad offered to pay the rent on my apartment, because he knew how much I loved the neighborhood. I didn't want to be a burden, but moving back home was less appealing. As for my rent, he said, 'Don't worry about it,' which I've heard far too many times."

"I guess your parents are always positive people. Most family members look really stressed out in court."

She held out her hands. "Yeah, I know. I'm certainly not like that. Sometimes I tell people I was adopted, just as a joke. There's one good thing about their attitudes: I've never heard them argue with each other, ever. I don't know how they do it, but Mom and Dad always look at life as the glass being half-full. For me, it's hard to see it that way."

"Well, believe it or not, there's a positive side. You were released on bail. Do you get along with them?"

Amanda tilted her head. "I guess so. Growing up, I was closer to Dad than Mom, but they didn't play favorites. Dad took me to hockey games, both the Rangers and the Islanders." She released a half-smile. "Those were really good times. We also saw the Mets, and Dad had a good buddy who sometimes gave him free tickets."

"It seems your father has many good buddies."

Amanda smirked. "Yeah, I know. Dad could walk down the street anywhere in the city – Harlem, Staten

Island, Tribeca, wherever – and someone might say, 'Hi, Paul' or 'Hey Pauley, how's it going?' Everyone likes Dad because he's a people person."

"Your father was a union rep; what exactly did he do?"

Amanda held up her hands with the palms facing out. "No clue. I asked once or twice, and he didn't provide me with any details, just some vague comments. When I was a kid, Dad took me to construction sites a couple of times. He shook hands with the workers and introduced me, like he went there to socialize. One time, he took me to an unfinished floor of a high-rise. We stood close to the edge as he talked to some construction workers and plumbers. It was really high, and we were exposed to… you know. It was terrifying!"

The food arrived, and they ate in polite silence. David enjoyed every juicy bite of his medium-rare burger and found the fries to be fresh and crispy. Meanwhile, Amanda took three bites of her burger and left most of her fries on the plate. When they finished eating, the crowd had thinned out, and there was no one waiting for a table, so David figured there was nothing wrong with continuing their conversation at the restaurant instead of returning to the office.

"Amanda, tell me a little bit about your mom. She owned a travel agency, right?"

"That's right. She sold it for a 'tidy sum,'" she said with air quotes. "No idea what that means. After Mom bought the business, she hired some of her friends from the neighborhood, including Debra. My folks have known Pete and Debra so long that when Daniel and I were growing up, we called them aunt and uncle. Still do, I suppose."

"So, your mom was a good businessperson?"

Amanda raised her eyebrows. "Seems hard to believe, doesn't it? She's always been scatterbrained."

"When you were growing up, did you do any mother-and-daughter activities?"

"Yeah, sometimes. After I joined Thorton, Mom came to the office about once a month, and we went to lunch, which was nice. In the weeks before the... you know, Mom and I had lunch about once a week. Sometimes she came with Debra. Maybe she came more often after she sold the travel agency because she was bored. Mom stopped coming to the office after the... incident. Kind of hard to blame her. We still had lunch, but we met at a restaurant."

Amanda looked at the table and swirled the straw in her glass of water. "There's something else bothering me. I don't know. Maybe I shouldn't tell you. It's not that important."

"No, it's fine," David said. "Go ahead."

"There's something about Pete and Debra, but I don't know what it is. Sometimes I get the feeling they're talking in code in front of me, like they don't want me to know something. Maybe it's my imagination, or maybe they still see me as a little kid."

"I don't know. Sometimes the older generation is like that. What about your brother? Is Daniel older than you?"

She frowned at the mention of his name. "Yeah, by four years."

"I got the impression you and Daniel were close. Did you know he allowed his house to be used as collateral for bail?"

Amanda leaned forward. "What? Are you serious? That's surprising, and trust me, we're not close."

"Does he have a family?"

"Yeah. A wife and three kids. He's an architect and lives in Westchester County. When the economy slowed down, it didn't hurt him. Daniel and his college friends had invested in another friend's business, and that friend invented a cheaper, stronger, and lighter version of bulletproof glass. The economy went down, but the glass money started rolling in." Amanda scoffed. "That's typical for Daniel. *Everything* goes his way."

"So, there's a lot of money in bulletproof glass?"

"Are you kidding me? They put that stuff in police cars, armored cars, limos, maybe even in military vehicles. Then there's the worldwide market, including embassies in certain countries."

"Sorry, I didn't know, but I guess you do." David detected more than a hint of jealousy.

"No choice. I heard about it many times during family get-togethers. The company's now working on a better version of storm windows. They want them to withstand a Category 5 hurricane. I'm sure another ton of cash is coming Daniel's way."

"I think I saw his wife at the initial hearing."

She clenched her jaw. "Yeah… Trudy was there. Yes, that's her real name, but her blonde hair is fake. She's a little too perky, *and* she's a kindergarten teacher. Guess what she did in high school?"

"Cheerleader?"

"Bingo." Amanda pointed at him. "She still is, sort of. Most of the time she's happy peppy, and then she has other moments. I once told Daniel that Trudy was bipolar, which led to a really uncomfortable Thanksgiving dinner with the family."

David received another call on his cell phone, checked the number, and again let it go to voicemail. "How have you been spending your time lately?"

"Besides hanging out in jail? Not doing much. I've been sleeping in, and I'm in the middle of Geoffrey Ward's book on FDR. I was a history major in college and still enjoy it. On the weekends, I get together with Valerie or other friends. Sometimes I go shopping with Mom."

"It might be a good idea to exercise. I run when I have the chance."

"Yeah, I've been thinking about that. I ran the mile in high school."

David smiled. "Really? So did I."

"What was your best time?"

He paused and tried to remember. "Not sure. It was 4:40 or 4:41, something like that. And you?"

"Not that fast. I could run, but you can't do it all day. Maybe I could work again as a model, but I'm probably too old."

David was caught off guard. "You worked as a model?"

"Yeah. Only a couple of times while I was in college. Back then, I was in really decent shape, better than now." Amanda gazed at her glass and swirled the straw again. "The first time, a student studying photography hired me for a project. It was no big deal."

"What about the other one?"

She frowned and waved her right hand. "It was ridiculous. Some company wanted to create a calendar called *Country Girls*, and all twelve girls of the month lived in the city. The photo shoot was on a farm upstate, and we were supposed to be wholesome and a little sexy. They dressed me in a red plaid shirt, denim shorts, and cowboy boots. I had to sit on top of a hay bale and smile. It was hard to fake a good time since it was really cold outside. I mean, I was freezing! Besides, do you see me as a country girl?"

She pulled her hair out of her ponytail. She made pigtails with her hands, tilted her head, and gave a fake smile.

David chuckled and noticed her facial expression called attention to her high cheekbones again.

Amanda's smile disappeared, and she put her hair back into the ponytail. "Yeah, I know. Really lame, right? Modeling seemed so phony, and I had enough of that."

Even though Amanda was not in the best of moods, David still enjoyed their conversation, but more pressing matters awaited him.

"Sorry, I need to get back to the office. I almost forgot to give you this." He pulled a business card out of his shirt pocket and handed it to her. "My cell number is on the back. One other thing, and please don't take it the wrong way. I'm not trying to run your life, but you should find a job, any job, to keep yourself busy."

Amanda raised her eyebrows. "And what will they ask me during a job interview? 'Why did you leave your last job?' Oh, it was nothing much. They fired me after one of my bosses was shot to death, and I've been indicted for his murder."

"Try to leave that part out," he said with a wink. "I'll get the check on the way out."

* * *

When David returned to his law firm, Irene was missing, which improved his morale. He made a beeline to Bev's office so he could chat with her before she left for the day. While it was barely the middle of the afternoon, she only worked part time.

"How was this morning's hearing?" David asked.

"Just as expected," she said without a hint of emotion. "My motion to suppress was granted, and I'll move to dismiss first thing Monday morning."

David nodded. "Sounds good. I'm sure the client will be pleased."

"Indeed. How was your working lunch, or was it a date? You were gone for some time."

"It wasn't a date, and she's not my type."

Bev raised an eyebrow. "Oh, why is that?"

"Amanda's attractive... Okay, she's gorgeous, but it's nothing like that. She's not my type because she's a client. You told me never to cross that line with one, and I never have." He tilted his head. "Although I have to admit there haven't been too many female clients."

"Are you going to bill her for lunch?"

"Nope."

"Good man. Did you learn anything useful?"

David bobbed his head back and forth. "Perhaps a few things, and I received a text from Marc. Remember when I told you what Paul said about wanting to hire Marc? Well, take a look."

Bev viewed the text message and frowned. "Morelli's father lied. Let's hope it's not a family trait."

"No kidding."

"What are your plans for the weekend?"

"Before leaving today, I'll try to call Marc and bring him up to speed."

"Don't you usually brief him in person?" Bev removed her glasses to clean them.

"Yes, but I'm busy this weekend. On Saturday, I'll be in the office to prepare for my DUI trial on Monday. On Sunday, I'm meeting with Morales at the federal jail in Brooklyn. Man, he is such a pain! After that, it's dinner with my family. Do you have any plans?"

Bev returned her glasses to their rightful place. "It'll be mostly a quiet weekend at home, but tonight, Stanley and I are having dinner at Le Cirque. We've been looking forward to it for a month." She turned off her computer and grabbed her satchel on the floor. "Now if you don't mind, it's time to pack up for the day."

"All right. See you next week."

Chapter 5

Sunday, September 20

David's extended family gathered at his parents' Brownstone home in the Upper West Side of Manhattan to celebrate his younger sister, Courtney, obtaining her PhD in economics. While David and his sister were on good terms, they had little in common except for their tall, slender builds, complexions, and senses of humor. Nevertheless, David relished the opportunity to catch up with her.

Besides getting her degree, Courtney could also celebrate the reputation she had begun to build. While completing her dissertation, an investment group called Peabody Gleason had hired her as a consultant. She had convinced Peabody in early 2007 that a recession was on the horizon, so they sold most of their stocks and real estate in more risky markets. Then, after the economy tanked, they bought low, and two years later, Peabody had more than doubled in value.

After dinner, David guided Courtney to the small patio off the living room so they could talk without interruption.

"Congratulations again," he said while raising his second glass of champagne of the evening.

"Thanks." She clinked her glass with his.

"Now that you have your PhD, what's your game plan?"

Courtney cocked her head and gave a big smile. "I have some good options. Four out-of-state universities are considering hiring me as a professor, and Peabody wants me to come on board permanently."

"Sorry to hear about your suffering."

Courtney smirked. "Yeah, it's been terrible."

"As for a career choice, I suggest you take the one that makes the least amount of money, which will disappoint our parents the most."

She smiled and lightly slapped his chest. "That's not a bad idea, if we're only considering your entertainment. I think I've decided what to do. While I'd love to be part of the academic world, Peabody are offering a generous salary and an obscene signing bonus. It's more like a big thank you for my past consulting work. Plus, there's one other important consideration."

"Which is?"

Courtney took a step closer. "I'm in a serious relationship," she whispered, "and Chris lives in Manhattan."

David's mouth dropped open. "What! Why didn't you tell me about him sooner?"

She grinned and had a gleam in her eye. "Give me a break. Do you tell me all the details of your social life? I don't think so. Besides, I wasn't ready to tell you or anyone else until the relationship became more serious. It is now, and… I have a feeling he might propose. If I take another job out of state, I can't stay in the city, and his practice is here."

"He's a lawyer?"

"Oh no… much better. Chris is an orthopedic surgeon, and he just finished his residency."

David chuckled. "Geez. Thanks for the little shot. So, he has a great job, but does he look like a troll?"

"No, sorry about that. I tried to find an ugly white guy who's a disreputable used-car salesman, and it didn't work out."

David held up his hands. "Okay, okay. When do you think Dr. Loverboy will pop the question?"

"I don't know. Maybe I should drop a hint or two."

"Well, you could do that, or you could ask him."

She momentarily froze. "What? You mean I propose?"

"Why not? I don't see a problem. Do you? It's not like we're stuck in the 1950s."

Courtney stared into the distance. "Hmm… I'll get back to you on that one."

Chapter 6

Monday, September 21

Late Monday morning, David placed a call to his law partner.

"Hey, Marc. Got any time for me today?"

"What do you think? Steph's at work, which means we can get into a lot of trouble. What'd you have in mind? Skydiving?"

David smirked. "Sure, why not?"

"Hey, wait a minute. I thought you had a DUI trial this morning."

"Yeah. I did, but it went away. As soon as the judge took the bench, the ADA dismissed the case."

Marc chuckled. "Do you know why?"

"Nope, and frankly, I don't care," David said, "So, I have plenty of free time on a weekday, which probably won't happen again for months. Can I come over, or do you have plans?"

"My lunch date with the queen isn't until tomorrow, which means I'm free. I planned to watch a movie with Steph tonight. We can watch it this afternoon instead."

"Sure. I'll leave the office in a bit, and I'll pick up lunch on the way to your place."

"Great! Can you get Chinese?"

David sighed. "You want the crummy soup again, right? Yeah, sure."

* * *

David arrived at Marc and Stephanie's apartment in Lenox Hill, and the door was answered by "The Creature," a nickname Marc gave himself due to chemotherapy's side effects. Although David and Steph never used the nickname, it was fitting, as Marc's hairless head sat on top of his unusually pale and thin frame. While he lacked energy, he maintained a positive outlook.

As they ate, David brought Marc up to speed on the events of the last few days, and they cracked jokes about their caseload.

"From what you told me," Marc said, after he'd finished his soup, "Simpson was a real piece of work."

David nodded as he swallowed the last bit of his tasteless noodles. "Yeah. He was a sexual harasser on steroids." He snapped his fingers. "There's something I forgot to tell you earlier. Simpson called himself Big Bobby, but the women at the firm called him Big Bastard."

"Big Bastard? Did they get it from Fat Bastard?"

"From what?"

Marc rolled his eyes. "You know, Fat Bastard from the *Austin Powers* movies."

David smiled. "Oh yeah. What a horrible character." His smile then disappeared. "Oh, no. This isn't an excuse for you to do another Austin Powers impression. I'm so tired of it."

Marc chuckled. "But Steph still likes it."

"She's just used to you and had all her shots. We really need to change the subject. What movie are we watching?"

With his right hand, Marc retrieved a DVD hidden behind a sofa cushion. He held it at shoulder level and placed his left hand on his chest. "On tap for this afternoon is *The Silence of the Lambs*."

David's anticipation was quashed. "Really? Can't we watch something else? You know I'm not into horror movies."

Marc put down his hands. "Come on. It's a great movie, and I haven't seen it in forever. It's one of only three movies to win Best Picture, Director, Actor, Actress, and Adapted Screenplay."

"Yeah, but in 1991, which was a really weak year for movies."

"I've heard some people argue that, but I don't agree. You don't think Jodie Foster and Anthony Hopkins are great actors? Besides, it's a psychological horror movie, not a cheap, slasher flick like *Halloween* or *Friday the 13th*."

"I get it, but can't we watch something else?"

Marc shook his head. "It's either Hannibal Lecter or the two of us cuddling on the sofa. Your choice."

David threw up his hands. "Hannibal Lecter it is!"

* * *

Despite his initial reluctance, David found himself enjoying the film to an extent. When it ended, he noticed Marc was asleep, and David had no idea how much he missed. It didn't matter as he could watch it again with Steph.

David examined the rest of Marc's movie collection, which sat on three shelves bolted to the wall. Almost an entire row consisted of classic movies, including *Bonnie and Clyde*, *Some Like it Hot*, *Psycho*, and *The Great Escape*. Another row featured movies from the 1980s. He sighed when he noticed *Back to the Future*. "Sorry, Marc," he said to his sleeping friend, "I would've definitely preferred to watch that instead."

Chapter 7

Thursday, September 24

Thursday morning brought a sentencing hearing for another rich kid with a drug problem. As soon as it concluded, David returned to the office.

As he passed by Irene, she said, "David, we got–"

"Sorry, not right now. Have to pee."

While dashing off, out of the corner of his eye, David thought he saw Irene scowl and put her hands on her hips. He didn't understand why she was upset but acknowledged he could be mistaken. He returned to her desk after finishing in the restroom.

"What's up?"

"The DA's office sent over the discovery for Morelli. It's in the conference room."

"Okay, thanks."

There were twelve numbered boxes covering most of the glass-top table. While the sense of organization pleased him, Irene's decision to place the boxes on the table was a different matter. She had previously scratched the glass by doing the same thing, so David had instructed her to place future deliveries on the floor, and once again, she had not listened to him.

Bev arrived at the office moments later and joined David in the conference room.

"Hi, Beverly. How was your appointment with the doctor?"

"I just had my annual physical and can't complain. Neither could my doctor. Mind if I look with you?"

"Of course not."

They took the tops off the boxes, and their contents were impressive. For many "discovery dumps," the prosecution had thrown the documents together with the apparent attitude of "let them figure it out." This time, however, the boxes were well organized. Someone had placed each item in a separate folder with a label, except for the subject matters with voluminous paperwork. A large, sealed envelope contained videos on disks, and phone and bank records for the deceased filled two boxes. Jacqueline Marshall had also provided documents concerning cell tower data from the night of the murder. David found a table of contents in the box marked "1."

"Have you ever seen discovery delivered in such an organized fashion?" he asked Bev.

"Not very often. I suspect this is an exact duplicate of Marshall's files. Perhaps she believes she has nothing to hide. The police must've thrown considerable resources into the case to create all of this in only three months."

David nodded as he examined the first box's contents. He removed a magazine with a middle-aged attorney on the cover.

"Oh look, an alumni magazine from a second-rate law school in the Midwest. That must be Simpson on the cover. Look at his pose. What an arrogant jackass." David tossed the magazine back into the box. "Do you think we can argue justifiable homicide?"

Bev frowned and glanced upward at him through her stylish glasses. Her white bangs almost touched the top of the frame. Based upon past experiences, he expected she would visit a hairdresser in two weeks.

Irene stood at the door frame and leaned into the conference room. "David, Judge Chavez's clerk is on the phone."

"Which Judge Chavez, state or federal?"

"Federal. Remember the hearing scheduled for 1:30 next Thursday? The judge wants to move it up to eight. Can you make it?"

He gave a dismissive wave. "Not a problem."

"Are you sure? Can you get up early enough?" Irene asked sarcastically.

"Just tell her I'll be there at eight."

As Irene left, David clenched his jaw and closed the conference room door, preventing himself from slamming it in a fit of anger.

"Did you hear that? Ever since Marc had to take a leave of absence, I've had to put up with her crap, and I'm getting sick of it."

Bev raised an eyebrow. "Will you do anything about it?"

"I don't know yet," he said as he crossed his arms. "Ordinarily, I'd fire her in a heartbeat, but I can't make a unilateral decision, and she's part of Marc's extended family. Marc has talked to her multiple times, and it's made no difference. Maybe her behavior will improve once he starts working again, but I doubt it. Any suggestions?" His cell phone rang. "Hold that thought, please."

Bev nodded.

"This is David," he said.

"It's Jacqueline Marshall."

"Oh, hello. I'm here with Beverly Cohen. Can I put you on speaker?" David switched over and placed the phone on the table before receiving a reply.

"That's fine. I'm calling to make certain you received some of the discovery we sent over this morning."

"I'm looking at it right now. Did you say 'some'?"

"Yes. We sent over twelve boxes, and you'll get another four tomorrow, which have phone records for Morelli and her parents, plus some miscellaneous items. Get back to me once you've reviewed everything. I might allow your client to plead guilty to murder two. Frankly, if I'd worked for Simpson, I might've blown him away."

David tilted his head and looked down at Bev, who again raised an eyebrow.

"Okay, thanks," he said. "We'll get back to you."

"Not a problem. Goodbye."

David kept his focus on Bev. "Marshall's a hard charger, and I've never known her to offer a deal right after an indictment. Something's up. What do you make of it?"

Bev removed her glasses and tapped a temple tip on her right cheek. "Perhaps there's a weakness in her case. Only time will tell."

"Care to be my trial partner, if it gets that far?" he asked.

She donned her glasses and gave a subtle shake of her head. "I'm not as young as I used to be, and I can't work the many long-hour days needed before and during a trial."

David was disappointed and about to drop the matter when he had another thought. "How about carrying about twenty percent of the load? Maybe a little more or a little less? By the time we get to trial, Marc should be back, and he can also work on the case."

Bev stared at the wall for a couple of moments. "A smaller percentage of the load? Fair enough. You have a trial partner."

"Excellent!" he said as he pumped his fist.

In some ways, it would be like old times except for their reversal of roles. This time, he would take first chair for the defense.

"Just remember," said Bev, "if we go to trial, it'll be my last. When the Morelli case is over, Stanley should be ready to retire, and we can start on our bucket list."

"Sounds good."

They continued to examine the boxes' contents for several minutes. David found the crime scene photos and the coroner's report, which he decided to review first.

"We'll need Freddie to look into a few things if he's available," David said. "We'll also need someone to examine Simpson's financial records. Any ideas?"

Bev stared at him. "You don't have a clue? What name just popped into my head?"

"Stanley? I didn't think he does this kind of work, which would include potentially testifying as an expert witness."

"I believe he would this time. He seems interested in the case."

"All right, great! So, I'll finally get to meet your husband. I imagine his services won't come cheap. I'll have to run it past the Morelli family, but I'm sure they'll approve. We'll also need someone to review the phone records. If I have to do it, I'll get a massive headache."

David's cell phone rang again, and it was Paul Morelli.

"Hey, David. Lorraine, Amanda, and I are in Murray Hill, and we just finished brunch. We want to stop by your office and see how things are going."

David was uncertain whether all three had the same desire. Nevertheless, he believed Paul should see all the boxes so he would realize Amanda's problems would not vanish in the near future.

"Not a problem," he said. "Come anytime. I don't have any appointments or court appearances for the rest of the day."

* * *

When the Morellis arrived, Bev was on a call in her office and waved to them. David guided them to the conference room and asked them to remain standing so they could better observe what was in the boxes. He surmised Amanda was in a somewhat better mood, because she cracked a smile when she saw him. David referred to the table of contents and explained how each portion of the discovery could relate to the overall case. He also mentioned the boxes scheduled to arrive the following day. Paul and Lorraine remained attentive during David's ad hoc presentation, while Amanda appeared bored and leaned against a wall.

"Paul, look at box number six," Lorraine said. "There's a file with your name at the top, and the one next to it has mine."

"The police spoke with both of you, right?" David said. "Every time they interview someone, they create a report, and the ADA has to provide copies of them to defense counsel." He noticed Paul's file was much thicker than Lorraine's. "In addition to reviewing the discovery, we'll need to conduct our own investigation and look for any holes in the prosecution's case. In the past, I've hired Frederick Ferguson, who's an excellent private investigator and a retired NYPD detective. We'll also need an accountant to look through Simpson's finances, and Beverly's husband might make himself available. I strongly recommend hiring both, but this will increase the costs."

"Don't worry about it," Paul said. "Just give our daughter the best defense you can."

Amanda took her shoulder off the wall and stood straight. "What about a jury consultant? The lawyers at Thorton used them all the time."

David held up his right hand. "Let's not get ahead of ourselves. Any possible trial is way off in the distance. Besides, jury consultants are a waste of money. Beverly wrote the book on how to pick a jury, literally, and there's a copy in my office. You can borrow it if you like."

"Sure, why not?" Amanda said.

Irene returned to the conference room again. "David, the Morelli case has been assigned to Judge Perkins, and a status conference is scheduled for this coming Monday at 11:30."

Paul looked in the air as if he were viewing a calendar on the ceiling. "11:30, huh? We might not be able to make it."

David shook his head in disbelief. "With this judge, checking your schedule is irrelevant. Unless you have a hearing in federal court, you're in the hospital, in jail, or dead, you better appear in his courtroom. Sometimes, even jail isn't a good enough excuse. Irene, tell the judge's clerk Amanda and I'll be there. Paul, I don't want to be too blunt, but if you and Lorraine can't attend, there's not much I can do about it."

Chapter 8

Monday, September 28

David, Amanda, and her parents arrived early for the hearing with Judge Sherman Perkins, who had presided over David's civil rights case against the NYPD. Perkins had been a federal prosecutor, but on the bench, he did not favor the district attorney's office and had no tolerance for police misconduct.

Judge Perkins set exacting standards for himself and could quote chapter and verse of any aspect of the law. He was always prepared and expected the same from the attorneys. When a lawyer made a frivolous argument or appeared clueless, Perkins did not yell, but no one doubted he was upset. The fact that he never raised his voice made him more intimidating than other judges.

David had heard about one occasion in which a defense attorney had irritated Judge Perkins too much. The attorney went on a rant, which resulted in Perkins holding him in contempt and fining him $500. The attorney refused to calm down and continued his rant. Perkins responded by glancing at his bailiff and giving an imaginary slap. Before the attorney realized what happened, he was spending the night in jail.

David had recently seen a ten-year-old picture of Sherman Perkins taken at an NAACP dinner to honor his elevation to the bench and was surprised the judge looked the same, except for faint wrinkles and bags developing under his eyes. Over the years, Judge Perkins had kept the same short Afro and thick mustache. David once spotted Perkins outside of the courthouse and was surprised to discover the judge was much shorter than him – he always seemed taller on the bench.

When David and the Morellis entered the courtroom, three elderly men sat in the gallery's fourth of six rows. The man in the middle held his index finger to his mouth and said, "Shh."

"Thanks," David whispered. "I already know." He motioned for Paul and Lorraine to sit in the first row, while he and Amanda went to the defense table.

Marshall entered and took her seat at the opposite table. An African American woman in her thirties typed at the clerk's station and nodded to acknowledge both attorneys. The bailiff, a middle-aged and overweight Caucasian man, sat in a corner. His eyelids kept closing and reopening as if he were trying not to fall asleep.

The "quiet rule" is ridiculous, thought David as he waited for Judge Perkins. No one else demanded almost complete silence before a hearing started. Above and to the left of the bench, the judge's portrait hung from the wall. Perkins rested his chin on his right hand and gave an eternal downward gaze upon all those who entered his realm. David had met many judges and attorneys with large egos, but the painting reflected Perkin's highly inflated view of himself, which fell into another category.

Promptly at 11:30, David heard a side door open, which caused the sleepy bailiff to jump to his feet and announce, "All rise! The Supreme Court of the State of

New York is now in session, the Honorable Sherman Matthias Perkins presiding!"

Judge Perkins stomped into the courtroom. "Good morning," he said in a raspy voice, without the slightest hint of warmth.

David never failed to notice his droopy eyelids, which gave him a look of permanent disappointment. His demeanor intimidated most attorneys, but not David, who instead took it as a personal challenge to never upset him. If it did not occur, it would be his own little victory.

"Ms. Marshall, what's the current status?" Judge Perkins asked after all parties had taken their seats.

Marshall rose to her feet. "Your Honor, the People turned over sixteen boxes of discovery, and no more is forthcoming. If the People conduct any additional investigation, which produces more evidence, they will notify the defense immediately."

Perkins paused and gave a slight wave of his right hand, which indicated some level of disapproval. "Do you mean to tell the Court you indicted before finishing the investigation?"

Marshall did not flinch. "Not at all, Your Honor. The People are simply not foreclosing the possibility of additional discovery should anything arise prior to trial."

The judge put down his hand, and his expression did not change. "Anything else?"

"No, Your Honor." Marshall took her seat.

"Mr. Lee, should I expect any motions in the near future?"

David stood. "No, Your Honor."

"Anything else?"

"No, Your Honor." He sat down.

"Very well. We'll have another status conference on Monday, November 16, 2009, at 11:30. Both parties shall follow the rules of this Court to the letter and without exception. Any motions shall be filed at least one week prior to the next hearing. We're adjourned."

After the judge departed, Paul looked at David with a confused expression. "That's it?" he asked.

David took him aside and further away from the microphones at the defense counsel's table.

"Yes," he whispered, "for now, and careful what you say. Those microphones could still be on. If so, the judge can hear you from his chambers."

"Got it," Paul said in a hushed voice. "Why'd we have to show up?"

"Judge Perkins requires it, which is reason enough. If both sides have nothing to discuss, he's fine with it. Besides, I wouldn't ask why we have short hearings. The judge can do just about whatever he wants. Other hearings will take longer."

Paul's distaste for court disappeared as he clapped his hands together. "Now that we're done, care to join us for lunch?" he asked in a louder voice.

"Sure," David said with a smile. "There's a great Chinese restaurant only three blocks away. It's called the Red Chili House. Sound good?"

"Let's go."

* * *

The Red Chili House had yellow walls and a dragon sculpture hanging at the back. Photographs and signatures of well-known people, including the current and two past mayors, hung on the right wall. Nearly all the tables were taken, and the room was filled with the chatter of loud conversations.

Mr. Chen, a diminutive Chinese man with wire-frame glasses and a bad comb-over, spotted David. He rushed over, vigorously shook his hand, and greeted him as if he were an old friend. Mr. Chen seated David's party at the first available table, even though others had arrived before them. After he left, David explained the special treatment.

"That was the owner. I come here frequently, and his son was a client."

"For a criminal case?" asked Amanda.

"Yes. Fortunately, the DA agreed to reduce the charge to a misdemeanor, and his son was sentenced to probation. Obviously, Mr. Chen's still grateful." David held up his hands. "What can I say?"

After the waiter provided the menus and later took their orders, the conversation continued.

"David, why'd you become a lawyer?" Lorraine asked.

David considered whether he should answer. He preferred not to discuss his personal life but surmised there was no harm in telling the story.

"Well, during my freshman year in college, I was home during spring break. Early in the week, I wandered around the city and ended up in front of the federal courthouse. I went inside and found a criminal trial in progress. It was a white-collar crime case with three defendants."

Paul and Lorraine inched forward while Amanda seemed disinterested.

"I didn't fully understand what was happening, but it was fascinating. During a recess, I tried to speak with one of the defense attorneys. Two of them did their best to ignore me. However, the one representing the third defendant gave me a few minutes of her time. She said she'd answer more questions if I joined her for lunch at the courthouse cafeteria, which I did. During lunch, the lawyer brought me up to speed."

"That was sweet of her," Lorraine said.

David grinned. "Yes, it was. I watched the afternoon session, came back the next day, and we had lunch again. I was back for a third day, and during the morning session, the defense rested. There was no rebuttal case. I made a comment about the case during lunch, and the attorney used it in her closing argument. That was really something. I never expected it."

Paul nodded while pouting his lower lip.

"While waiting for the jury verdict, the attorney invited me to her office and introduced me to some of her colleagues. Little did I know I was on a job interview. A few days later, the attorney called and told me the jury convicted the two other defendants and acquitted her client. She also offered me a summer job, and I accepted. I worked at the law firm every summer until I graduated from law school. During that time, I attended about ten hearings and a couple of trials. I guess after all that, it was inevitable I'd become a litigator."

"That's really nice," Lorraine said. "Did you stay in touch with the lawyer?"

"Oh yes. She's Beverly Cohen."

"How about that!" Paul exclaimed. "Is she going to help you out with Amanda's case?"

"Absolutely."

Chapter 9

Tuesday, September 29

David set aside a large block of time to study the crime scene investigation for the Morelli case. He reviewed the materials in the conference room, where he had more room to spread out the documents, and the boxes now sat on the floor. Among other items, one box contained the crime scene photos and the schematics for the tenth floor of the O'Connell building.

The schematics held no surprises as it listed each paralegal's cubicle and each attorney's office by name. Amanda's former office was on the right side, and Valerie Fernandez's cubicle sat directly in front of it. Old Man Thorton and the other senior partners had offices across the back row. As expected, Simpson had the largest office, in the northwest corner, which formed an L shape. The conference room was in the center, and other attorney offices fell in a row along the left side.

David turned to the crime scene photos, which were high-quality color copies. The first photograph showed the receptionist's desk and the space behind it, but Simpson's office was not visible. The next several photos depicted the area behind the receptionist, including the conference room, various cubicles, and possibly all the attorneys' offices. He did not understand why so many photos showed areas with seemingly no connection to the murder.

Next were images of the crime scene, starting with Simpson's office from a distance. The glass wall would have allowed for a clear line of sight to the inside if not for two black leather chairs blocking the view of the deceased, a rather large man in a business suit slumped over a black leather couch. David could still see a dark-red stain on the wall behind Simpson's head, however. For some unknown reason, the next few photos showed the floor outside of his office, which only revealed short, thick beige carpet, typical for office buildings.

The next several photos supplied a closer view of the office's interior. The far left contained Simpson's black leather chair and oversized mahogany desk, both appearing more expensive than the rest of the law firm's furniture. A computer screen and keyboard sat on one corner of the desk, and two small stacks of papers lay on another. Other than that, the desk's surface was bare. There were no pens, notepads, or any other items indicating Simpson had regularly worked at his desk. Perhaps he had kept any necessary materials inside a drawer.

To the right of the desk sat the black leather couch and matching chairs. A small navy-blue pillow was propped up on the side of the couch closer to the desk. Next on the couch was Simpson. Since his head had fallen forward, David could not clearly observe his face. He instead viewed the top of his head, which was covered in blood.

He tried to hold back his nausea and knew he would see more graphic images.

Simpson's right hand rested on his right thigh, and his left arm hung down. Another photo showed a closer view of the dried blood splatter and the corresponding blood streaks on the solid off-white wall behind him. In addition to its repulsive appearance, the splatter's location caught David's attention in another way. Most of Simpson's office had floor-to-ceiling windows, but the section behind the couch did not, indicating part of the building's superstructure ran through it. He wondered whether the killer picked this location to shoot Simpson so a bullet would not shatter a window and rain down bits of glass, calling attention to the grisly scene above.

David rifled through another box to find the autopsy report, which said Simpson was fifty-three years old, six feet two inches tall, and weighed 216 pounds. Upon viewing the corpse again, he concluded Simpson carried an extra three to four inches around his waist.

The next few photographs depicted Simpson's clothing. Thanks to a close-up image of his watch, David read the manufacturer's name: Cartier. He also determined Simpson had worn a dark-gray Armani suit, a silk striped tie, a silk dress shirt, and Prada shoes.

Artwork hung above the couch, a quasi-impressionist painting of two sailboats racing. With a magnifying glass, David made a closer examination of the bottom right-hand corner, and as he suspected, the painter was Leroy Neiman. Two specks of blood had dried near the bottom.

The next two photos depicted the area to the right of the couch, which included a mahogany liquor cabinet with glass doors and a floor-to-ceiling window behind it. A glass tumbler etched with Simpson's initials had a small amount of liquid and rested on top of the cabinet. The inside had various bottles of Scotch, bourbon, and other hard liquor.

The corner was solid, and David surmised it was also part of the building's superstructure. To the right was the rest of Simpson's office, which had another giant window and a solid wall to the far right. A small mahogany conference table and four matching chairs with black leather seats sat in front of the liquor cabinet.

There was a large photograph hanging on the wall behind the table. It featured Simpson holding high a champagne glass in his right hand, while he stood on the stern of a small yacht called *The Apex*. David scoffed at the entire scene and wondered if there had been no limit to Big Bobby's ego.

The next few photographs showed much closer views of Simpson's body and the area surrounding it. At first, David thought Simpson's left hand held a second dark-blue pillow, but then questioned whether a dead hand could grasp anything. Perhaps the pillow stood upright on its own and leaned against the hand.

Closer views of the pillow revealed two bullet holes, one slightly higher and to the right of the other. One side had gun muzzle imprints and powder burns surrounding the two holes, and several specks of blood stained the other side. David tried to determine what had happened. Simpson could have tried to shield himself with the pillow, which did not make sense. Maybe the killer had used the pillow to muffle the sound of the shots, indicating an amateur's work. A professional hit man would have brought a silencer.

David studied a few more photographs and once again believed the crime scene photographer had taken too many unimportant pictures, including images of the floor in Simpson's office from multiple angles. He only saw beige carpet and the furniture legs, not even shoe prints. Then he realized there were no shell casings on the floor and imagined two possible explanations: the shooter had used a revolver, which did not eject shells, or they had used a semi-automatic pistol and retrieved them before making their escape.

David grimaced as he examined the next several images, which provided an even closer view of the dried blood splatter and streaks on the wall. One photo had two blue ink circles drawn amid two large, dark-red patches, which highlighted the slugs' locations. He gasped at the sight of scattered, tiny gray bits on the wall, which were probably pieces of Simpson's brain and skull.

Additional photographs had closer images of Simpson's face and head. His assassin shot him through the right eye, and slightly above and to the left. The distance between the bullet holes appeared consistent with the distance between the holes in the throw pillow. David then recoiled upon viewing the back of Simpson's head, which had been blown apart.

The crime scene investigators had also taken photographs of the slugs after they had removed them from the wall. The forensic report said the bullets were fired from a .38-caliber weapon at a slight downward angle, approximately five degrees lower than horizontal. The report also concluded the gun was in contact with the pillow when fired, and the pillow was within inches of Simpson's face. A lab report said the only DNA on the pillow belonged to the deceased.

Another report stated the police had found several fingerprints in Simpson's office. Both door handles had been wiped, however, resulting in no identifiable prints. David thought the lack of shell casings and fingerprints indicated a professional hit man committed the crime but knew those two facts were not conclusive.

David turned to the autopsy report and the corresponding photos. The first photo showing Simpson on the autopsy table was horrific, and the subsequent images were even more graphic. While holding back nausea, David flipped through the images to make certain he didn't miss any more crime scene images. He knew Judge Perkins would allow the jury to view some images of

Simpson's body, but the autopsy photos were too shocking for the ordinary citizen.

The cleaning crew had found Simpson's body at about 3:30 a.m. Soon thereafter, the police, the medical examiner, and the crime scene investigators had arrived. Based upon the body's lividity, the medical examiner concluded no one moved Simpson since the time of death, which occurred between 9:30 and 10:30 the prior evening. The examiner established the estimated time of death based upon multiple factors, including the temperature of Simpson's body at the time of examination, the amount of rigor mortis, and the extent of his stomach contents' digestion.

Simpson's last credit card charge had occurred at a restaurant earlier during the same evening as the murder. Two detectives went to the restaurant, which was about five blocks away from the building housing the law firm. They obtained a copy of the receipt, which someone originally printed at 9:16, and the manager confirmed the credit card machine was in good working order.

The detectives had also spoken with the server who waited on Simpson's table. He said the deceased had been a difficult customer. He also remembered the tall blonde woman who had accompanied him. According to the server, Simpson insisted they sit in a back corner so he could face towards the rest of the restaurant, which meant the server mostly saw his date's back. He could not provide a detailed description of the woman and only recalled she was tall with long, straight blonde hair. He paid little attention to her because he preferred redheads.

David jumped upon hearing a knock on the conference room's door frame. He looked over his shoulder and saw Bev.

"I'm sorry. I didn't mean to startle you."

"It's okay," he said and spun in his chair to face her. "I'm fine. What's on your mind?"

"Remember Susan Thompson?"

"Who?"

"The college student caught with cocaine at the Statue of Liberty."

David chuckled. "Oh yeah, right. What about her?"

"I just got off the phone with her parents. Susan's hometown newspaper published a story about her arrest and has continued to report on the case. The university is certainly not pleased, and Susan's sorority is more upset. The National Council told her to straighten herself out, or they'd ask her to leave."

David rolled his eyes. "So, let me get this right. A sorority has no problem with binge drinking, but snorting coke at a national treasure is another matter."

"Apparently so," Bev said with a straight face. "Susan's now open to enrolling in a rehabilitation program as part of a plea deal for a lesser sentence. I don't know if she agreed so she may remain in her sorority, or if she really intends to be drug-free. Perhaps the AUSA will reduce the charge to a misdemeanor. Whether it's a felony or not, the sentencing exposure is about the same."

"Sounds good. Please keep me posted."

Chapter 10

Wednesday, September 30

David heard a knock on his open office door. Before him stood a muscular, light-skinned African American whose shaved head almost touched the top of the door frame. Despite the lighting bouncing off his dome, David noticed the roots of his speckled gray-and-white hair.

Frederick Douglass Ferguson gave a wide, toothy smile. "Good afternoon," his baritone voice proclaimed. "Hope you don't mind I let myself in. Didn't see Irene."

David smiled. "Of course not. Please have a seat." He gestured toward a chair. "I gave Irene the day off. Marc hasn't returned to work yet, and Bev's out too. So, it's just me." After Freddie sat, he asked, "Hey, how's Helen doing?"

Freddie let loose another wide smile. "My sweetie is *just* fine, thank you. Every day with her is a blessing. You should've seen Helen work her magic two weeks ago during the black-tie fundraiser for the children's hospital. No doubt her speech convinced a donor or two to give even more. Oh, let's not forget one other important thing. I looked good in a tux, you know, really good."

David chuckled. "I'm sure you did. I'd love to hear more about it, but we need to discuss Morelli."

"Right, right. In your email, you said she's charged with murder, and the deceased was Simpson, another lawyer."

"Yeah, and he was shot in his own office."

Freddie's eyebrows raised. "What? Someone had a lot of nerve."

"No kidding. Could you start working on the case right away?"

"As a matter of fact, I can. Just turned in a final report about a cheating husband." Freddie exhaled. "Sorry to say that's going to be a *very* nasty divorce. Also finishing up another assignment and can make you my top priority real soon."

"Terrific." David slid four thin folders across his desk toward Freddie. "The top file contains a summary. You got a pen handy? I have a to-do list for you, including maybe some paralegal work."

"That's fine, but I thought you had a paralegal. What was his name? Quincy? Don't believe I ever met him," Freddie said.

"You didn't, and he wasn't here very long."

"Oh, why not?"

"I fired him due to a lack of work ethic. We also caught him using the office phones and email for other purposes, such as chatting with his friends and setting up a side business on our time.'"

"Oh boy." Freddie shook his head.

"Yeah. Getting back to Morelli. First, please look into Simpson's two ex-wives and see if NYPD missed anything. Their information is in one of the files I gave you. They probably weren't involved, but it doesn't hurt to check them out."

"Will do," Freddie said. He took notes on a small pad he had removed from a pants pocket.

"I also want you to investigate Simpson's clients for the past two years and see if any of them had a motive to kill him. I doubt it, but you never know. Same goes for the opposing parties. Maybe someone had a shady background. Simpson represented a pharmaceutical company called Bennington when he was part of his last two law firms, and another file has the info on Bennington and them."

"Okay, what else?"

"Please talk to security for the O'Connell building. That's where the murder took place. No one saw the killer enter or leave the building. How come? I also need you to review security camera footage. The disks are in the conference room along with the rest of discovery."

Freddie nodded and continued writing. "Sounds like quite a bit to do, which is just fine with me."

David leaned forward and put his elbows on the desk. "There's something else I want you to quietly investigate and bill separately. I won't charge my client for this part. For now, don't mention it to anyone, including Amanda, her parents, and especially Irene."

Freddie stopped taking notes and looked up.

"I need you to investigate Amanda's father, Paul Morelli. A copy of his file is on the bottom." David casually pointed to the ones on the desk. "NYPD took a good, hard look at him, and they contacted the FBI, who gave them no answers. Maybe the FBI has something on Paul, or maybe they have nothing – who knows?"

Freddie inched forward in his chair. "What's the deal?"

"Well, Paul is a retired union rep, and the police suspect he has ties to the mafia. They questioned him about it, and he vehemently denied it. Paul told the police he knew some wise guys, and that was it. He also said the mob took its cut from the unions, construction companies, and so on. Nothing we don't already know, but I'm not convinced he was honest with the police. He's already lied to me once by claiming Marc was the nephew of a good friend. So…" David raised his eyebrows and held out his right hand.

Freddie pointed to him. "Gotcha. Maybe Amanda was wrongfully charged, and this was a mafia hit."

David leaned back. "Well, I don't know, could be. It's worth considering that angle. Simpson was murdered in his own office, and there were no witnesses. The shooter wiped down door handles to his office and left no shell casings behind, both of which have the mark of a professional. On the other hand, it looks like the killer used a throw pillow as a silencer."

"What?"

David raised his hands. "I swear. It was a throw pillow."

"Anything else?"

David mulled it over for a moment. "Do you have time to examine the crime scene photos? I might have a question or two for you."

"Am I on the clock right now?"

"Yeah."

Freddie chuckled. "Then I have the time."

David escorted him to the conference room and grabbed the folder containing the crime scene photos. He spread them out on the glass-top table.

"Simpson was six two, and the forensic report said the bullets were fired at a slight downward angle, about five degrees. In addition, the gun contacted the pillow, which was right in front of Simpson's face. From this information and these photos, can you make an educated guess regarding the shooter's height?"

"It's possible. Please point me to the report's section on the bullets' trajectory."

"Okay." David found the forensic report, turned to a specific page, and placed it on the table. "Would you like any coffee? I made a fresh pot a couple of hours ago."

"Please," Freddie said as he sat.

David went to the breakroom and poured coffee into two plain white mugs. He then returned to the conference room and set Freddie's cup on top of a coaster. "Here you go."

Freddie was so engrossed in the crime scene photos he failed to notice the coffee. For a few minutes, he studied the forensic report and the corresponding images while David patiently sat and waited.

While still staring at the photos, Freddie said, "All right… Need to figure out if Simpson was sitting upright when he was shot. We could then figure out the shooter's height from the position of Simpson's head and the angle of the shots. Best guess, probably not slouching at all. I'd pay close attention and sit upright if someone pointed a gun at me. Hold on." Freddie turned his head towards David. "Did the autopsy report mention Simpson having any back issues?"

"Not that I recall."

"Okay, and the killer had his full attention." Freddie closed his eyes. "Yeah… Upright and wasn't leaning towards the killer. Only a complete fool would get closer to someone pointing a gun at him… Assuming the killer took a proper shooting stance with the knees bent…" Freddie opened his eyes and again looked at David. "Just an educated guess, no promises, right?"

"Right."

"The shooter was short, probably five three or five four. Five five, maybe. Definitely not taller than that. How tall is Amanda?"

David groaned. "Five four. What if a taller person, say five ten or so, held the gun lower? You know, with one arm or both bent at the elbow?"

Freddie gave a slight nod. "Get it and not likely. Simpson's head started to drop right after the shot, which meant the second one had to follow very quickly. If the shooter's arm was bent, it would've been difficult to manage the recoil and fire again accurately. Also, doesn't make much sense to shoot that way."

"What about a taller person sitting down in a chair?"

"Anything's possible, but it would've been awkward. The shooter would've had to move the chair really close to Simpson to be able to fire into the pillow. Who'd do that?"

"What about a taller person crouching and holding their arms straight out?"

"Yeah. See where you're going," Freddie said. "Again, anything's possible, but why crouch? Would've been more difficult to fire the gun. Maybe someone would do it to disguise their height, but who'd think of it? Doubt even a pro would. In all my years as a cop and a private investigator, never heard of that one. Based upon what I see, the killer was between five three and five five. Sorry."

David sighed. "Yeah, I know. Even so, the murderer could've been a short contract killer."

"Could be. Didn't anyone at NYPD take a guess at the shooter's height?"

"Yeah," David said with a certain amount of disappointment. "Their expert said five four, give or take."

"If you want to be sure, you could hire your own expert. Can the client afford it?"

"I thought about hiring one… I don't know. It might not be worthwhile. Amanda's parents are paying the legal bills. They act like money isn't a problem, but something's fishy."

"Oh?"

"They have money in the bank, but it's not an endless supply. Get this. They're paying me in cash, and like I said, the police questioned Paul about mob ties. See why I want you to investigate him?"

Freddie casually pointed at him. "Got it. Anything else?"

David glanced at the boxes with the phone records. "Since you asked, there's one more thing. Someone needs to review the phone records for anything suspicious or unusual." He gestured toward those boxes. "They have the phone records for Simpson, Amanda, and her parents. I feel a little guilty dumping it on someone else, but I'd rather not do it. Do you know someone who likes to wade through a lot of numbers?"

Freddie grinned. "That would be me."

David was caught off guard. "Really?"

"Hey, why not? Know it's tedious, but have you ever been on a stakeout at night in the middle of winter? Shoot. Going through phone records is nothing."

"Sounds good. You're hired again."

* * *

After Freddie departed, David needed a break from the Morelli case and turned his attention to other matters. About thirty minutes later, Beverly Cohen arrived at his office door. Her short white hair and glasses with white rims blended together.

"New glasses?" he asked.

"No, these are my back-up pair," Bev said in her usual stoic manner. "I accidentally scratched a lens on my other one, and I should have a replacement lens in a few days."

"Okay. What's new? I didn't expect to see you today."

"I finished my errands and decided to work for a couple of hours. I also wanted to drop off Stanley's analysis of the victim's financial situation. Here's his report and his bill." She laid a manila folder on his desk.

"Stanley went through the records already?"

"Yes, he was here last weekend. As you know, we'll be out of town next week to visit friends and attend a wedding. He didn't want to wait until after we returned."

"You know, this means I missed another opportunity to meet your husband."

"Apparently so," Bev said. "I read Stanley's report, and here's the *Reader's Digest* version. He found nothing terribly unusual. Simpson owned two homes, one in the city and one on Long Island, but not in the Hamptons. Financially speaking, he was doing fairly well. He had a mortgage on the Long Island house, and the other he owned free and clear. You already know about the yacht. Simpson made substantial alimony payments to his second ex-wife and had manageable credit card debt, at least manageable for his income."

"Okay. Any evidence of debts to a bookie or loan shark?"

"Stanley found no reason to suspect an unconventional loan, so to speak. Simpson had expensive tastes in clothes, shoes, and liquor. He owned two Mercedes with no outstanding loans and used his credit cards at the better restaurants. Bottom line, he could handle all his expenses without much difficulty. He didn't have a retirement account, which was rather foolish. Obviously, it doesn't matter anymore."

"Yeah, obviously. So Stanley didn't have any concerns, nothing at all?"

"I'm sorry to disappoint you, but there was nothing out of the ordinary."

David sighed. "All right. Please give your husband my thanks."

"He was happy to assist, and your prompt payment of his bill will be thanks enough."

Chapter 11

Thursday, October 1

Following a hearing in federal court, David once again buried himself in the discovery for the Morelli case. After about one hour, he read one document and shouted, "Shit!" He slammed his right hand onto the conference room table and immediately regretted it. He checked the glass top for any cracks. Upon finding none, he breathed a sigh of relief.

David then realized he had left the conference room door open. He peered towards the reception desk and saw Irene, Bev, Marc, and his wife, Stephanie, standing next to it and staring at him. Bev's frown lines were evident, while Irene was scowling with her hands on her hips. On the other hand, Steph and Marc were trying to contain their laughter. While a bit embarrassed, David ambled towards the front desk.

"That was some greeting," Marc said. "It's nice to see you too."

"Sorry about that. I just found something rather disturbing in the discovery. You're looking better. Gained a little weight?"

"Good news," Steph said as she tucked a few strands of her long, strawberry-blonde hair behind an ear. "We just came from the doctor. He said Marc can start working part-time next week, maybe a few hours a day."

Marc gave a wink. "That's right, but we'll need to keep Nerf basketball on hold. So, what's with the profanity?"

"I'll show you."

Marc and Bev followed David to the conference room, and they sat down. Marc pushed back the hood on his sweatshirt, which revealed his bald head.

"Okay," David said, "Marshall told us about the 'Let's kill him' email, and there's more to it. Take a look." He turned a paper around for their benefit.

> From: Valerie Fernandez
> Sent: June 15, 2009 2:08:32 PM
> To: Amanda Morelli
> Subject: Re: Big Bastard
>
> Sure
>
> On Mon, 15 June 2009, at 14:08:05, Morelli, Amanda wrote:
>
> Discuss over drinks and dinner?
>
> From: Valerie Fernandez
> Sent: June 15, 2009 2:07:21 PM
> To: Amanda Morelli
> Subject: Re: Big Bastard
>
> Are you serious?
>
> On Mon, 15 June 2009, at 14:06:49, Morelli, Amanda wrote:
>
> Let's kill him.

Marc shrugged. "What's the big deal? We already knew about it."

David held up his right hand with a gesture indicating stop. "Wait, there's more. You need to read one of the detective's reports." He paused for a moment. "On second thought, I'll tell you what's in it. After work, Amanda and Valerie went to a restaurant a short distance from their law firm and sat at a table near the bar. The place wasn't busy, and the bartender overheard almost their entire conversation. According to him, Amanda and Valerie plotted how to kill 'Big Bastard', and he thought they weren't joking, for the most part. He also said they imagined many ways to kill him, such as throwing him off a roof, stabbing him, poisoning him, and so on. Take a guess at which method they finally chose."

"Shooting him," Bev said with an eyebrow raised.

"And…" David said while waving his hand like an orchestra conductor.

"Twice in the head."

"Exactly! Thus, the expletive."

Marc turned towards Bev. "Is this the part where you say *oy vey*?"

Bev did not react and instead addressed David. "Time to have a little chat with Amanda?"

"That's what I was thinking. I'll call her right now."

"Wait a minute," Bev said. "Wouldn't it be better to wait until you're a little less emotional?"

David gave a dismissive wave. "No, I'm fine. I can keep it under control. Besides, I won't mention the email and what happened later. I'll only ask her to come to the office to discuss a few matters."

David called Amanda on his cell phone and put it on speaker. She answered after three rings.

"Hello."

"Hey, Amanda. It's David. I've been going over the discovery, and we need to chat about a couple of things. Can you come to the office, say sometime tomorrow morning?"

"Um, not really… Mom, Dad, and I are in Charleston, South Carolina right now."

David's eyes bugged out as he mouthed, "What the hell?"

Marc raised his eyebrows and his hands, while Bev appeared unfazed.

"Charleston?" David said calmly. "What are you doing there?"

"Mom always wanted to visit Charleston and Savannah. We're going there next."

David frowned and shook his head. If he were an older man, he thought, this family would give him a heart attack.

"As part of the terms of your release from jail, you're not supposed to leave the state or even the city."

"Oh... we didn't think it was a big deal. We're flying back on Monday. How about I come by Tuesday at three?"

David sighed. "Fine. See you then. Bye."

"I'm sorry. Bye."

Marc slumped in his chair. "It looks like we'll have to wait until Tuesday for some answers."

"I don't think so," David said. "Her little friend was also at the restaurant. Time to call her?"

Bev gave a slight wave, which indicated her approval.

David called Valerie Fernandez and again put it on speaker. "Hi, Valerie. It's David Lee. Can you talk right now?"

"Not really," she said politely but firmly. "I'm at work. You know how it is."

"Yeah, I do. Any time tomorrow good for you?"

"No. Friday's bad too. Working all day. Sorry."

"Okay. Can you come by my office this Sunday afternoon, maybe around two?"

"I... think I'm available. What are we going to talk about?"

David inhaled and glanced at Bev. "Well, we need to discuss what happened during the week of the murder, including the 'Let's kill him' email and what you and Amanda later discussed at the restaurant."

"Oh... yeah... that," Valerie said. "I'll be there."

"Okay, bye."

David shook his head. "Did you hear that? 'Oh yeah, that.' Hey, not a big deal, just an itty-bitty detail that helped get Amanda indicted."

"I know it's bad," Marc said as he leaned forward and put his hands on the conference room table. "But don't think about it too much. We'll get some answers on Sunday. The doc said I can start working next week, and Sunday's next week. We can even wear matching underwear as a sign of mutual support."

David smirked. "I'll pass on the underwear thing. Beverly, I believe you'll be out of town?"

"Correct. We're leaving Sunday morning. Now, if you don't mind, there's another matter needing my attention."

* * *

After Marc and Steph departed, David continued to review the discovery for the Morelli case until well into the evening. He specifically read about two dozen files concerning some of the attorneys and paralegals at the Thorton law firm. During their initial interviews, NYPD detectives had asked them to provide their locations at the time of the murder and state whether they had owned or used any firearms.

One report contained a summary of Amanda's answers. She had disclosed that when she was growing up, on several occasions, her father had taken the family to "a good buddy's" two-story cabin in upstate New York. The cabin had been in a wooded area and had been stocked with rifles, shotguns, and handguns. Her father's friend taught her and her immediate family how to shoot them. While Amanda found firing a .22-caliber rifle to be tolerable, she hated the shotguns and more powerful rifles. She also learned how to use various types of handguns, including a .38 revolver, the same caliber as the murder weapon. She never enjoyed these family outings but believed she was too young to object.

The detectives had also asked Amanda whether her parents ever owned any firearms. She had acknowledged her father had owned a .38 revolver and had kept it in the house for protection. As an adult, Amanda disliked firearms even more than when she was a child, and as her parents grew older, she became more concerned about the revolver in their home. She feared one day there could be a tragic accident. About three to four years beforehand, she repeatedly asked her father to get rid of the gun, and he finally relented. Amanda didn't remember what happened to the revolver and did not care. She said she was simply relieved it was out of the house.

During another interview, Amanda had told a detective she did not own any firearms, and two weeks later, the police had searched her apartment. In the back corner of her bedroom closet, the police had found a .22-caliber pistol inside a gun case. Since the pistol was not the murder weapon, the police did not seize it and instead took photos of the closet, the case, and the pistol. The detectives never informed Amanda they found the pistol or asked follow-up questions about it.

There were more damaging statements. Amanda told the police she had worked on the Bennington case and had interacted with Simpson regularly. According to one detective's report, she had said she never went into Simpson's office and tried to avoid him as much as possible. However, a forensic report said a fingerprint found on the lower right corner of Simpson's desk matched her right thumbprint. David compared the two fingerprints, which had been copied into the report, and they indeed appeared identical.

The police had questioned everyone at the Thorton firm about their opinions of Simpson. The women's responses had ranged from reluctant admissions of disapproval to outright disgust. Valerie's blunt answer came as no surprise. Amanda provided a much different viewpoint by stating, "He wasn't so bad." The report suggested that Amanda had lied given she had been the author of the "Let's kill him" email. No one asked her to further explain her opinion, however.

David read another police report concerning an interview with Leslie Van Martin, who worked for the Equal Employment Opportunity Commission. Exactly two weeks before the murder, Amanda had visited the local EEOC office to file a complaint against Simpson for sexual harassment and creating a hostile work environment. Van Martin remembered Amanda calling him Big Bastard and saying he would be "better off dead." She explained the lengthy EEOC process, which frustrated Amanda. The next day, Van Martin started a two-week cruise. After she returned to the office, she caught up on the latest gossip, including the murder of an attorney, which the news had mentioned. She put "two and two together" and called NYPD.

Amanda's statements to the police irritated David because he did not believe any potential suspect should be so forthcoming without counsel. Even an innocent person's statement could create an unfavorable impression upon a jury. However, upon further reflection, David thought there could be a silver lining. He could turn her cooperation into an advantage at trial by arguing she had spoken freely with the police as she had nothing to hide.

Later in the evening, David realized he was tired and had read enough for one day. He considered calling Marc and Steph to determine if they were available for dinner. Before doing so, he glanced at his watch and discovered he had worked past eleven o'clock. He chuckled to himself. It had been months since he had worked so diligently that he forgot to eat dinner.

Chapter 12

Sunday, October 4

David was asleep when his phone rang. After the third time, he answered.

"Hello?"

"Hi, it's me!" Courtney said excitedly. "What time is it? 1:30, oops. Sorry about that. Were you asleep?"

David yawned. "Yeah, but it's okay. Why'd you call? Is something wrong?"

She gave a little laugh. "No, no, nothing like that. Earlier this evening, or I guess yesterday, I did it. I did it!"

"Did what?"

"I proposed to Chris, and he said yes!"

David became fully alert. "Wow! Congratulations! When's the wedding?"

"No date yet. You won't believe what else happened?"

"I don't know. You're going to appear on *Jeopardy*?"

Courtney laughed again. "That would be fun, but I've got better news. Last Friday, when was that? Oh yeah, two days ago, Peabody sweetened their offer. I can also teach so long as they come first. I won't be able to join a prestigious out-of-state university, well, out of most states, and I might be restricted to an adjunct professor position, but how can I pass up Peabody's offer? That gave me the push to propose to Chris. Now I can stay in the city, get married, and work for one, maybe two great employers! I can't tell you how happy I am right now!"

"That's great, really great!"

"Any ideas where to go on a honeymoon?"

David ran his fingers through his hair. "I don't know. How about Paris or the south of France?"

"Maybe, maybe. Both are excellent choices. When can we get together? I want you to meet Chris. Are you available for lunch tomorrow, I mean today?"

"Sorry, I can't make it. I have a date. We'll get together real soon. Promise."

"Okay. See you soon. Bye."

David was truly happy for his sister and wanted the best for her, but also noted his *younger* sister would marry first, which did not sit well. He made a quick assessment of his own life. He was dating Beth, the flight attendant from Air Canada, but their relationship was not serious. Over the past few weeks, he'd been on a few first dates, which had not led to second ones.

David flashed back to a recent afternoon when he had seen an elderly couple holding hands. Their body language spoke volumes about their devotion to each other, and they cared for each other in the same way as Amanda's parents. These long-lasting relationships contrasted with the lives of some of his friends, who had been married and divorced within a few years. He wondered if he would ever get married, and if so, whether it would last until "death do us part."

* * *

On Sunday afternoon, David found Marc in the conference room, reviewing documents for the Morelli case. Marc had planted an elbow firmly on the table, and his chin rested in his hand. He wore a Yankees cap to hide his bald head and missing eyebrows.

"So, what do you think?" David said.

Marc let out an exaggerated sigh. "It's a lot to take in. I read your summary of Amanda's statements to the police. I've had better news. How was your lunch date with Beth?"

"Terrific," David said with a half-frown. "She's quitting her job to become a wedding coordinator in Toronto."

Marc's eyes widened. "Are you serious?"

"Yeah. She became a flight attendant to see the world and no longer wants to live her life out of a suitcase. She's going into business with her cousin."

"Sorry about that. Are you disappointed?"

David glanced up and flicked his right hand. "To some extent, I guess. We were never that serious, but we had some fun."

"Yeah, I get it. Hey, I checked the table of contents for the boxes. One file labeled 'Office Evidence' is supposed to be in box ten, and it's missing. Is it in your office?"

"No, I review everything in here."

Marc and David rummaged through the sixteen boxes of discovery, but they couldn't locate the file. Marc then shrugged his shoulders.

"Huh," David said. "Marshall wouldn't hide evidence. So, I guess it accidentally got left out."

He called her cell phone, and she answered on the second ring.

"You know it's Sunday, right?" Marshall sounded annoyed.

"Sorry, and yes, I know. We just noticed the Office Evidence file is missing."

"I'm not sure how that happened. I'll have it sent over first thing tomorrow morning. It should've been placed in the first box, not the tenth, so you would have looked at it earlier. I strongly suggest that when you get it, you should stop whatever else you're doing and read it thoroughly. Your next step will be to call me about your client pleading guilty."

Marshall abruptly ended the call.

"I forgot to put the call on speaker," David said. "Did you hear that?"

"Oh yeah. Loud and clear. Any guesses what's in the file?"

David shook his head. "You want to handle it?"

"Sure, why not?"

* * *

About five minutes later, Valerie Fernandez arrived in a Mets T-shirt and had pulled her long, wavy black hair into a loose ponytail. David stepped out to greet her.

"Thanks for coming," he said. "We'll chat in the conference room."

"Fine with me."

A few steps later, David said, "Valerie, this is my law partner, Marc D'Angelo."

"Nice to meet you. Sorry for the way I look," he said sheepishly.

"You should be," Valerie deadpanned. "Your Yankees cap is really offensive."

David unsuccessfully tried to hold his laughter.

Marc looked surprised at first but then chuckled. "Tough. The cap stays. I meant the way I look. I recently went through chemo."

"Amanda told me about it," Valerie said. "You don't look too bad. A friend of mine dealt with it a few years ago, which means I sort of know what you've been going through."

David held out his right arm with the palm facing up. "Please, have a seat."

Valerie took the chair closest to her, while David and Marc sat on the opposite side of the table. David also grabbed a pen lying on top of a notepad.

"Before you called, I knew Amanda was out of town," Valerie said. "I guess you couldn't wait for some answers."

David nodded. "Something like that. So, let's go back to the Monday before the murder. What happened that day and why did Amanda send the 'Let's kill him' email?"

Valerie exhaled and gazed at the blank television screen in the conference room, as if she could use it to view images in her memory.

"Let's see. Monday was like every other day, Simpson being an a–hole. Amanda and I were assigned to Bennington, which meant constant exposure to him. I can think of better things to do than dealing with him, like getting a cavity filled without Novocain. You know what I mean?"

"So, what happened?" David asked. "Please, start with Monday morning."

"Nothing much, just the usual work. Amanda and I went to lunch at a coffee shop, and we complained about work, again. We wanted to find something else, but the job market stunk, and I couldn't quit. My son's a junior in college, and my daughter started this semester. They have scholarships, but there are other expenses."

"Okay," Marc said. "What happened after lunch?"

Valerie's mood darkened, and she folded her arms. "Big Bastard was in Amanda's office. I couldn't hear their conversation because the door was closed, but I could see them. Obviously, Amanda was not enjoying herself, and after he left, she made this face. At first, I thought maybe she was ticked off at another crude comment. I sort of said, 'What's going on?' without actually saying it." Valerie perked up. "Then Amanda sent me the email about killing him. It was really funny."

Neither the email nor Valerie's comment amused David. "What happened at dinner? Did the two of you really plot to kill him?"

"Yes and no," Valerie said, with a smile that almost appeared as a grimace. "We were only blowing off steam. Come on, Amanda's not a violent person. I guess I've had my moments, but I never wanted to kill anyone, not even him."

"The bartender thought you were serious."

"We weren't laughing that much, but we weren't being serious. I guess he overheard us, and we didn't care. Maybe it was the alcohol, even though I only had a couple of glasses of wine. Same for Amanda."

David stopped taking notes and considered what he just heard. Valerie's version of events seemed plausible, and he wondered what a juror would believe. "What happened Tuesday and Wednesday at work?"

Valerie twisted her mouth for a moment and continued to cross her arms. "Same old stuff. Probably a crude comment or two from Big Bastard."

David scribbled a few notes. "Anything unusual happen on Thursday, the day of the murder?"

"The morning was the same as always. Amanda and I went out for lunch again. Around two, Amanda said she wasn't feeling good, and she was holding her stomach. Maybe it was something she ate. So, she went home." Valerie shrugged. "I think that was about it."

"Where were you that afternoon and evening?" Marc asked.

"At work the rest of the afternoon. I called Amanda later on to see how she was doing. She didn't pick up, and I left a voicemail message. I went out to dinner with my mom and kids. The police asked for the receipt, and I gave it to them."

David had already read Amanda's version of what transpired on Thursday. Amanda had told a detective she went home mid-afternoon and had gone to bed early. She did not call anyone that evening, and no one could confirm she was in her apartment all night.

David inched forward in his chair. "Valerie, the murder took place late in the evening. Did anyone ever work late at Thorton?"

She shook her head. "Not most of the time. We came in early if we needed to put in any extra hours. That way we could still have the evenings with our families. A few times, I got in around six, and some people were already there. Several attorneys sometimes worked in the office on a Saturday. Of course, the hours got longer when we were preparing for trial, but we didn't have one pending last June."

David nodded and stopped taking notes. "Okay. What happened the day after the murder?"

"I got to work around… 8:20, I guess, and the cops were in the lobby. They didn't let anyone go to the tenth floor. So, everyone went to nine, and that's where the cops were interviewing people. Betty told me Simpson had been killed in his office. I was shocked and not sure what to think."

"I understand," David said. "A police report said you called Amanda that morning and told her about Simpson's death."

"Yeah." Valerie nodded. "At the time, I was a little freaked out. At first Amanda thought I was joking, but she also freaked out once the news sunk in."

"How are things at Thorton right now?" Marc asked.

Valerie offered a sour frown. "Still going down the drain. It looks like a handful of us will join another law firm… Harrison Day, I think. It's only going to be Caldwell, six other attorneys, and a few paralegals, including me. I think we're moving at the end of the month. Three junior partners kept some of Thorton's clients, and they're forming their own firm. Two paralegals might join them. Anyone who's left must fend for themselves. It's really sad, you know."

"Of course," David said. "So, you'll still work for Caldwell and have to deal with his attitude."

"Probably, but he's not so bad. You caught him on a bad day."

"What about Charles Thorton?"

Valerie shook her head. "Don't know. I haven't seen the Old Man for a long time. I feel really bad for him because none of this was his fault."

David pulled out two lists from a folder in front of him. "I got the first list when I visited you at the law firm, and it shows who worked at Thorton as of January 1, 2009. The firm gave the second list to the police, which was current as of June 2009, when the murder occurred." He handed Valerie the older list. "I highlighted the names of two people who were no longer with the firm by June. Do you know what happened to them?"

"This first one," Valerie said as she studied the list. "Jason…" She looked in the air and then smiled. "Yeah, I remember him. Nice kid. He's the Old Man's nephew, and he took a semester off from college. He worked in the mailroom for a little while and then went back to school."

"So, he was long gone by the time Simpson arrived?"

"Yeah, lucky him."

"What about the other one, Donna Conway?"

"Donna… Donna…" Valerie gazed at the ceiling for a couple of moments. "I kind of remember her. She wasn't with the firm for very long. I think she was Walter's friend from high school, maybe? Donna was a paralegal on the ninth floor, the one below me, and she was the last person hired before Big Bastard arrived. One day, she was just gone. I think something really bad happened. The senior partners were really quiet about it, and no one gave me the details."

David smiled. "Okay, that's it for me. Marc, do you have any questions?"

"Nope."

"All right. Thanks a lot for stopping by."

"Not a problem," Valerie said. "If you need anything else, just let me know." She smiled as she rose from her chair.

David noticed her dimples and wondered why he had not previously seen them. Then he realized there was nothing to smile about when they first met.

* * *

"Hey, Marc," David said, after Valerie left the office, "I don't think the police interviewed Jason and Donna. Maybe they never knew about them. I don't care about Jason, but Donna's another matter."

Marc smirked. "No kidding. I'd like to know why Donna left the firm. Maybe she was a malcontent or had a drug problem."

David checked the table of contents Marshall had provided with the discovery. "Just as I thought. There's no mention of the police interviewing Donna Conway." He examined the tabs for the files concerning Thorton's paralegals. "No file on her either. Bill Saxer can probably tell us what happened to Donna. I'd also like to know how the police got copies of the firm's emails."

"So would I," Marc muttered.

David called Saxer and put it on speaker. "Bill, it's David. I'm in the office with my law partner, Marc, and we have a few more questions. Is this a good time?"

"Sure, go ahead," Saxer said in an agreeable tone. "I've got a few minutes."

"Okay. As part of discovery, we received a stack of Thorton's emails. How'd the police get them?"

"We made an arrangement. NYPD paid for an attorney to review the firm's emails from the month before the murder to the week afterwards. The attorney acted like a special master and never disclosed most emails. He only printed the ones that were non-privileged and non-work product. He also withheld emails concerning personal matters between family members. It took him some time to review all of it."

"What the hell?" Marc whispered.

David shook his head because he would have never allowed the police to go through his firm's emails without a court order.

"Why did the firm agree to release any emails?" he asked.

"We already had financial difficulties, and we didn't want to lose any more clients. We wanted to show them we were fully cooperating with the police, within reason."

"Okay. Do you remember a paralegal by the name of Donna Conway?"

"Oh sure, she was Walter Bennett's friend. I think they grew up in the same neighborhood. Donna enlisted in the Air Force, and I heard something happened while she was serving overseas. I don't know the details. After she was discharged, Walter asked the Old Man to hire her."

"Why'd she leave?"

"Oh, that… she had to leave."

David's eyes widened. "You mean she was fired?"

"Uh… yes."

"What happened?"

"The senior partners wanted to keep it quiet. To make her termination a little less harsh, the Old Man gave her a generous severance package."

Saxer's evasiveness began to irritate David. "Come on, Bill. What happened?"

Saxer gave a heavy sigh. "Okay, okay. According to Simpson, Donna threatened to slit his throat."

David exhaled, and Marc jumped back in his chair.

"Was that true?" David asked.

"Probably. Donna was in Simpson's office, and from a distance, I could tell they were having a heated argument. Donna made some gesture, which I couldn't see clearly. Right after she stormed out, I walked into Simpson's office and asked him what happened. He was furious and cursed her out. He said she made a death threat with a slashing gesture across her throat. When I asked Donna about it, she didn't confirm it, but she didn't deny it either."

The wheels in David's head spun, and he realized the police had missed a viable suspect. This could be significant, in fact very significant, even a game changer.

"When did the death threat happen?" he asked.

"Mid-May, I believe."

"Did the police ever ask you about Donna?"

"Well… I don't think so… Oh, wow, do you think–"

"Maybe, but let's not jump to conclusions," David said. "By the way, how tall is Donna?"

"Five four or five five. Why do you ask?"

"Just curious."

"So, Donna could've done it? It never dawned on me."

"Don't dwell on it, and don't get carried away," David said. "We'll look into it. That's it for now, and thanks for your time."

"You're welcome," Saxer said awkwardly.

After David hung up, he and Marc stared at each other for a few moments.

"Holy crap!" Marc eventually said. "Donna Conway's about five four, the same height as the killer, and she made a death threat! Wouldn't it be great to spring those nice little tidbits during trial?"

David cocked his head. "Or?"

"Yeah, yeah, I know," Marc said with his hands raised in the surrender position. "We investigate, and maybe Amanda doesn't have to go to trial. Time to call Freddie?"

"Yup. I'll ask him to make finding Donna his top priority. Do you want the pleasure of reviewing all the Thorton emails? I haven't gone through them yet."

"Sure. Let me have all the fun," Marc said sarcastically. "I'll get started tomorrow afternoon, after reviewing the 'Office Evidence' file. I'll flag any containing negative comments about Big Bobby. As compensation, you need to bring me Chinese takeout for lunch."

David scoffed. "Not that crummy soup again? I'm embarrassed to even order that dreck. Geez, can't I introduce you to some real Chinese food? You know, authentic Chinese that tastes great?"

Marc feigned being hurt. "Would you deny a poor man recovering from leukemia his favorite comfort food? You're cruel and heartless."

David chuckled. "And you're a pain in the ass. Fine. I'll get the crummy soup."

Chapter 13

Tuesday, October 6

David arrived at the office just after 9:30 in the morning.

"Look what the cat dragged in, finally," Irene said from behind her desk.

He clenched his jaw and walked past her, then stopped and spun around. Irene apparently sensed it and swiveled in her chair to look at him face to face. He stared at her and her smug expression.

"Let's get something straight," he barked. "This is my firm, not yours. I can come and go as I please. So what if I arrived late today? I sometimes work late and on the weekends. I carry my own load plus some of Marc's. I *don't* want to hear any more nasty, little comments coming out of your mouth. Do I make myself perfectly clear?"

Irene bowed her head and looked at the floor. "I was just having–"

"Having what, a little fun at my expense? Keep your stupid comments to yourself."

Before she said anything else, David marched to his office. For the next thirty minutes, he worked on matters unrelated to Amanda Morelli, which gave him sufficient time to cool down. Then Marc appeared at his office door. His complexion had returned to normal and stubble was present on top of his head and where his eyebrows would grow back.

"How'd last night go?" Marc asked.

"How'd what go?"

"Hello! Didn't you have dinner last night with your sister and your future brother-in-law?"

David chuckled. "Sorry about that. It slipped my mind. Dinner went fine."

"Fine? That's it? No details? What'd you think of Chris?"

"Well… he seems like a good guy. I couldn't find any faults with him."

"And that's why you hate him."

"Exactly," David said with a grin.

* * *

Early afternoon, Marc again interrupted David. This time, he had a very serious expression, which was quite unusual.

"David, I wanted to review the 'Office Evidence' file before Amanda got here, and oh boy, we've got a problem. I got everything laid out in the conference room."

The conference room table was filled with photos and police reports. Some photos contained more images of the blood splatter on the wall in Simpson's office, while others depicted an attorney's office and a white takeout box on the desk.

"Okay," Marc said. "Someone took a very close look at the blood splatter on the wall. Look at this extreme close-up, you can see a little smudge at the upper right edge of the splatter."

"Yeah, I see it," David said. "It looks like someone's finger touched it."

"Right. Now look at the next photo. There are black marks above the smudge."

"Got it. Someone dusted for prints."

Marc nodded. "Correct, and none were found. This means the killer was wearing gloves."

Marc then pointed to the next photo to the right, which had a close-up view of the bullet holes in the wall. Scratch marks were visible in the track for one bullet.

"So, here's my best guess," he said. "Maybe Freddie was wrong about Simpson dropping his head after he was shot. Maybe it instead lurched back. The killer wanted to retrieve the bullets from the wall so the police would have less evidence. They pulled Simpson forward to move his head away from the wall. I'm not sure how that happened without any more blood transfer.

"Then the killer had to be some kind of contortionist to avoid Simpson and get at the bullet holes. Someone used their right hand to brace themselves against the wall while using a tool to retrieve the bullets. For whatever reason, the killer stopped trying. Maybe they heard something. Who knows?"

"Possibly," David said. "Since the right hand was used for bracing, does this mean the killer was left-handed?"

Marc shrugged. "Hard to tell. Being left-handed doesn't mean too much. About ten percent of the population is or something like that. Is Amanda left-handed?"

David flashed back to their lunch. "Yes, she is."

"Then maybe it does, but none of the reports that I read came to that conclusion."

"Okay, anything else?"

Marc groaned. "Oh yeah, I saved the worst for last."

He turned over a photo with a closer view of the white takeout box sitting on a desk. David sat in the nearest chair and grabbed the photo. A red speck was on a corner of the box. There was nothing else on the outside, not even food stains. Marc then turned over another photo, which had an even closer image of the red substance. No doubt it looked like blood, and it was the same color as the smudge on Simpson's wall. It was not a drop or another smudge. It looked like someone had swiped the blood across the box's hinge, probably accidentally.

"That's Simpson's blood, isn't it?" David asked.

"That's what the DNA report says."

"And the takeout box was in Amanda's office."

"Yeah. Houston, we have a problem."

David slumped in his chair and put his right hand over his eyes.

"Aw, crap!" he exclaimed. "Why don't you take a seat and let's think this thing through."

"No need. There's not much to think through." Marc took a seat anyway. "The blood on the box was in plain view, or as Jacqueline Marshall will tell a jury, in plain sight. Even though the transfer is really small, it's really obvious. The police and forensics were walking back and forth between the front entrance and Simpson's office, processing the crime scene. Amanda's office was on the same row of offices as Simpson's. So, they could've constantly passed by her office and eventually saw the blood on the box."

"Terrific. Any way we can get around it? Can we claim the spot on the box was not obvious enough to be blood?"

Marc scoffed. "Let's not get too carried away. When we both first looked at the spot, we knew it was blood."

David lowered his hand. "Yeah… I know. The police saw it, which gave them a valid reason to enter Amanda's office and seize the takeout box. Maybe we can argue the killer planted it to throw suspicion off him and onto Amanda."

"Good luck getting anyone to believe it," Marc said. "Besides Judge Perkins won't let us present that theory to a jury unless we have something solid to back it up. There's more bad news. One of the senior partners, Richard Caldwell, allowed the police to search the entire tenth floor for evidence, including the gun. So, the police rifled through all the attorneys' offices and paralegals' cubicles, including opening all the drawers."

"You've got to be kidding me! What about all the documents covered by attorney-client privilege?"

Marc rolled his eyes. "Yeah, I know. Caldwell and two other attorneys followed the police around so they wouldn't grab any of that."

David shook his head. "I had a run-in with Caldwell, which didn't go well. Now, I have another reason to dislike him."

"Oh, and there's one more thing… Except for Simpson's office and the takeout box, forensics found no blood anywhere else, not even on the floor."

"That's just great," David said sarcastically.

"Yeah," Marc said. "I guess this is something else we'll have to discuss with Amanda."

* * *

At three o'clock, a notice flashed on David's computer, reminding him of his meeting with Amanda. By 3:15, she had not arrived. Since late arrivals were uncharacteristic of the Morelli family, David was somewhat concerned. He placed a call to Amanda's cell phone, and she answered after the fourth ring.

"Amanda, this is David. I thought you were coming to the office at three."

"Oh… right," she said as her voice cracked. "I'm, I'm sorry. Uh, I forgot." She sniffled and made a shallow cough.

"Hey, what's going on?"

"I… I can't talk right now. I'll call you tomorrow. Promise." Amanda ended the call.

David didn't know what to think. Perhaps a family member was seriously ill, or there had been a death in the family. He hoped neither scenario was correct. David considered calling Valerie, but she might not have an answer. If that were the case, Valerie could become upset with Amanda for not reaching out to her, and he didn't want to create friction between friends. Instead, he walked to Marc's office, where he found his partner sitting behind his desk.

"Hey, where's Amanda?" Marc asked.

"I don't know. Something's up. I called her, and she seemed really upset. She said she'll call tomorrow."

Chapter 14

Wednesday, October 7

Early morning, David finished breakfast and got ready for a meeting with a client who was housed at the federal jail in Brooklyn. Prior to leaving his apartment, his cell phone rang.

"Hi, it's Amanda. I'm really sorry about hanging up yesterday."

"No need to apologize. Is something wrong?"

"Yeah. Mom had a really bad accident and needed surgery."

"What happened?!"

"We were in Savannah, and Mom tripped while walking down some stairs. She came down hard on her left wrist and fractured it along with doing other damage. You could tell right away she was badly hurt."

David grimaced while an image of what occurred flashed in his head. "That's terrible. What's the extent of her injuries?"

"I was kind of freaking out and don't remember what they said at the hospital. You can ask Dad about it. Of course, he stayed calm and asked the doctors a bunch of questions. Nothing rattles him. He kept reassuring Mom and me that everything would be fine."

David ran his left hand through his hair. "Is she going to be okay?"

"She should fully recover, but it didn't seem that way at first. The doctors said Mom needed a hand specialist to operate on her immediately. So, they flew her to another hospital in Jacksonville. The surgery went fine, and she'll probably need another one once the swelling subsides.

Mom told the doctors she'd been having pain in her left shoulder for about a month, and she thought it was arthritis. Turns out she has a partially torn rotator cuff, and we don't know how that happened. It can be repaired arthroscopically, which isn't as big of a deal. She's also going to need physical therapy for her wrist and shoulder."

David had difficulty processing how a simple fall required emergency surgery, even though he knew stranger things have occurred. "Sounds like a long road to full recovery. Has your mom had any similar accidents?"

"Oh no, not even close. Mom's known for being scatterbrained, not a klutz. Anyway, I'm moving out of my apartment and back home to help out. I'll have to do the cooking until Mom's wrist gets better; Dad in the kitchen is maybe the one thing that could put a strain on their marriage. At least I won't feel guilty anymore over Dad paying my rent."

David was uncertain what to say and remained silent.

"Yeah, I get it," he said eventually. "I know your mom comes first, but you still need to come into the office for an interview."

"Yeah, I know. We're still in Jacksonville, and we'll be back home in a couple of days. After that, I'll need to move and help settle into a new routine."

"That's fine. After I get in the office, I'll look for a date and time sometime fairly soon when we can get together."

"Yeah, sure."

* * *

Marc arrived in the office in the early afternoon and David briefed him on why Amanda didn't show up for the interview. Marc seemed just as concerned about Lorraine as him.

"Now, I want to get back to the takeout box and the blood transfer," David said. "Besides Amanda, someone else could give us some answers."

"Valerie?"

"Yup, Valerie. Let's give her a call."

David and Marc took their usual places in David's office. David made the call on his cell phone and made certain it was on the speaker.

"Hey, Valerie, it's David Lee, and I'm here with Marc again. We have a few more questions for you."

"Not now," she grumbled. "I'm at work. Can this wait until later?"

"Not really. We'll make it quick."

"Okay, fine. What do you want to know?"

"On the day of the murder, where did you and Amanda go to lunch?" David asked.

"What? Is that important?"

"Yes," he said firmly. "I'll explain later. Where did you go?"

"To this Mediterranean place a couple of blocks away."

Marc gave a thumbs-up, and David knew what he meant. They had read the same police report, which stated Mediterranean food was in the takeout box.

"Did either you or Amanda take any leftovers back to the office?"

"Um… Let me think… I didn't but Amanda brought some back."

"Did she forget to take the box home when she left early?" David asked.

"Yeah," Valerie said with more certainty in her voice. "Now that you've mentioned it, I remember. I saw it after she took off, which wasn't very smart of her, even if she was sick."

"Why not?"

"It's against the firm's policy. Two senior partners were really paranoid about ants and cockroaches. They told the early morning cleaning crew to throw out any leftovers on people's desks. Anything else? Are we done?"

"Yes, we're done," David said. "Thanks for your time."

"That's right," Marc said after David hung up. "We're done!"

David rubbed his forehead. "It's bad, but it's not that bad."

"Bad enough. No one planted the box, and the blood transfer on it belonged to Simpson. The blood was in plain view, so we can't get the evidence tossed out. The police had a very good reason to be in Amanda's office; the blood on the box stood out like a red nose on a clown."

David nodded. "Yeah, I know. Still, there's nothing to show Amanda stepped into her office that night. We can say it was someone else."

"I guess so. We're going to double-check the DNA results, right?"

"Of course. My old firm used a private lab in Connecticut, and they're well respected. We'll hire them."

* * *

Later in the afternoon, David checked on Marc before leaving for the day. He was sitting in the conference room, reviewing emails from Amanda's old law firm.

"Are you taking off soon?" he asked with a smile.

Marc chuckled. "Yes, Mom."

"Any interesting emails?"

"I've only read some of them, but I've got the general idea. Even though no one else threatened to kill Simpson, it's obvious he wasn't well liked. I set aside a few of the more notable comments. Get this. One paralegal called Big Bobby's death 'a gift from Heaven.'"

David shrugged. "Yeah, it doesn't surprise me."

"I found something else. Some emails reference a female attorney secretly organizing the women at the law firm. They didn't mention her by name, but I know the mystery woman was scheduled to meet with Old Man Thorton on Friday, the day after the murder."

"Any indication Valerie or Amanda knew about this secret group?"

Marc shook his head. "Not that I can tell. You know, this creates another issue for us. The prosecution can show there was another reasonable option, taking legal action against Big Bobby, instead of blowing him away."

David crossed his arms. "Yeah, maybe. Someone must've identified the mystery attorney, and it should be somewhere in the discovery."

"I suppose you want me to go through all that?"

"Well, not just you. We also need to figure out why the police eliminated everyone else as a suspect."

Marc let out an exaggerated, fake sigh. "Yeah, okay. I'll get to it."

Chapter 15

Tuesday, October 13

David was pleased to see Bev in the office and noticed she once again wore her stylish glasses instead of the ones with white rims.

"How was your vacation?" he asked.

"Great, Stanley and I enjoyed ourselves, and it's always good to visit old friends. The wedding was tasteful and elegant, but the food at the reception was a bit of a disappointment."

"Well, I suppose you can't have everything. It sounds like it was a pleasant trip though. What's the status of your workload?"

"Mostly winding down. Can I assume you want me to start working on Morelli?"

David gave a wry smile. "Am I that transparent? Marc and I have gone through some of the discovery. This week, he's reviewing all the documents concerning the law firm's employees. Could you give him a hand?"

"That's why I'm here," Bev said without emotion.

"Marc's not yet one hundred percent, and he's only working in the afternoons Monday through Thursday. Could you switch your hours from mostly mornings to mostly afternoons? That way, you and Marc can better coordinate your efforts."

"Can do, except for a day here and there."

* * *

Later in the day, David was reviewing materials concerning a rich kid accused of dealing drugs when he heard a familiar baritone voice state, "Greetings."

David grinned and saw Freddie Ferguson casting a wide smile. "Hey, how are you doing?" David asked.

"Very well and having an excellent day. Thanks for asking. Stopped by to drop off three reports. Got a few minutes to discuss?"

"Of course. Please, sit down." David held out his arm.

Freddie put the files on the desk and parked himself in a guest chair. "Before we get started on anything else, Helen wanted to know if you, Marc, and Beverly can join us for our annual Christmas celebration on Sunday, December 20."

"I know I'm available but don't know about Bev and Marc. I'll find out."

Freddie nodded. "All right."

"Why are invites going out so early? It's just a dinner party, right?"

Freddie chuckled. "Oh, no, not this time. Helen and her friends are making it a big deal this year, renting a hall and whatnot. They need a head count pretty early."

David leaned back and crossed his legs. "Sounds like fun. Anything I should bring?"

"Nah. Just be ready for a fun time with family and friends."

"Great, I'm looking forward to it. Now, let's get down to business."

Freddie rubbed his hands together. "Okay, let's get started. Simpson was first married to Nancy Hammond. I met her and her second husband, Brian, at their home in Westchester County. Great people, a genuine pleasure. Nancy's the manager of the Crate & Barrel store in White Plains, and–"

David perked up. "Nancy works at Crate & Barrel? I love that place!"

Freddie's amiable demeanor disappeared. "Are you really going there?" His right hand brushed across his shaved head. "Another one of those. Next time Helen wants to go, you can take my place."

David chuckled. "Sounds good to me. Getting back to Nancy Hammond."

"Yeah. She married Simpson right after college. Then they moved to New York after he graduated from law school. Nancy saw him slowly change for the worse, becoming increasingly obsessed with making money. He also started making inappropriate comments about women. Nancy disliked the man he became, but he was the one who filed for divorce. During the middle of it, Nancy met her current husband. Years ago, she regretted marrying Simpson. Now she believes without first marrying him, her life would've taken a different course, and she might never have met her 'soulmate.'" Freddie made air quotes.

"Okay. Was she ever a viable suspect?"

"No way. She wasn't aware of her first husband's murder until the police contacted her. They hadn't spoken to each other in seven years. Nancy said she worked on the day of the murder, and she gave me a copy of her pay statement. She also gave me a copy of a credit card statement, which had a charge for a restaurant in White Plains for that evening. Confirmed the place was only open for dinner on weekdays. Not enough time for her to pay the bill, get to Manhattan, and shoot Simpson, given his time of death. Besides, Nancy had no motive to kill him."

David tilted his head while leaning back in his chair. "Okay. What about Simpson's second ex-wife?"

Freddie shook his head. "Oh, you know the saying 'if you can't say anything nice, don't say anything at all'?"

"Yeah?"

"I'm done."

David laughed. Simpson's second ex-wife must be an awful person if Freddie didn't care for her. He liked almost everyone.

Freddie chuckled at his own joke. "Man, got to laugh. She's absolutely horrible!"

"You got to meet her, and better you than me," David said with a smirk.

Freddie pointed at him. "Just for that, I'm telling Helen, and you might be disinvited to the Christmas party." He chuckled again.

"Why was she so horrible? What was her name, Victoria something?"

"Victoria Devereaux. Met her at her apartment, which set new standards for rich people throwing their money away on tacky and gaudy décor."

"Oh yeah?"

"Yeah. She was also arrogant and completely self-absorbed, bragged a designer created the outfit she was wearing just for her."

David grimaced. "How wonderful."

"That's one way to put it. Victoria said her marriage to Simpson lasted 'five long and difficult years.' Blamed him because he never fully catered to her needs. Simpson wrote the alimony checks, and she was upset the judge didn't make him pay more. At the time of the murder, Victoria was living with her boyfriend and refused to remarry so the alimony checks would continue to flow."

"What a piece of work!"

Freddie exhaled. "Tell me about it. Money's her only true love. Victoria said she was in her apartment during the murder. I tried to confirm it with the doorman, but he didn't remember. Victoria claimed she might've made a call or two from her home during that night. I asked to take a look at her phone records, and she refused to sign a release – very nasty about it too."

"Terrific," David said.

"Bottom line, I don't believe Victoria killed Simpson or hired someone else to do it. She had a motive to keep him alive."

"Makes sense. I imagine the third report concerns Simpson's prior law firms, the executives at Bennington, and so on."

"You got it."

"Was there anything noteworthy regarding the lawyers and executives?"

"Nah," Freddie said with a dismissive wave. "Just a bunch of mostly white people suing each other and no shady backgrounds. One disturbing thing, though. The executives at Bennington loved Simpson."

"You're messing with me, right?"

"Nope. They thought he was a great lawyer for their company."

"Geez. Were all the executives men?"

"Guess what? One of them was a woman, and she sang praises of Simpson the most."

David leaned forward. "Seriously? What about all the sexual harassment?"

"Mentioned it, and they looked at me like I was some space alien who landed on Earth five minutes ago. They said he never did that stuff in front of them."

David shook his head. "So, he could behave himself but chose not to most of the time."

"Guess so. That's it for now. I'll get back to you in a couple of days about other stuff. We'll be getting together with Marc and Beverly for the meeting, right?"

"Yeah. Thanks for coming by, and please tell Helen I said hello."

"You got it, my friend," Freddie said while casually pointing to him.

After Freddie departed, David strolled to the conference room to speak to Marc, who had documents and folders spread over two-thirds of the glass-top table.

"Freddie was just here. As expected, we can't pin the murder on Simpson's ex-wives or former associates. How are things going with you?"

Marc exhaled through his nose. "Wading slowly through it all. I still don't have the drive or energy I had pre-leukemia, but I'm making progress. So far, I've reviewed the files for about one-third of the attorneys and staff at Thorton, and I'm comparing their statements to their work emails. I'm also creating a spreadsheet and brief summaries to keep track of everyone."

"Okay. What have you determined so far?"

Marc shook his head. "What a bunch of bozos. Nearly all of them spoke to the police without counsel. One paralegal asked for a Thorton attorney to be present, which was a good idea, but not a great one, because they didn't practice criminal defense. One junior partner only spoke with the police in the presence of his criminal attorney. He already had a possession of cocaine conviction and was probably a little paranoid."

David smirked. "Yeah, maybe he was still snorting coke, which caused the paranoia. Anything else?"

"NYPD conducted background checks, asked everyone if they owned any firearms, and ran database checks for firearms registration. So far, I found six who owned guns. One attorney owned a .38 revolver, and someone stole it about five years ago. We received a copy of the corresponding police report. Another attorney owned a .38. However, on the night of the murder, he was on vacation in California, and when he's here, he lives alone."

David frowned. "Any way we could point the finger at him?"

"Uh-uh. He's Mr. Clean. The detectives interviewed Old Man Thorton and inspected his firearms collection. He owned a variety of antique and modern weapons, which were on display at his home outside the city. The Old Man told the police since the onset of arthritis, he can't fire a gun and last held one about three years ago."

"Yeah… makes sense. Thorton's getting up in years."

"There's something else interesting about the Old Man. He said he was at his country home when the murder occurred, and his driver confirmed it. But the driver doesn't live on the property, and I doubt he stayed at Thorton's side night and day."

David was discouraged but not surprised. "Anything else interesting or noteworthy?"

"Yup. NYPD looked for evidence to back up alibis. Some people used their credit card around the time of the murder, and the location of their purchases put them too far away. Some made phone calls from their home phones, and others were simply home with family members. Having a loved one vouch for you isn't the most unbiased source, but it's better than nothing."

David frowned again. "I suppose so. Anyone without a concrete alibi?"

"Some had shaky ones, and for one reason or another, the police ruled them out. It's part of my summaries."

"Right, any idea as to the mystery attorney's identity, the one who was organizing the women?"

"Two paralegals mentioned her to the police. It's Kelly Holcomb."

"What?" David said as he raised his eyebrows. "The former Cleveland Browns quarterback is now an attorney?"

Marc laughed a little. "No, it's a different Kelly Holcomb, and she's a woman. Then again, the former quarterback could've undergone a sex change operation. Want me to make a few phone calls to check on it?"

David smirked. "Let me get back to you on that. Anything else on her?"

"I haven't read Holcomb's file yet. I'm going through them in alphabetical order, and I'm finishing G."

"All right. Keep wading through it."

Chapter 16

Monday, October 19

During the mid-afternoon, Frederick Ferguson returned, and from his office, David watched him give a pleasant greeting to Irene, who appeared to respond in kind. They also engaged in conversation, which David could not hear. Nevertheless, he surmised Freddie gave a compliment about her hair because she touched her gray shoulder-length locks. Irene then laughed at something. After Freddie and Irene chatted for about five minutes, David broke it up.

"Hey, Irene. It looks like there are no pressing matters for you. Why don't you take the rest of the afternoon off?"

"Huh?" she said with a quizzical expression.

"That's right. You can leave and still get paid for the entire day."

"Are you serious?"

"Of course. You mean you don't want to go home two hours early?"

"What? I mean yes," Irene said as her eyes brightened. Thanks." She placed a couple of items in her purse and hurried out the front door.

Once she had left, Freddie chuckled. "That was fairly gracious of you. Perhaps I should work here too."

David smiled. "Not so generous of me. Think ulterior motive. You're here to talk about Paul Morelli, among other things, right?"

"That's right."

"I'd rather not have Irene around when you do. She likes Paul and Lorraine and would probably blab to them."

"Whatever you say," Freddie said as he held up his hands.

"Before we get started, would you like some coffee?"

"No, thanks. I'm good. Hey, how was your interview with Amanda? Wasn't it this morning?"

"Supposed to be, but she called and said she was sick." David shrugged. "What are you going to do?"

David gathered Marc, Bev, and Freddie in the conference room, and they took their seats. David noticed a large paper cup in Marc's right hand and detected the aroma of his latte. Bev brought a legal pad and pen, ready to take notes even though Freddie had always submitted written reports.

Freddie clapped his hands once. "Thought it'd be better to update you in person about Paul Morelli. So far, we've only got what's in the NYPD file. Reached out to my contacts in the department, and either they don't know anything, or won't tell me. Best guess is the FBI never shared info on Paul, which is typical. Mitch Stanton's a former partner on the force, and he knows a couple of agents. Mitch promised to contact them, but doubts he'll get answers. Haven't looked at Paul's phone records yet, and it'd probably be a waste of time. If he's connected, he won't be foolish enough to call a wise guy on his own phone. No pun intended."

David took the news in stride. "Okay, just keep looking, or have Mitch keep looking. Do you have anything on Donna Conway, the paralegal who threatened to slit Simpson's throat?"

"Hey, about that." Freddie rubbed the back of his neck. "Sorry to tell you, haven't been able to contact Donna.

Even in this day and age with everyone leaving a paper trail, no luck. It's not as if she vanished off the face of the Earth, but pretty close. Her last known address is an apartment in Brooklyn. Spoke with the apartment manager, and he said she no longer lives there. Donna might be living with her parents in Philly. Three credit card companies and her cell phone company send bills to their address. I called her father, and he wasn't helpful, refused to tell me anything. Told me to contact their attorney and rudely hung up."

"Did Donna's father provide the attorney's name?" Bev asked.

"Yeah. Some guy in Philly."

"Should we tell the ADA about Donna and let the police track her down?" Marc asked.

David shook his head. "Let's talk to the Conways' attorney first. Anyone want to volunteer and possibly take a trip to the City of Brotherly Love?"

Bev briefly held up her right hand. "I'll do it. If the Conways will play ball, Stanley and I'll take the train to Philadelphia and visit with friends while we're there. I'll only bill the client for my round-trip train fare and one night's stay at a decent hotel. We'll cover our meals, Stanley's train fare, and local transportation. Approve?"

"How could I not?" David said. "Oh, Freddie, you don't mind, do you?"

Freddie let out a wide smile. "Of course not! Do you have any idea how much business Beverly threw in my direction when she worked for her old firm? How could I possibly deprive her of a nice, little trip?"

Bev gave a nod of acknowledgment.

"All right," David said. "Getting back to Freddie's to-do list. Except for further looking into Paul Morelli, what's left? Oh yes, building security, the videos, and the phone records."

"Right," Frederick stated. "I'll speak with security first and save the phone records for last, if you don't mind."

David snapped his fingers. "I almost forgot. There's one other thing. Eventually, you'll need to investigate the backgrounds of the detectives and other potential witnesses for the prosecution. You can put it on the bottom of the list, after the phone records. After all, at this point, we still don't know if we're going to trial."

Chapter 17

Tuesday, October 27

Marc rushed into David's office. "Sorry I'm late. I got stuck in traffic for a while. Did I miss the interview?"

David frowned. "No, Amanda couldn't make it. She had to take Lorraine to the doctor."

"Paul couldn't do it?"

"No, he had to take off somewhere with his friend, Pete. Amanda wasn't too clear about that."

Marc took a seat. "Are you sure about that?"

"What do you mean?"

"I'm not jumping to any conclusions, but maybe Amanda is trying to avoid us."

David scoffed. "That's ridiculous."

"Oh, really? Please hear me out. So far, she's dodged us three times. The first time, I get it. It was after Lorraine's accident, she was moving, and all that stuff. Then she was sick. Was she really? The interview for today was scheduled at least a week ago, and she didn't know about her mom's doctor's appointment in advance, really?"

"I think you're reading a little too much into all of that. Besides, we've been looking into everything about her case, and speaking to her hasn't been an urgent matter. It's not that big of a deal."

Marc held out his arms in front of him. "If you say so." However, the lilt in his voice indicated he was not on the same page as David.

* * *

Later in the afternoon, David, Marc, and Bev again gathered in the conference room to hear Freddie's report about the O'Connell building, where the Law Offices of Thorton, Saxer & Caldwell was located and probably for not much longer. He arrived with a long cardboard tube in his right hand.

"Are you going to begin with a song?" Marc blurted out.

Freddie chuckled. "Any requests?"

"Gentlemen," Bev said. "May we please get started?"

Freddie nodded. "Right. Only asked for a copy of the first floor, and it's the most important one for today's discussion," he said.

He opened the tube and removed the architectural plans. As he rolled them out, Marc placed a book on each corner. All the markings on the plans were too much for David to absorb, and thus, he was glad someone could explain them to him.

"Okay," Freddie said. "As we can see here, the O'Connell building is a little longer going north and south than east to west. Streets run next to the east and west sides, and alleys run parallel on the other sides. The lobby is on the east side, and the parking garage entrance lies to the west. For the lobby," he said as he pointed to it, "there are two cameras. They were in place last June, when the murder happened, and there are no cameras anywhere on the building's exterior. In addition to the four elevators, there are interior staircases on each side of them." He motioned toward the middle of the drawing. "To enter these staircases on the ground floor, someone needs a key card to get in but not to get out."

David thought so far Freddie provided no surprises.

"There are several law offices in the building. Since some attorneys work all kinds of crazy hours, security keeps a presence 24/7. Three guards are stationed in the lobby during the day and swing shifts. Only two cover the graveyard shift." Freddie shook his head. "Boy, I'd hate to be on duty at three in the morning."

Marc chuckled. "No kidding. Do the guards patrol the higher floors?"

"Now they do but they didn't last June. Near the entrance to the parking garage, another guard is stationed in this little booth." Freddie pointed to the location on the architectural plans. "It's right next to the driveway leading to parking on two lower levels. After the gate closes at 7 p.m., a guard is stationed in the general area until it reopens at 6 a.m. When the gate's closed, someone needs a key card to open it, and that's how the cleaning crew gets in early in the morning. From the little booth, a guard should see everyone going to the parking garage, assuming he's paying attention, and a security camera records all entries by car."

"Okay," David said. "Let's get back to the elevators. I saw security cameras in them, both the regular ones and the freight elevator. Was that always the case?"

Freddie shook his head. "They were installed after the murder."

David made a half-frown. "That means back then, security wasn't aware of anyone's presence on any other floor, unless they patrolled the upper floors."

"Which they didn't at the time of the murder," Freddie said.

"When I was there, the freight elevator wouldn't work. I needed a key card, right?" David asked.

Freddie pointed at him. "You got it. Regardless of the time of day, it won't move without a key card, and it's been that way for years. You only need a card outside of normal business hours to use the regular elevators. Security told me the cards are programmed by floor. During the off hours, someone from Thorton could only access the parking garage, the first floor, and the two floors for the law firm."

Bev put down her notepad. "Do you have anything else to report about the building? Perhaps other manners of entry and exit?"

Freddie smiled. "I was about to get to it. Let's examine the first floor's layout some more." He pointed to the top of the plans. "The north side has two fire exits near the northeast and northwest corners. The freight elevator is also near the northeast corner. Same thing for the south side, two fire exits and another freight elevator. No one can open the fire exit doors from the outside because there are no door handles, keyholes, or key card slots. I suppose someone could pry the door open with a crowbar, but building security and NYPD checked all the fire exits after the murder and found no evidence of tampering."

"What about the freight elevators?" Marc asked. "Can someone access them from the alleys?"

Freddie smiled and pointed at Marc. "Nice try, my friend. The freight elevators open on both sides. However, to access them from the street, someone first needs to roll up a large metal door. You can only open it from the inside manually or by pressing a button. Best guess, on the evening of the murder, someone left the building through a north side fire exit, but the police found no fingerprints on the inside door handle for either one."

"Can anyone access the stairs leading to the fire exits from any floor?" Marc inquired.

"I thought I told you about that," David said as he looked at Marc. "On the tenth floor, anyone can gain access to the stairwells. It's probably the same for the other floors above ground level. Right, Freddie?"

"Right. Now let's go over the videos."

With a remote, David turned on the television and video recorder in the conference room. He then handed the remote to Freddie.

Freddie put a disk in the recorder and let it play. "This is from a security camera in the main lobby on the night in question. Both cameras depict about the same thing from different angles. Watch the time stamp in the lower right-hand corner." He let the recording run for about one minute.

David leaned toward the television screen. Simpson entered the lobby and proceeded to the elevator banks. David thought he observed nothing noteworthy.

Freddie stopped the recording. "Okay, let's watch it again with some commentary." He rewound it and played it again. When Simpson entered the lobby, he pressed the pause button and pointed at the screen.

"See, right there. It's 9:31 p.m. and change. There's a tall blonde woman with Simpson, but you can't get a glimpse of her. You can only see a little bit of her hair, her arm, and her hand touching Simpson's shoulder, while our victim glances back and smiles. He keeps that grin on his face until he gets to the elevators."

"Uh-huh," David said. "The police interviewed the security guards, and they recalled the woman's shapely legs and long blonde hair. Unfortunately, they didn't get a good look at her face. According to them, she told Simpson she needed to step outside to make a call. She also told him to go upstairs, and she'd be there shortly to have some fun. Any guesses how Big Bobby interpreted the comment?"

"Nope," Marc said. "It's loud and clear."

"According to the guards, the blonde woman stepped outside and never returned," David said. "Simpson had dinner with a tall blonde woman earlier in the evening. She must be the same person we sort of see. Any footage of her stepping back into the front lobby?"

Freddie shook his head.

"Was she seen at the building earlier in the day?"

"I checked the videos from all three security cameras, and never saw her."

Marc's eyes got wide, as if he had a sudden revelation. "Please, play back the recording from 9:30 to maybe 9:32."

Everyone watched the video again, and David unsuccessfully tried to spot something unusual.

Marc pointed at the screen. "Did you see it? She stopped right before she got into the camera's field of vision. It's almost as if she'd been in the lobby beforehand and knew how to avoid them."

The wheels in David's mind spun fast. "A tall blonde woman… could've been there before… yeah… Wait a minute! I think I know who she is, sort of. Bill Saxer talked about a tall blonde messenger coming to the office about two weeks before the murder. Her appearance caught Simpson's attention, and his libido took over. He abandoned a meeting to speak with her. I bet the messenger and the woman with him two weeks later are the same person. Does building security still have footage for early June?"

Freddie thumped the table once. "Good thinking, my friend, but no. Asked about old video footage, and security said they only keep the recordings for ten days. If nothing bad happened or no one filed a complaint, they recorded over the old video. That means footage for two weeks before the murder is long gone."

David frowned. "Damn."

Freddie shrugged. "Nothing we can do about it. Remember Simpson entered the building at 9:31. You don't see him getting into the elevator, but how else did he get upstairs? The woman went outside to make a call. The nearest cell tower handled several calls around the same time, and I reviewed the data. About one minute after Simpson appears, there's a fifteen-second call from one cell phone, which I call Cell Number 1, to another cell phone, Cell Number 2. The same person bought both phones sixteen days before the murder, and coincidentally, the phone numbers end in 7881 and 7882. Seven minutes later, Cell 2 called Cell 1 for twenty-two seconds. Now hang onto your hats. Cell 2 was only in use during that evening and only for those two calls."

"So, Cell Number 2 sat for sixteen days, was used twice, and then dumped!" Marc said.

Freddie gave a wide smile. "Sure looks like it."

"What about the call history for Cell Number 1?" Bev asked.

"Good question. For two weeks, it communicated with only one other phone, which belonged to Simpson."

"What?" David said.

Marc's mouth dropped open.

Bev remained stoic and glanced in their direction. "Now, gentlemen. That should've come as no surprise." Returning her focus to Freddie, she asked, "Who purchased the cell phones?"

"Bonnie Parker, or someone using the name. Probably an alias, and she paid in cash."

Marc laughed a little. "I'm sure the name was phony. Recognize it, David?"

"Yeah, I do. Bonnie Parker was one half of Bonnie and Clyde."

"Yeah, and it was also a great movie starring Warren Beatty and Faye Dunaway."

David held up his right hand. "Stop right there, Cowboy, and let's stay on track. Freddie, do you have anything else for us regarding the cell phones?"

"Nah," Freddie said. "I spoke with two employees who were working the day Bonnie Parker bought the phones. For future billings, they needed a credit card number, and the one Bonnie provided was bogus. Neither employee remembered what she looked like."

"Huh, too bad," David said. "Did the cell phone store have any security cameras?"

"Afraid not."

"Did the police check the phone records for the law firm around the time of the murder?" Bev asked.

Freddie casually pointed at her. "Good question, and they did for every landline in the law firm. The last call ended about 8:25, and it was made by a junior partner. The cameras in the lobby saw her leave the building minutes later. There were no other calls on the firm's phones until after Simpson's body was discovered."

"Which means no possible witnesses," David said.

"And no indication another attorney or staff member was involved in the murder," Marc said.

Bev removed her glasses and tapped a temple tip on her cheek. "I believe we can make some reasonable assumptions. Bonnie Parker was the tall blonde messenger and the blonde woman with Simpson on the night of the murder. She essentially escorted Simpson to his waiting assassin, who knew how to get in and out of the building undetected. Anyone want to dispute my theory?"

Three heads shook.

David crossed his arms. "So far, none of this clears Amanda. Any other good news, Freddie?"

"If you mean more bad news, getting to that." He switched out the disks and played another one. "This is footage from a camera pointing north and attached to the building directly south of the O'Connell building. It recorded the area in front of both buildings on the west side. There's a lot of foot traffic. Keep your eyes on the far corner… and we're coming up on 9:43." Freddie paused the recording and pointed at the screen. "An older woman with a cane exited the alley north of the O'Connell building. She turned right and disappeared into the crowd."

David frowned. "I couldn't see her too well. There were too many people on the street, and she was too far away from the camera. I'm surprised you noticed her."

Freddie grinned. "Didn't the first time around." He switched disks again. "Someone at NYPD must've stared at the last video too long and finally noticed her. They made another one with some enhancements and focused on the older woman." He pushed the play button. "The camera never captured her face. She could've shot Simpson and hurried down ten flights of steps. But best guess, she had a key card, took the freight elevator, and got outside through a fire exit." Freddie stopped the recording.

"Hang on," Marc said. "Why not go downstairs in the freight elevator, open the metal door, and leave?"

Freddie gave a thin smile. "Another good guess, my friend, but no. Opening the rolling door next to the freight elevator would've triggered an alert on the security board. Why were the rolling metal doors alarmed and not the fire exits? No clue. Plus, once she got outside, she couldn't have closed the door, and it was closed when the police arrived. Did you get a good look at this woman?"

"Not her face, but overall, yeah," David said. "Long gray hair in a bun, frumpy clothes, a large purse, and a cane. I think she's five three or five four."

Freddie pointed at David. "Right. Anything else?"

"Like what?"

Marc perked up. "She didn't fit in with the rest of the crowd?"

Freddie shook his head. "That's not it. Let me play the enhanced video again."

While the recording played on the television screen, Bev leaned forward. "She's not using the cane correctly. It's only a prop."

Freddie clapped his hands once and pointed to her. "That's right! You got it!"

David groaned. "Ah crap. So, here's the DA's theory of the case. The tall blonde woman, also known as Bonnie Parker, arranges for Simpson to take her to his office, and it's a setup. She ducks out to call the killer, who's somewhere in the building. After Simpson's shot, the killer calls her back, but why? Just to say she did it? Maybe Bonnie was also the getaway driver, and if so, where was her car? The killer's a short woman who wore a disguise to make herself look older, and the DA believes it was

Amanda. Since Amanda worked in the building, she knew how to avoid the security guards and cameras. We also know she went home early, and no one can vouch for her whereabouts until the following day. Did the cameras in the lobby catch her leaving?"

"Absolutely," Freddie said.

"Any footage of her coming back later that day?"

"Nah. Checked the footage from the lobby, the parking garage, and the other camera."

"Did any camera spot an elderly woman entering the building through the lobby?"

"Strike two."

David rubbed the back of his neck and considered other possibilities. "What about Bonnie Parker driving into the parking garage? If so, did she have any passengers?"

Freddie nodded. "I looked for that too. Quite a few women drove into the building. Some had passengers, but nobody had long gray hair. Two female drivers who arrived late in the afternoon might have been taller. One was Asian, and the other one was a white brunette with large sunglasses. Could have been Bonnie with a wig, but she had no passengers."

David crossed his arms. "Well, assuming the woman with the cane was the killer, she could have gained access to the building by someone on the inside opening a fire exit door. Security would've been unaware because the fire exits don't have alarms."

"Right," Freddy said. "Unless you have more questions, that's it for now. I'll get back to you soon enough on the other matters."

Chapter 18

Friday, October 30

The blaring alarm caused David to wake up startled. He glanced at his clock – it was 6:30, and he couldn't remember why he needed to get started so early. He grabbed his cell phone on the nightstand and found a text message Bev had sent late yesterday:

> Spoke with Conway and her attorney. Email to follow.

David coughed and then shuffled to his small dining-room table, where his laptop sat. He turned it on and accessed Bev's email.

> From: Beverly Cohen
> Sent: October 29, 2009 9:58:07 PM
> To: David Lee, Marc D'Angelo, DAL firm
> Subject: Donna Conway
>
> I met with Conway and her attorney, and her contempt for Simpson was obvious. Conway admitted that after he'd made another crude comment, she threatened to slit his throat but only wanted to scare him so he would leave her alone. Conway claimed that in hindsight, she knew the threat was inappropriate and alleged she had been in a considerable amount of pain (which is not a sufficient excuse in my book). While on active duty with the Air Force, she suffered a significant injury and never fully recovered.

> Conway said that after she was fired, she returned to Philadelphia, and eight days prior to the murder, she had back surgery at the local VA hospital. Four days later, she was discharged to a rehabilitation center and claimed she was still there when the murder occurred. However, Conway's attorney refused to send us copies of her medical records to back up her story.
>
> I asked Conway whether she would testify for us if Morelli went to trial. She said she would think about it, but I sincerely doubt it. Her attorney's body language indicated he would advise her not to do so.

David groaned upon reading the last paragraph. He knew the firm could not compel her to appear in court because she lived out of state. If Conway were a viable suspect, he would have been tempted to file a motion to dismiss, but this was probably no longer an option. He was also concerned that if Conway refused to testify, the jury would never hear about her death threat, and her testimony was necessary to counteract the impact of Amanda's "Let's kill him" email.

* * *

Later in the morning, David watched security footage from the O'Connell building in the conference room. Marc's arrival provided a somewhat welcome reprieve.

"Geez, Davey. You look terrible with those bloodshot eyes."

"Thanks a lot. Aren't you in the office a little early today?"

"It's not early, about 10:30. Besides, I'm getting better and almost back to my old self."

"Oh really? Your old self? Is that a good thing?"

Marc chuckled. "Probably not. How long have you been staring at that screen?"

"Too long."

"Learned anything interesting?"

"Not really. I watched the videos from the lobby and tried to get a glimpse of the blonde woman's face. When you can see some of her, I reviewed the videos frame by frame and saw only her arm and a few strands of hair."

"Anything else interesting?"

"Well, during the thirty minutes before Simpson arrived, there were three food deliveries. One of them was definitely pizza, and the other two were probably deli food and Persian. Exciting enough for you? On another note, did you read Bev's email?"

"Yeah, I did. I guess we'll have to rule out Conway as the killer. Oh well."

David stared at Marc in disbelief. "*Oh well?* What if Conway doesn't testify? It could really hurt our case."

"You've been staring at the TV too long, and your brain's turning to mush. Think about it. How can we get Conway's threat into evidence?"

David threw up his hands. "Okay, I'll play along. Two people were present when the death threat was made. One is dead, and the other probably won't testify. Now what?"

Marc bent over and used his right hand to make the motion of a wheel turning round and round. "Come on. Get the hamster moving and think it through. Who else knew about the death threat?"

David stared at the wall. "Bill Saxer saw something but didn't hear it."

"Keep going."

After a couple of moments, David smiled as he realized a senior partner could testify that they fired Conway due to the threat.

Marc patted him on the shoulder. "And now we're up to speed. You probably missed one other thing."

"What's that?"

"If Marshall can't get Conway's medical records, she can't exonerate her. If that happens, we can send Freddie to Philly, and hopefully, Conway and her attorney won't cooperate again. Then Freddie can take the stand and testify about it."

David smiled. "Very nice."

Chapter 19

Monday, November 16

Another rich kid with a drug problem, David thought as he watched Marc usher a pretentious teenager and his parents into the conference room. David was relieved he could take a break from the steady stream of the privileged and entitled. More importantly, he was glad Marc was regaining his strength, but he still didn't have the endurance for the rigors and stress a full-blown trial presented. Nevertheless, Marc was working almost full time and could handle most of the firm's clients, which meant David could focus almost exclusively on Amanda Morelli. Unless a significant development occurred, which seemed unlikely, he and Bev would soon be drowning in pre-trial preparation.

Despite Frederick Ferguson's best efforts, no new leads presented themselves. David, Bev, Marc, and Freddie had reviewed all sixteen boxes of discovery from the district attorney's office and found no decent basis to support a motion to dismiss. Meanwhile, Freddie's examination of the phone records revealed nothing noteworthy, except for Simpson's communication with "Bonnie Parker" during the last two weeks of his life.

By this time, David understood NYPD detectives had narrowed down their list of suspects through a process of elimination. The police had obviously concluded Amanda was the most likely one but uncovered no direct evidence linking her to the murder. David's team could not identify any other possible suspect, but this didn't faze them. The prosecution had to prove its case beyond a reasonable doubt, and the defense did not have to prove anything. If necessary, the defense would only need to discredit portions of the DA's case, and David saw multiple possibilities.

* * *

Later in the morning, David arrived at the courthouse for another status conference with Judge Perkins. He had looked forward to it because he had seen no member of the Morelli family in weeks. He had instead given them updates over the phone and via email. While David had initially dreaded dealing with Amanda's parents, their personalities had grown on him, even though he still didn't trust Paul.

As usual, David arrived at the courthouse well before the scheduled hearing. While waiting to pass through security, he observed a petite woman in line ahead of him. Her dark-brown hair flowed down past her shoulder blades, and she wore a burgundy business suit with a knee-high skirt and matching two-inch heels.

David also noticed the woman was alone. She carried a purse, as opposed to a briefcase or satchel, indicating she was not an attorney making a court appearance. David checked his watch and confirmed he could spend a moment or two with this woman. If she made a good first impression and they seemed to click, he would give her his business card. After all, he was single and unattached, and there was no harm in introducing himself.

David passed through the metal detector and strolled toward the woman, who stopped in front of Judge Perkins' courtroom. She glanced left and then right, as if she were searching for someone. When David was about ten feet away, she turned around. It was Amanda! She saw David and released a big smile. She put her hands on her hips and made a pose stating, "Look at me now."

"Howdy, Stranger," Amanda said, with a gleam in her eye. "You come here often?"

David chuckled. "Good morning. Did you go back to your original hair color?"

"Yes, thanks for noticing. We really need to catch up. How about lunch after the hearing?"

"Sure, I'm available. Where are your parents?"

Amanda gave a dismissive wave. "They're not coming. They figured not much would happen today, and Dad had a doctor's appointment this morning."

* * *

David and Amanda entered Perkins' courtroom where the same three elderly men sat in the gallery's last row. The one on the right put his index finger in front of his mouth and said, "Shh!"

David smiled. "I know," he whispered. "Thanks."

As he sat down, he wondered why the retired men chose to observe in this courtroom, as opposed to any other, where the judges created a more tolerable atmosphere. He once again noticed the painting of Perkins casting an eye on him from above and hoped his ego would never become as inflated as the judge's.

As expected, the hearing was brief.

"What's the status of the case?" Judge Perkins asked in his raspy voice.

"The People have provided no additional discovery to the defense," Marshall said, "and we don't anticipate providing anything else before trial."

The judge turned his gaze toward the defense table.

"Your Honor, the defense has reviewed the discovery from the prosecution and has complied with our obligations by serving reports concerning our investigation," David said. "The defense will file pre-trial motions shortly."

Perkins remained expressionless except for his droopy eyelids, which made him appear disappointed. He had no questions, comments, or scathing remarks, which meant he was satisfied. No attorney would ever hear the slightest bit of praise from him.

"We'll meet again for another status conference on December 14," he said. "Hearing is adjourned."

* * *

David and Amanda decided to eat at a Japanese restaurant two blocks away. As David left the courthouse, he checked his phone for any messages and then turned it off to give Amanda his undivided attention. After a server took their orders, he studied her large brown eyes and high cheekbones. He also noted she was wearing makeup but did not need it.

"You know plenty about what I've been doing lately," David said, "and you know Marc's back in the office. It's not a good idea to talk about the case right now, because others might try to eavesdrop. So, please tell me what's new with you."

"What's new?" Amanda smirked. "Does anyone really talk like that?"

He shrugged.

Amanda gave a light chuckle. "As I said before, I thought about getting into shape and got tired of sitting around and doing nothing. I've been running and working out at a gym, and I've lost about ten pounds. I now fit into my skinnier clothes, including this outfit. It's almost like I'm back to my college days when I was in shape."

"That's great. I'm glad to see you're in a better mood, and I'm really sorry about your mom's accident. How's she doing?"

Amanda's smile disappeared. "It's been a tough road for her. Both surgeries on her wrist went okay, and she recovered from the arthroscopic on her shoulder sooner than expected. She's still in physical therapy for her wrist. She won't admit it, but the exercises have been painful. A couple of times, I took her to therapy and could see she was trying to hide it."

"Sorry about that. I guess it's a good thing your mom already sold the travel agency. That's one less thing to worry about."

Amanda shrugged. "Yeah, suppose so. The doctors also advised Mom to get regular exercise, and now Mom and Dad go walking together every morning."

David nodded and acknowledged he needed to exercise more often. "Sounds good. What about when winter sets in?"

"No problem," she said with a dismissive wave. "Dad already planned for it. He bought a matching set of exercise bikes and put them in Daniel's old bedroom. It's kind of cute: his-and-her bikes.

"Oh, there's been one good thing. Since Mom's accident, we've had many guests over to the house, and of course, Pete and Debra are the most frequent visitors. All of them have helped to lift Mom's spirits, and she really enjoys entertaining. As a bonus, their friends frequently bring food or invite us over for dinner. That's a little less time in the kitchen for me."

David chuckled. "I'm not much for working in the kitchen either."

"It's not so bad if you don't have to cook every meal," Amanda said. "Another thing – believe it or not, Daniel and I are on better terms, and his family's been over to the house more often. Also, we finally coaxed Mom to go with us to a hockey game. The Rangers lost, but it was still fun. Mom said she liked it, and I suspect she was just humoring us. Dad and I hope to see a few more games this season."

"That's nice. So, your folks are enjoying themselves as best as they can."

"Yeah. Halloween helped too. I thought after Mom's accident, they would have cancelled their annual party, but they threw it anyway. This time, they hired a caterer. You won't believe what Mom and Dad chose as their costumes."

David slightly shook his head.

"Indiana Jones and Marion Ravenwood, an injured version of Marion with her arm in a sling."

"From *Raiders of the Lost Ark*, right? So, what was your costume?"

"I didn't have one," Amanda said. "It was an older crowd, and I didn't want to stick around. I went over to Valerie's place, and her kids wanted to watch a very scary movie. So, Valerie rented *The Exorcist.*"

"I'm not into horror films. Is it really scary?"

"If you believe in Heaven and Hell and were raised Catholic, oh yeah," Amanda said as she raised her eyebrows. "It's probably the most frightening movie of all time. Think you can handle watching it with me, Big Boy? I've never seen a grown man completely freak out." She flashed a devilish grin.

David chuckled and raised his hands. "No, thanks!"

Despite the creepy look, David was pleased to see Amanda in a better mood. Perhaps her true personality was coming through. More than once during lunch, David had to remind himself Amanda was a client, and he did not date them. Nonetheless, he appreciated her company in more ways than one. After they finished eating, the conversation continued.

"Getting back to you and your family. Anything else interesting at home?" David asked.

Amanda's eyes widened. "Yeah! After I read Beverly's book on jury selection, Dad read it twice. Sorry, I forgot to bring it with me. Dad's been asking me many questions about lawyers and trials. He always supported my decision to become a lawyer, and he's more interested now for obvious reasons. He really wants to know what could happen during a trial, and I've been teaching him the rules of evidence."

David was astounded. "The rules of evidence? Really? I found them confusing the first time around and the second."

"Yeah, I know. It was the same for me, but Dad's a pretty sharp guy, and he's picking it up fast. I don't know if it was intentional, but it was a brilliant idea to show Dad the boxes of discovery. It made him realize the case wasn't going away. He hasn't kept asking the equivalent of 'are we there yet' over and over, right?"

"Nope. He asks questions, but not that one."

The check arrived, and Amanda reached into her purse.

"Don't even think about it," David said. "I don't make clients pay for meals with me."

She smirked. "At least not directly. We're paying your fees."

"*Touché*," he said with a grin. He then placed a credit card on the tray holding the bill.

Amanda laughed a little. "Hey, did my parents tell you the reason they hired your firm? Marc was a nephew of a good buddy, right?"

David was amused and anticipated the punch line for a joke. "Yeah. We checked it out, and it's not true. So, you know the real reason?"

Amanda laughed some more. "Uh-huh. Dad told me yesterday. He and Mom checked the phone book for defense attorneys with Italian last names, and D'Angelo must have been the first one they spotted."

David laughed as well and had difficulty stopping.

"I guess you're not mad at my folks?" Amanda asked.

"Gee, I wonder why you'd said that?" David chuckled. "Well, they could've hired a lot worse. I know some attorneys with Italian last names who are so dumb I'm surprised they passed the bar exam. No offense. I also know attorneys from other ethnic backgrounds who are complete morons."

Amanda smiled. "I didn't take offense, and I know some of those attorneys too. Maybe someone took their bar exams for them."

"Yeah, maybe. Anyway, about your case. I need to talk to you and your parents about a public relations strategy, and we need to discuss other matters alone. Can all of you stop by the office tomorrow afternoon at three?"

"Uh, sure. I'm off Mondays and Tuesdays. What public relations strategy?"

"Sooner or later, your case will be in the news, and we should set the agenda." David's mind stopped in its tracks. "Wait, what? What do you mean off Mondays and Tuesdays? You're working?"

"Oh yeah, I forgot to mention it. I've been working the lunch shift at a Greek restaurant not too far away from the house. The owner's another good buddy of my dad's, of course." Amanda smiled and rolled her eyes.

"How's that going?"

"Not too bad. I don't want to work in a restaurant forever, but it's better than sitting around doing nothing."

"Does the owner know about your situation?"

"Oh yeah, and he thinks it's good for business. According to him, lunchtime has been busier since I started."

David suspected the uptick in business had less to do with Amanda's criminal case and more to do with her being very attractive. He wanted to give her the compliment but didn't do so because he didn't want to run the risk of her feeling uncomfortable around him.

Chapter 20

Tuesday, November 17

As expected, the Morellis arrived early for their meeting, and they briefly chatted with Irene. David noticed the brace on Lorraine's wrist and a tray covered with aluminum foil in Paul's hands. Since he had not seen Paul and Lorraine in some time, he had forgotten the extreme difference in their sizes. Paul was about one foot taller than Lorraine and outweighed her by at least 120 pounds.

David went to Marc's office, where his law partner was staring at his computer screen. "Hey, the Morellis are here. I want to introduce you."

Once they reached the front desk, David said, "Paul, Lorraine, and Amanda, this is Marc."

"It's nice to meet you," Marc said. He could not take his eyes off the tray.

"Yes," Paul said, "it's nice to finally meet you."

"Likewise," added Lorraine.

Marc pointed to the tray in Paul's hands. "What'd you bring?"

Lorraine giggled. "Why don't we show you. Where can we set it down?"

David gestured toward the conference room. "Over there."

As Lorraine passed him, he noticed her lavender perfume.

Paul set the tray on the glass-top table and removed the aluminum foil.

"Cannoli!" Lorraine said. "There's plenty for everyone. I should have brought something sooner, but oh, I don't know why I didn't. Since we're coming anyway, I thought why not? Enjoy!"

Shells stuffed with ricotta cheese and dusted with powdered sugar lay before David and the others. He was not fond of any dessert containing cheese but tried one cannolo to be polite. Upon his first bite, his knees nearly buckled. The shell had a nice crunch, and the powdered sugar added sweetness. The ricotta had a smooth texture and was just sweet enough, complemented by hints of vanilla, lemon, and orange.

"Lorraine, this is spectacular!" he said.

Marc's closed eyes and the "mmm" coming from his mouth indicated he was impressed. Paul and Amanda had their mouths full, and both gave a thumbs-up. Irene's rapid consumption of one cannolo and then another reflected her approval.

Lorraine was beaming. "Thanks."

"You were able to make this with your banged-up wrist?" David asked.

"Oh sure. It was really nothing."

"Oh no, it's a lot more than nothing," Marc said. "This might be the best cannoli I ever had, and there are some excellent cooks in my family. It's too bad Bev took the day off and can't have any."

"Are you kidding?" David uttered. "With her super healthy diet, she wouldn't touch them."

Marc smiled and grabbed another cannolo. "True, true. Too bad for her, and more for the rest of us."

After the last piece had disappeared, Irene returned to her desk. Everyone else sat in the conference room, and David was ready to discuss more important matters.

"So, Paul. I heard you went to the doctor yesterday. How'd it go?"

Paul waved his right hand. "Fine, fine. Don't worry about it."

David saw Amanda shake her head, which her parents apparently did not notice. She mouthed, "Tell you later."

"All right. Let's talk about the case," David said. "Simpson's murder was in the news a little bit. Marc and I searched for any coverage of Amanda's arrest or indictment and found nothing. Amanda, I take it the police never did a perp walk."

"A perp walk?" Lorraine asked.

"Yeah, perp walk, Mom. It's when the police parade someone in front of the cameras right after an arrest. No, it didn't happen."

"Okay, good," David said. "Jacqueline Marshall doesn't like to cozy up to the media, but her boss, the district attorney, is another story. I'm a little surprised the DA's office never issued a press release. We're not sure what to make of that. Anyway, sooner or later, there'll be media coverage, and many people follow murder trials. Besides, Amanda's case is more interesting than one gang member killing another one."

David noticed Paul and Lorraine were paying close attention.

"This type of case sells newspapers and drives up TV ratings. So, I suggest we get Amanda's name and face out there, so that we can set the agenda. Any coverage should reach some potential jurors, which will work in our favor. During jury selection, they'll be asked if they have any prior knowledge about the case, including whether they heard about it from any TV show, the radio, *The New York Times*, whatever. Even if someone says no, he or she will still be on notice of Amanda's celebrity status, and celebrities receive more favorable treatment from juries. So, what do you think?"

Paul tilted his head and raised the left side of his mouth. "Have you done such a thing before?"

"To an extent, yes, but not the massive exposure I have in mind. I plan to contact many media outlets, and we'll see who's interested. We'll give as many interviews as possible, within reason, of course. Marc and I already have some contacts, and Beverly has a few more."

Paul nodded. "Uh-huh, uh-huh. What would you say?"

"More like what would Amanda say," David said. "We'd present her side of the story. She was sick and in bed when the murder happened. The police and the district attorney made a terrible mistake and went after the wrong person. I also want to provide Amanda's backstory, which means telling the public where she grew up, her family, that kind of thing. Her life will make a good human-interest story, and she'll become likeable in the eyes of potential jurors."

Paul tapped his right index finger on the table. "And you think this can help Amanda during a trial?"

"Absolutely."

Paul turned to his wife. "Honey, what do you think?"

Lorraine shrugged. "I guess so. I can smile and wave at a camera if I have to."

David nodded. "Paul, okay to proceed with a PR strategy?"

"Okay by me," he said.

"Amanda?"

She smiled. "Sure, why not?"

"Great!" David grimaced and snapped his fingers. "Oh yeah, there's one other thing I forgot to mention. Amanda, since you're attractive, some members of the media will play up that angle *a lot.* You're probably going to hear or read many comments about your appearance. Some will be favorable or rather innocuous, while others will be demeaning and sexist. Even if you try to ignore all the buzz, you won't be able to tune it out completely. Can you handle it?"

Amanda pursed her lips for a few moments while looking at the conference room table. She then raised her head. "I guess it's better to be viewed as a sex object than a cold-blooded killer. I'm still in. When do we get started?"

"Today. I'll start making phone calls, but first you and I have a few things to discuss."

Paul slapped the arm of his chair. "I guess that's the cue for Lorraine and me to leave."

"Oh sure," Lorraine added. "Next time, I'll bring another dessert."

"Please, do," Marc said. "If you can't, I can make the sacrifice and come to your house to eat them."

The Morellis laughed and waved goodbye. Once they departed, Amanda leaned toward David.

"Here's what's happening with Dad. A little while ago, he had a check-up, which revealed he has high blood pressure. His doctor ordered blood tests and an EKG, and yesterday he went back for the results. His heart is fine, which is great. However, he has high cholesterol, really high. Exercising helps, and he is supposed to take medication. Of course, with him, it's always 'Don't worry about it.' He'd like to ignore his doctor's instructions." Amanda tapped the table with her right index finger. "I'll make certain he takes his medication every day until it becomes routine for him. The Italian desserts don't help matters. Hopefully, the medication will work, and Dad doesn't have to take what he'd consider more drastic measures, such as eating healthier."

"I'm sure he'll be fine," David said.

While not mentioning it aloud, he was not pleased Paul had lied to him a second time. Lying about one's health was not the greatest sin in the world, but it gave David one more reason not to trust him.

"Now, for another matter… we need to have a trial prep discussion."

Amanda's pleasant demeanor disappeared. "I've been trying not to think about it. When I do, I get a little sick to my stomach. Is it really going to happen?"

"It certainly looks that way," David said, "and I'm confident the jury will rule in your favor."

Amanda sighed. "Yeah. Trial prep… okay. I know you talked to Valerie about that email and what we said at the restaurant. I guess we both have a sick sense of humor. We were only blowing off steam."

"Yeah, I know," David said. "I want to cover a few other things. Let's start with the gun. You told the police you didn't own a gun, but they found one in your apartment. How do you explain that?"

Amanda looked down and exhaled through her nose. "At the time they asked me, I had forgotten about it." She looked at David in the eyes. "Really, I did. When the police executed the search warrant, they never mentioned finding it. I didn't realize I had it until I was packing up to move back home with Mom and Dad. I sold it to a gun store, and I think I still have the receipt if you need it."

"How'd you end up with the gun in the first place?" Marc asked.

Amanda scoffed. "My crazy ex-husband gave it to me after we broke up about… five years ago." She shook her head. "What a mess it was. My ex came over to my place shortly after we separated, and he gave it to me. He said I needed it for protection. I didn't need it, and the gun wasn't much of anything. It was a .22 semi-automatic: a tiny little thing. If I wanted a gun for protection, I would've bought a larger-caliber revolver or a shotgun. I just took the .22 to avoid another argument and threw it in the back of my closet. I guess I forgot about it."

David thought Amanda gave a credible explanation. "Why didn't you tell me about the pistol?"

She shrugged. "I thought it didn't matter because it wasn't the murder weapon."

"Okay. When you were a kid, you learned how to fire a variety of guns, right?" David asked.

"Yeah," she said with a confused look. "What's your point?"

"Do you still go shooting?"

Amanda frowned and rolled her eyes. "You've got to be kidding. I really hate guns and told the police that. Isn't it in one of their reports? I haven't fired a gun in over ten, maybe fifteen years."

"Do you still keep in touch with your ex?" Marc asked.

"No way. His presence only brings up bad memories, such as the times when he was completely neurotic. Would you believe he was a stockbroker? He probably had a complete meltdown when the market went into panic mode last year."

David nodded. "I'm sure the same thing happened to many other stockbrokers. On to the next topic. According to one detective's report, you said you never went into Simpson's office, but they found your thumbprint on his desk."

Amanda appeared stunned. "What? That's not right. I don't remember exactly what I told the police, but I never would have said that. I was assigned to Bennington, you know, the pharmaceutical company, which meant I had to work with Simpson. Sometimes I spoke to him in his office, and when I did, I made certain the door was always open. Other times, I dropped off paperwork early in the morning, before he arrived, so there would be one less opportunity for him to make a crude comment."

"Okay. Sounds reasonable," David said. "How did the police match your fingerprint to the one found in his office? Did you have a prior arrest?"

"No. The police asked several of us at the firm for our fingerprints. I didn't see the harm, and they brought a fingerprint kit."

Even though David found the last comment disturbing, he maintained a poker face. Meanwhile, Marc's astonishment was written on his face.

"Anything else?" Amanda asked.

"A few things," David said. "The police asked the attorneys and the staff their respective opinions of Simpson. Many comments were rather unkind, and apparently, you said, 'He wasn't so bad.' Is that true?"

Amanda looked at the table for about five seconds. "Not sure. I don't remember exactly what I said… it could be right. He was a really awful person, but he wasn't so bad that I thought someone should've killed him."

"And you told someone at the EEOC that Simpson was better off dead."

Amanda sighed. "Yeah, I said it. I was pretty mad and didn't want to deal with him anymore." She grimaced. "All of this doesn't look good, does it?"

"Not on the surface," Marc said. "However, it doesn't mean you shot Simpson twice in the head. A trial won't be fun, but I really like our chances."

"*Our* chances?" Amanda asserted. "You're not the one on trial. Care to switch places? You'll probably look fabulous in prison stripes."

Marc grinned and turned towards David. "I like this one. Can we keep her? You know, make her a partner?"

"Cute," David said.

"Anything else?" Amanda asked.

"Nothing from me," David said. "Marc?"

"More cannoli, please."

Amanda smirked. "I know! They're delicious. I have to stop Mom from making them all the time, or I'll blow up like a balloon."

Chapter 21

Wednesday, November 18

It had been another long day in the office. David was exhausted and wanted nothing more than to eat leftovers and go to bed. Nevertheless, he sat in the conference room with Marc and Bev. Freddie had big news and refused to divulge it over the phone.

"He didn't give any indication what's going on?" Marc asked.

"No, sorry," David said anxiously.

"Seems a little out of character. When was the last time Freddie was like this?"

David shrugged his shoulders.

"Never," Bev said. "Both of you need to be a little patient. He'll be here soon enough."

Minutes later, Freddie arrived with a serious expression, more serious than David had ever seen on him. He had no smile and did not give his usual, friendly acknowledgment. Instead, he closed the conference room door.

"Just in case Irene or some client shows up," he said.

Although Bev gestured for him to sit, he remained standing.

"Sorry about getting together so late in the day," Freddie said. "Remember when I mentioned my former partner, Mitch Stanton? He was working his contacts at FBI, and they still won't give him anything about a possible investigation related to Paul. It's not surprising because either they have nothing or can't disclose for obvious reasons."

Freddie paused and wiped his forehead. David anxiously rubbed his right foot against a leg of the conference room table.

"I take it Mitch found something else," Bev said calmly.

"Not exactly but close enough. One of his contacts, he wouldn't say which one, let something slip that was not FBI-related. About thirty-five or forty years ago, the police in Miami interviewed Paul in connection with the accidental death of a fellow New Yorker."

"Was the deceased a mafioso?" Bev asked with a raised eyebrow.

"Possibly but never confirmed," Freddie said.

"Holy shit!" Marc said.

David rubbed his right hand over his forehead, attempting to process what he had just heard.

"Did you get the name of the deceased or the date of death?" Bev asked.

Freddie shook his head. "Mitch said his contact didn't tell him anything else, and I don't have anyone in Miami. I can fly down there and maybe poke around. Any records from that far back are probably not on a computer. That means there's probably nothing logged under Paul's name, and searching records over a five-year span might be a complete waste of time." He rubbed the back of his head. "Maybe I can find a retired detective who was at the scene, but it'll be tough."

"Yeah, I get it," David said. "No chance we can get even a portion of the FBI's file and take it from there?"

"No," Bev said. "I tried to do the same a few years ago, and the Bureau told me to pound sand."

Marc slammed into his chair's backrest and threw up his hands. "That's just great, terrific! The accidental death might not have been an accident, and Paul might've been involved. Marshall could be sitting on this info, and she's under no obligation to disclose."

"Correct," Bev said.

"Yeah, you got that right," Freddie said. "It's a long shot in finding something, but you never know. Should I get down there and do some poking around?"

The room fell silent for a few moments.

"No," David said, "let's try another route first. I already have a meeting scheduled with Paul for tomorrow, and I'll bring it up."

Chapter 22

Thursday, November 19

David arrived at the Morelli residence in Bensonhurst, Brooklyn. Despite the cool, brisk weather, he took a minute to view the neighborhood, consisting mostly of rows of houses with the same façades and color scheme. The Morelli home was a detached, two-story, single-family residence. It was long and narrow, and driveways ran on both sides. The home's exterior had a hodgepodge of architectural styles. Bricks covered the first story, and a brick chimney rose above the left side. A bay window jutted out to the left of the front door and clashed with the brick. The second story's exterior was made of gray horizontal boards, which didn't match anything else.

David spotted a low, white metal fence, and when he opened the corresponding white metal gate, it made a faint squeak. To the left of the walkway laid faded red brick surrounding a bare area, which was probably filled with flowers during the spring and summer. He approached the white front door and rang the doorbell.

About thirty seconds later, Paul opened it and held out his right arm. "David!" he said with a wide smile. "Please come in."

"Thanks."

"We'll talk at the kitchen table."

The big man escorted David through the living room, where the tan carpet showed years of wear and tear. The room also featured aging and overstuffed furniture, and the wallpaper appeared faded. If plenty of natural light didn't fill the room, its ambience would have been too depressing. Paul and Lorraine's wedding photo sat inside an elegant silver frame on a small table next to the couch. David also noticed many family photos on the walls, including those depicting Amanda and her brother over the years from early childhood to various graduations.

A round table and four metal chairs with a yellow flower pattern on the seat cushions sat next to the kitchen. Cheap plastic with more flowers pretended to be a tablecloth. David took a seat opposite Paul and wished they would have sat at the dining-room table. Given its apparent quality, David suspected it had been imported from Italy, and its top shined after a recent polishing. A modest chandelier hung above the table, and not a speck of dust was on it. In fact, everything within his field of vision appeared clean and tidy.

The dated kitchen and its cabinets needed an extra coat of paint. The dishwasher was new, but the avocado-green oven featured a mechanical clock, not a digital one. Even though David's legal fees were reasonable, he felt guilty over taking money that could have been used to remodel the house and buy new appliances and furniture.

"What do you think of the place?" Paul asked.

David wanted to be positive and still honest. "It looks like Lorraine keeps up the house as well as she makes Italian desserts."

Paul smiled. "Thanks. It's mostly Lorraine, but I help a little. Amanda left for work, and Lorraine went out shopping with Debra, which means we're free to talk."

"Sounds good."

On previous occasions, David hadn't read Paul's body language to determine whether he was telling the truth. This time, he made a point to be more observant. He also tried to be as diplomatic as possible.

"We need to discuss some things that came up during the police investigation, okay? I believe you told a detective or two you had owned a .38-caliber handgun."

Paul appeared at ease and leaned back in his chair. "Oh sure, sure. I owned a Smith & Wesson, a snub-nose .38. I bought it for protection. Have you ever fired one?"

"Sorry, no. According to the police, you got rid of it some time ago. Is that right?"

"Oh yeah, sure, sure. Amanda bugged her mother and me to get it out of the house for the longest time. I don't know why she worried about it so much. I finally gave in and got rid of it… when was that?" Paul gazed at the ceiling as if it would help him remember. "Got rid of it three or four years ago."

"Did you sell it or give it away? Did you throw it away?"

Paul gazed at the ceiling again. "Huh… what happened?" He then looked at David. "I think I gave it to a good buddy who wanted it as a present for a nephew or a cousin. I'm not sure."

"Do you remember which buddy got the gun?"

Paul smirked. "No, not really. I've got a lot of good buddies."

Although David still didn't trust Paul, his posture and body language gave no hint of deception.

"Do you know why I'm asking about the gun?"

The big man nodded while continuing to lean back in his chair. "Oh sure, sure. The murder weapon was a .38. It's a coincidence but not much of one. There are probably thousands of them in the city, even more in the state."

David needed to move onto another topic but was uneasy about it.

Perhaps Paul noticed it. "Anything else?" he asked. "You can ask me anything. This is all about giving Amanda the best defense possible, right?"

David gave a half-smile. "Yes, it is. The police asked you about another matter, which we need to discuss."

The big man leaned forward and rested his arms on the table. "Yeah, I know what you're talking about. The police asked about the mob, right? They wanted to know if I knew any wise guys or ever worked for them."

"So, you're not offended about my asking?"

Paul chuckled and gave a dismissive wave. "No, no. I knew you were going to get around to it, eventually. Like I told the police, I was a union rep, and I dealt with all kinds of people. I knew quite a few wise guys, especially in the old days. I knew they took their cut, even though I was never part of that. Hey, everyone knew about it. Just because I knew some of them doesn't mean I was in bed with them."

He leaned back again. "You know, back in the day, life was better and less complicated. Suppose one of the families protected a construction site. Nothing unusual about it. The building owner and the construction company paid protection money. That might sound bad, but in return, *nobody* dared to touch the job site." He chuckled. "It would've been suicide. Do you know what I'm talking about?"

"Yes, I've heard."

"Now, it's a lot different," Paul said more negatively as he waved his arms in the air. "Now, an owner pays a private security company to protect a job site. The guards are supposed to watch the area when the construction crew isn't around, but who knows when the graveyard shift will be absent or asleep on the job? Thieves take whatever they want, lumber, pipes, copper wire. Don't forget drug addicts are looking for anything to steal and sell, and the guards could be crooks too. Many of them are ex-cons who have no decency, no honor." He shook his head in obvious disgust.

"I guess so," David said, simply to placate him. "So, if you weren't part of the mob, why does the FBI have a file on you?"

Paul chuckled. "Why does that not surprise me? Have you seen it?"

"No, I haven't. The FBI didn't turn over a copy to NYPD or the district attorney's office. Sometimes, the Feds don't work and play well with others. Back to my question. Any idea why they have a file on you?"

Paul pouted and shook his head. "Not really. Like I said, I knew some wise guys, and maybe the Feds did surveillance. You know, they targeted some guy, and I'm in the same photo. It could have happened a few times, and they opened a file on me. No big deal. Hey, wouldn't it be fun to get a look at my file, right?"

"Of course." David was hesitant to ask his next line of questions but knew he had no choice. "How well did you know the wise guys?"

"Some better than others. You know, I'd see them from time to time."

"What about more recently?"

"Oh, sure," Paul said with a smile. "You're probably too young to remember when the Feds went after the Five Families back in the day. They got a bunch of convictions, but they didn't get rid of the mafia altogether. They're still out there, just not as powerful."

"Okay. Did Amanda ever tell you about Simpson's personality?"

"Of course, Amanda and I are really close, and…" Paul's genial demeanor turned more serious. "You want to know if I told any wise guy about him."

"Well, yeah," David said sheepishly. "Sorry about that."

Paul held up his right hand with the palm facing out. "Don't worry about it. You've gotta do what you've gotta do." He put his hand down. "Amanda shared her feelings about Simpson with me in confidence, and I never told anyone, not even our good friends and neighbors. No wise guy did me a favor by whacking him. I didn't like the guy, but I never wanted him dead."

"Okay."

David considered what he had just seen and heard. Paul answered without hesitation and was forthright. He didn't sell his answers too much or too hard, as if he had added window dressing to cover a lie.

"Anything else?" Paul asked without a hint of anger or bitterness.

David squirmed in his chair and tried not to show his apprehension. "Sorry, but there is one other matter that we need to discuss. Have you ever been to Miami?"

Paul blinked and sat straight in his chair. "I don't know what this has to do with Amanda's case, but sure, Lorraine and I went there a few times. What's the big deal?"

"Well, were you ever in Miami a long time ago, when someone died?"

Paul chuckled again. "People die in Florida all the time. What are you getting at?"

"Maybe the police interviewed you about someone's death, and they said he–"

Paul almost jumped out of his chair. "Oh yeah, I remember that now," he said excitedly. "Lorraine and me were on vacation and stayed at this hotel where some guy died."

David did his best to remain calm, even though Paul's last answer was like a massive shot of adrenaline. "What happened?"

"Not sure," he said more calmly. "We didn't see what happened, and we didn't get a good look at the dead guy. I hung around with everyone else until the cops arrived. I think they saw me first and asked about it. I probably told them I didn't see anything and repeated what other people were saying. That was it."

"Uh-huh. What did the other people say?"

"The guy jumped from one of the higher floors and landed next to the pool."

"Did anyone push him?"

Paul shook his head. "I don't think so."

"Did the police interview Lorraine?"

"I doubt it," Paul said. "She never liked anything to do with dead bodies. She even asked for closed casket funerals when her parents died. She went up to our room as soon as we heard what happened and stayed there until it was all over."

"Did you know the name of the deceased?"

"No."

"Do you remember when it happened?"

Paul shrugged. "You mean the date? No, not really. I'm surprised I remember any of it. How'd you find out?"

"We have to do backgrounds on everyone involved in Amanda's case, and it just came up. No big deal."

Now it's not, David thought.

"Anything else? I got all day for you."

"No, that's it. We might have to chat again at a later date."

"Fine, fine." Paul gave a wide smile and smacked the table. "Hey, it's about lunchtime. How about Santorini? That's the Greek place where Amanda works. The food's excellent, and if I see anyone I know, I'll introduce you."

"Sounds good."

"Santorini's only a few blocks away. Let's walk."

* * *

Normally, David didn't mind travelling on foot. However, a stiff breeze blew as he and Paul crossed two larger streets. Between the wind and the cool temperature, David was miserable, while Paul appeared unfazed.

They arrived at a small and nicely furnished restaurant with white tablecloths. Views of various Greek vacation spots hung from the walls, and the aromas of olive oil, garlic, and onions wafted from the kitchen. Elderly customers filled most tables, which made sense because it was the middle of the week, and Santorini was in a mostly residential area.

A large man with thick, wavy gray hair spotted Paul and greeted him with open arms. "Paul!"

"Hey, Nico! How's it going?"

They acted as if they had not seen each other in years, though David suspected only a few days had passed.

Nico chuckled. "Business is good, really good, thanks in part to your daughter."

"Great!" Paul said. "Speaking of my daughter, this is her defense attorney, David Lee."

Nico shook David's hand forcefully. "Oh, yes. I've heard about you. Starting a media blitz, huh? Why don't you hold a press conference or do some interviews here, huh? Huh? It'd be good for business!"

David was not certain how to respond to the gregarious man, so he merely smiled. "Uh-huh."

Nico clapped his hands once and rubbed them together. "Okay! Paul, I have a very nice table for you."

"Fine, fine. First, I want to say hello to a few familiar faces and to my daughter." He looked to his left. "Oh, there she is."

Amanda exited the kitchen with two plates of food and wore the standard attire for the staff: a white top and black pants. Even though she sported a casual look with little makeup and a ponytail, David thought she looked stunning. Amanda could have dressed up for a walk on a red carpet, and he would not have been more impressed. She appeared to be enjoying herself, and her people skills were on full display. With her personality, a pleasant atmosphere, and apparently excellent food, all the patrons were happy.

Paul took David around and greeted those he recognized, which was at least one person at every table. As expected, he was engaging and introduced David. Paul occasionally made a comment such as, "Hey, give this one your business card. He's a troublemaker, and his luck's about to run out." Laughter followed such remarks.

Once they took their seats, David realized they were sitting at one of Amanda's tables. She chatted with them before handing out the menus, and there was something about the glint in her eye that caused David to wonder if she was flirting with him in front of her father. He told himself it was wishful thinking and needed to focus on his priorities. After all, she was a client, not a potential date. Nevertheless, during lunch, he glanced in Amanda's direction multiple times and noticed all the customers treated her well.

"Hey, Paul. Has Amanda had any problems with a customer?"

Paul chuckled. "Are you kidding me? No way! If someone did that, he'd have to answer to me, or worse, he'd have to answer to Nico Junior."

"Nico Junior?"

"That's right. He's not here right now, and he usually works in the back," Paul said as he pointed his thumb over his shoulder, "while his father works the front of the house. If he were here, you wouldn't miss him. He's a really big guy, bigger than his father or me. He's really great with the staff and the customers, but don't get on his bad side."

Paul leaned forward. "I heard about one jerk who gave a waitress a hard time," he said in a quieter voice. "Nico Junior wasn't working that night, but he and his family live about a block away. Somebody called him, and he got over here in a big hurry. He remained calm and politely asked the guy to step outside. What happened next?" Paul held up his hands. "Nobody told me. All I know is the jerk never came back. You know, they have a saying here. 'If anybody acts up, don't call the police. Call Nico Junior.'"

* * *

Later that day, David mulled over his recent conversations with Paul, and both raised red flags. He was nostalgic for the old days, when the mafia had freer rein in the city. Despite being a defense attorney, David was not a fan of organized crime and didn't buy into its hype and supposed glamour. On top of that, Paul had no issue with taking the law into one's own hands.

David considered whether Paul could have been involved in Simpson's murder. The physical evidence pointed to a shorter person as the shooter, and Paul was too tall. He could have shot Simpson from a sitting position, but as Freddie had said, that scenario was unlikely and would have been too awkward. Paul could have hired a contract killer, but the police had subpoenaed his bank records and found no suspicious withdrawals. Even so, David refused to rule out Paul as being part of a conspiracy to murder Simpson, although he acknowledged there was not a shred of evidence to support such a theory. On the other hand, with each passing day, David was more convinced Amanda was innocent.

Chapter 23

Monday, November 23

David arrived in the office shortly before 9:30 because he had a meeting with Marc and Bev regarding the Morelli case. They intended to discuss where they stood on the evidence and what further steps they should take.

While Irene was normally at her desk by 8:30, David saw no evidence of her presence. She had not draped her jacket on her chair instead of hanging it in the closet, as he had repeatedly asked. Her coffee cup was not sitting on her desk, and her usual coaster was missing. David didn't ask Marc about Irene's whereabouts and hoped she had taken the day off. Even after his law partner had returned to work, she had continued to get on his nerves, and he was uncertain how much longer he could tolerate her rotten attitude towards him.

The local media had begun to report on Amanda, largely as David had fed information to them. In addition to providing quotes for the print media, David and Amanda had made appearances on the talk show circuit. He first tested the waters on a horrible program with low ratings. To his delight, Amanda came across as comfortable, and perhaps more importantly, likeable in front of the cameras. She also repeated the mantra provided to every media outlet: she was sick and in bed at the time of the murder. Afterwards, David arranged for more television interviews on better shows with larger audiences.

For many criminal cases, a certain catchphrase or nickname circulated, but from what David had read, the media had not yet settled on a moniker. One reporter had used the term, "*La Femme Fatale*," which he did not appreciate, as it implied Amanda was guilty.

Many media outlets had made comments about Amanda's appearance, and a few had called her "The Bensonhurst Babe." David acknowledged the nickname was catchy and would probably stick. While it was rather sexist, he reasoned it was better than other nicknames referring to violence or murder.

One commentator opined J. Robert Simpson's murder was a victory for feminism. She discussed how women had suffered and claimed sometimes they needed to resort to violence to stop the oppression. David believed such action was acceptable in only the most extreme circumstances. A woman could respond to sexual harassment in other, less violent ways, including suing the pants off the offender.

Once Bev arrived in the office, David led her and Marc to the conference room.

Marc took a seat at the glass-top table with a latte in his right hand. "Okay. Where do we start?"

David passed a sheet of paper to each colleague. "I thought I should hand out an outline to provide some structure to the meeting." As he turned towards Bev, he added, "A wise sage once suggested it to me. The first item is Amanda's statements to the police. I don't see how we can get them excluded."

Bev put a check next to the first line on the list. "We could file one motion after another, and it wouldn't make a difference. Morelli gave consensual interviews."

"Agreed," Marc said and shook his head. "Would someone explain to me again why she did that?"

"Never mind," David said. "We can't travel back in time and stop her from talking. The next item is Amanda's comments to an EEOC employee, which included 'Simpson would be better off dead.'"

Marc groaned. "Another bad decision. It's really damaging but it's fair game because she gave a voluntary statement."

"Correct," David said with a half-frown. "Then there's fingerprint evidence: Amanda's thumbprint on Simpson's desk and the exemplars she provided to the police. They're clearly admissible."

"Agreed," Bev said as she checked off another item.

"Yeah," Marc said. "I can't remember a judge ever excluding prints found at a crime scene or an exemplar." He was about to take a sip of his latte but then paused. "What about Bonnie Parker?"

David smiled. "She's further down the list. We don't know the real identity of the tall blonde woman and have no leads. The authorities don't know her identity either, which might work to our advantage.

"Now, getting back to the list in order," David said with a smirk.

Marc chuckled.

"The next item is the blood transfer in Amanda's office."

Marc's jovial mood devolved into a groan. "Please, don't remind about this. We can't claim someone planted the takeout box in Amanda's office. We also can't argue the police planted the blood on the box, because they didn't focus on her until later. And we've got nothing on the detective who took the box, right?"

"No, or not yet," David said. "Freddie's still digging into the backgrounds of all the detectives and the uniformed officers who worked on the case."

"Let's not forget our lab confirmed the DNA on the box was Simpson's," Bev said.

Marc held up his hands. "I know, I know. It's a big problem."

"Don't get too overwrought," Bev said. "The prosecution still can't prove Amanda was on the tenth floor that night. Someone else could have entered her office for whatever reason."

"Correct," David said. "So, where do we stand? Do we go to trial or start plea negotiations?"

"Go to trial," Bev said without hesitation.

"Marc?" David asked.

He sighed. "I don't know. Besides looking into the cops' backgrounds, I'd like to investigate some more. Into what? Beats me. I guess I choose go to trial."

"So do I. Marshall only has circumstantial evidence, and it's not enough for a conviction. Since that's settled, the next item is pre-trial motions."

"Mine," Marc said. "I'll draft a motion to exclude the autopsy photos and the more graphic images of the murder scene. They're too shocking for the jury and too prejudicial to the defense."

"We should attempt to exclude the medical examiner's report in its entirety," Bev added.

"What?" Marc said. "It always gets presented to the jury."

Bev raised an eyebrow. "Think a little more creatively. The forensics expert can testify how Simpson was killed, which means the autopsy report and corresponding testimony won't be necessary. The medical examiner usually testifies about the estimated time of death, which we're not contesting. We could stipulate to it or allow another witness to inform the jury."

David was impressed. "If the medical examiner and his report are excluded, the jury might focus less on Simpson's death, which could help us."

"Exactly," Bev said.

Marc smacked the table. "Okay! I'll write it up. Beverly, could you review the first draft?"

"My pleasure," she said stoically.

"That gives me another idea," Marc said. "Perhaps we can do something similar with the DNA and keep another expert off the stand."

David smirked again. "Feeling better about the case? The next topic is any other motions."

"I've given it some thought," Marc said. "We could draft some of the usual motions filed by defense attorneys, but what's the point? Judge Perkins won't grant them."

"Agreed," Bev said.

"I know filing frivolous motions irritates Perkins to no end," David said, "and I'd rather remain in good standing with him. If there's a close call for a ruling, any little bit might help. Even though he tries to remain neutral and objective, his emotions could sway him one way or another."

"True," Bev said. "I'm fairly certain I know the answer to my next question, but you two know Jacqueline Marshall better than I do. Do you believe she'd hide anything?"

David shook his head slightly. "She was a straight shooter during my prior cases against her. Marc?"

"That was her reputation in the office. NYPD could have held something back, but I doubt it. Nothing gets by her."

Marc held out his hands. "So, here's where we are. We're ready to prep our witness and prepare for Marshall's cross-examination. We'll need to make copies of our exhibits, which Irene can take care of and won't take much time. We can be ready in about a month, tops. However, the Speedy Trial Act gives the DA six months to prepare, which means no trial until March. Are we just supposed to do nothing but spin our wheels for a while?"

"Not necessarily," Bev said with another raised eyebrow. "You should've done your homework on Judge Perkins, who's a stickler for the rules, but not all of them. The glaring exception is the Speedy Trial Act. In his opinion, the prosecution should be ready for trial immediately after the case is indicted. It might not take much of a push to force an earlier trial date."

"Nice!" David said with a wide smile. "I'll let a few reporters know that during the next hearing, we'll announce we're ready for trial. Marshall doesn't care about her public image, but the DA does. He'd look foolish if we say we're ready, and Marshall says she isn't."

Marc chuckled while Bev remained expressionless.

David continued with his train of thought. "If we start preparing for trial now, we'll probably give ourselves a little more time than Marshall. Given most defense attorneys drag things out, she probably hasn't switched gears and isn't in full trial mode yet. With less time, she might make a mistake during her preparation. It's unlikely, but it could happen. Anyone mind putting in extra hours around the holidays?"

Marc and Bev shook their heads.

"Good. We also need to consider the rest of our caseload. Marc?"

"It's not a problem. I can handle everything else while you and Beverly work on Morelli. If necessary, I'll ask to continue a hearing or two. If some other defendant wants to go to trial, I can stall the case for a while."

David nodded. "Okay. I'll still handle the sentencing hearing for Morales. What about the indigent defendants? I suggest we inform the federal and local courts we can't accept any more of them for a few months. Marc, are you okay with that?"

"Yup."

"Okay. Getting back to *The People versus Morelli*," David said, "once we get Amanda's approval to go to trial and to push for an early trial date, which I'm sure she'll give, we're officially going into trial mode. Her father wanted a quick resolution and might just get it. We'll ask Amanda, Valerie, and maybe Bill Saxer about other Thorton refugees who might make good defense witnesses."

Marc raised his hand. "Could you also ask Lorraine to bring us more desserts?"

Chapter 24

Friday, December 4

David had an unpleasant visit with Raul Morales, the indigent defendant housed in a federal jail, and on his journey back, the subway train experienced a mechanical problem between stations and didn't move for over twenty minutes, so he was in a foul mood when he arrived at his law office.

From her desk, Irene tilted her head down and bore her eyes into him. David had the clear impression she disapproved of his late arrival but did not inquire. If he did, he figured his rotten day could turn even worse. After working in the office for a couple of hours, he left for lunch, and when he returned, he headed straight to Marc's office.

"Hey, Davey. I'm almost at full strength right now. Are you ready to get your butt kicked in Nerf basketball?"

David chuckled. "Maybe. You might be getting better, but the Julius Caesar look must go. Your bangs look ridiculous."

Marc smirked. "Thanks, and I love you too. Is that why you came to my office, to criticize my haircut?"

"No, not really. It's something else. Do you want to attend a wedding?"

Marc feigned surprise and put his right hand to his chest. "Oh wow! Are you proposing? I didn't know you loved me that much. Can you wait? Divorcing Steph will take a long time and get really messy."

David chuckled again. "Hey, sorry to spoil your hopes and dreams, but I'm not proposing. I just had lunch with my sister, and we talked about her wedding."

"And?"

"Courtney and Chris want something simple and small in June, and they wanted to pay for it. As you know, in Chinese culture, the groom's side pays, but I guess my parents are more Americanized than I'd thought because they want to pay for it, and they're going all out. Both sides will invite a ton of people. Now, getting back to my question. Would you and Steph like to come to the wedding? I need at least two familiar faces in attendance."

"Sure, and you want me to be there so you can engage in pleasant conversation."

David tilted his head. "No, that's why I'm inviting Steph, and you'll just be… extra."

Marc smirked again. "I'm sure we have no plans for June. By the way, while you were having lunch, Bill Saxer called. He said Marshall wants to interview him next week, and he asked me what he should do."

David frowned and shook his head. "He's a law professor and was a partner in a law firm, now he wants to know what to do? Give me a break. What did you tell him?"

"Same thing you would've, it's up to him. I told him if he talks to her, that's fine. Tell the truth, don't leave anything out, and then tell us what you told her."

"Did he give you any more details about his conversation with her?"

"Nope. Maybe there weren't any."

David mulled over what he had heard while staring at a wall. "Yeah, maybe. Perhaps Marshall has gone into trial mode already, and she intends to call Saxer as a witness. We've talked with a few potential witnesses, but I didn't tell them about our big announcement during the next hearing."

"Neither did I. I'm sure Bev didn't, and we're keeping Irene in the dark."

David was lost in thought. "Yeah… right… probably doesn't matter. I'd still want to know what's happening at the DA's office. Got any spies you can call?"

"I left on good terms, and I still have friends over there. However, I doubt they'll tell me anything because I went to the dark side," Marc said.

"Suppose so. Have you had any luck setting up an interview with Old Man Thorton?"

Marc exhaled. "I'm still trying because he's hard to reach. Someone will probably have to interview him at his place. Want me to do it?"

"No. I should talk to him because, if we have to put him on the stand, he'll be my witness."

Chapter 25

Monday, December 14

During the past few weeks, the Law Offices of D'Angelo and Lee had been a hectic place. Marc had been dealing with most of the firm's caseload, while David and Bev had prepared for the Morelli trial, which included interviewing potential defense witnesses. They even brought in Valerie Fernandez to take part in a mock session. David questioned her on direct examination, and Bev played the role of Jacqueline Marshall and grilled her on cross-examination. Despite Bev's pretend assault on her character and credibility, Valerie never lost her composure. Just in case Marshall's co-counsel questioned her, Marc played that role, and he was intentionally too forceful and aggressive. Nevertheless, she remained cool as a cucumber.

Even though practice was no substitute for testimony in court, David believed Valerie would make an excellent witness. She could testify at length about Amanda's character, explain away the "Let's kill him" email, and discuss what transpired the following evening at the restaurant, when she and Amanda joked about killing Big Bobby.

David had usually asked witnesses to be themselves on the stand, but Valerie had referred to Simpson in harsh and vulgar terms. David had repeatedly reminded her not to swear on the stand, but even if Valerie let a curse word slip out, he believed her testimony would come across as natural and credible.

On Monday morning, David and Amanda arrived in court for another status conference with Judge Perkins. Amanda's parents and their good friends, Pete and Debra, sat in the first row behind the defense's table, while the elderly court watchers and the media filled the gallery's back half. Given the judge's quiet rule, David only heard murmurs in the back instead of the usual buzz before the start of a high-profile hearing. Meanwhile, microphone stands waited on the courthouse steps, ready for a press conference.

Prior to the hearing, various media outlets had discussed Amanda's case, and overall, the coverage was favorable to her. Most commentators were calling her "The Bensonhurst Babe" now and, in response, the district attorney had launched his own media campaign and had sat for interviews. David noticed Jacqueline Marshall's name rarely appeared in the news, which was not surprising, as she did not crave attention and was not fond of reporters. Nevertheless, Marshall caught his attention by changing her hairstyle again, back to a short Afro.

Last week, an unnamed source – none other than David himself – had told a handful of reporters that the defense would announce it was ready for trial, which would be an indirect message to the prosecution to force an early trial date.

As usual, Judge Perkins took the bench at the scheduled time. His facial expression and body language gave no sign the larger than normal number of court observers made any impact on him.

"The defense filed a motion *in limine* to exclude some of the crime scene photos and all those taken during the autopsy," Perkins said at the outset. "I've read your response, Ms. Marshall. Do you have any further comments?"

"Yes, Your Honor," Marshall said. She stood straight with her clasped hands behind her back. "It's customary to present photos to the jury to demonstrate how the victim died. Relevant case law clearly indicates such photos aren't too inflammatory or prejudicial."

Perkins had no reaction, and his eyes shifted towards the defense table.

"Nobody's disputing the deceased was shot twice in the head," David said. "We don't need one extremely graphic photo after another to drive the point home. As stated in the defendant's motion, a few crime scene photos would be sufficient."

The judge cleared his throat. "The defense's motion regarding the more graphic photographs of the crime scene and the autopsy is granted."

"Your Honor," David interjected. "We also moved to exclude the medical examiner's testimony and his corresponding report."

A vein on the side of Perkins' neck bulged while the muscles in his face became tense. "Mr. Lee," he growled, "the prosecution should be allowed to establish the approximate time of death."

"That's true, Your Honor, but in this case, there's no dispute. The defense will stipulate as to the estimated time of death, as stated in the examiner's report. In the alternative, a crime scene investigator may testify about it without objection."

Perkins pivoted to the right, while his neck vein and facial muscles returned to their normal state. He then turned his gaze toward Marshall and did not need to say another word.

"That's fine, Your Honor," she said.

"Very well. Does the defense anticipate filing any more motions?"

"No, Your Honor." David paused for dramatic effect. "And we're ready for trial."

Perkins remained expressionless. Perhaps the announcement didn't catch him off guard because he had read a news article quoting the unnamed source. "Ms. Marshall?"

Marshall tilted her head down, and her eyes drifted toward her forehead. David had seen this body language beforehand and knew it meant she was upset.

"Your Honor, the People are ready. However, I'd like to note the holidays are approaching and–"

"Yes, I'm fully aware. If we start the trial before the first of the year, we'll have difficulty seating a jury. Trial is scheduled for January 4, 2010."

"I'm sorry, Your Honor," David said. "I have a sentencing hearing in federal court that morning."

Without skipping a beat, Perkins proclaimed, "Trial is scheduled for January 11, 2010. Both parties shall follow the Court's standing orders regarding any further motions, exhibits, witness lists, and jury instructions. Given the expected length of trial, we'll seat four alternate jurors. Anything else from either party?"

"Nothing else," Marshall replied.

"No, Your Honor," David said. He chuckled to himself because four alternates were usually seated for a long trial, and he knew it would be a shorter one. David began to gather his paperwork, eager to bolt outside and step in front of the microphones on the courthouse steps.

Judge Perkins didn't rise from his chair, however. Instead, he examined all those in attendance, one at a time, which made David feel uneasy. After about twenty seconds of silence, the judge gave his final orders for the day.

"Everyone in this courtroom needs to listen very carefully. The Court acknowledges members of the fourth estate are present, and the parties have already been trying their cases before the public. It… stops… today. From this moment until the end of trial, a gag order is imposed upon the district attorney's office, defense counsel, all potential witnesses for both sides, the defendant, and her family members. There are no exceptions."

Perkins leaned forward, and the courtroom was so quiet that a faint squeak from his chair was like an eagle's screech.

"If anyone is foolish enough to violate the gag order in the slightest," he said in an even raspier voice than normal, "the Court *will* respond swiftly and harshly. Further, the reporters will want cameras in the courtroom during the trial, and someone will want to file a motion to allow them. Don't bother, because the Court will deny it. The trial shall be open to the public, and that's enough."

Perkins continued to lean forward, rested his arms on the bench, and clenched his jaw. "One final matter for the prosecution and defense. Given the nature of this case and the accompanying publicity, you might be tempted to push the ethical envelope. *Don't* even think about it. *This* Court will make certain you don't even see the edge. If you try, you *will* get slapped back. Let me make this perfectly clear. Both sides shall follow the rules of ethics, evidence, and trial procedure to… the… letter. We're adjourned." He then rose and stormed out of the courtroom.

Following the judge's departure, David heard the buzz in the back, turned around, and noticed several looks of bewilderment.

One reporter spotted David and mouthed, "What the hell?"

He shrugged in response. "Sorry."

As Marshall left, she gave David an icy stare. David, the Morelli family, and their friends, waited for everyone else to file out. While doing so, Paul gave David a thumbs-up. The twitch in Amanda's left leg and the tension in her face indicated she was less secure.

David put his right hand on her shoulder. "Are you all right?"

"I guess so… not really. I gave the green light, but I'm not ready for a trial."

He removed his hand and nodded. "I know. Give it a little time to sink in. It's still a month away."

"Yeah, but…"

"Don't worry about it," Paul said. "You'll get through this. You'll win, and you can get on with your life."

"Sure, it'll be fine," Lorraine added.

"Don't think about it right now," Paul said. "How about we all go to lunch?"

Amanda groaned. "Not me. I don't think I can hold anything down right now."

"Sorry, this time I have to pass," David said. "Too much to do today. Amanda, we'll talk again really soon, okay?"

* * *

David made a beeline to the office, and as he sat at his desk, Marc popped his head around the door.

"Remember when I tried to reach Donna Conway's attorney and left messages? While you were out, he finally got back to me and said she won't testify. Sorry about that."

David sighed. “Yeah, we figured she wouldn’t, and it’s not a big deal. We can work around it, and the jury will still hear about her death threat to Simpson.”

“What happened during the hearing?”

“Judge Perkins scheduled trial for January 11th and imposed a gag order.”

Marc chuckled. “Uh-oh. That means no more Mr. TV Celebrity for you.”

David smirked. “Guess not, but it’s fine. We’ll get some coverage today, and it’ll pick up again right before trial.”

* * *

Out of curiosity, David watched the local evening news and surfed the internet looking for articles discussing the court hearing. Many commentators made frivolous remarks, including those concerning Amanda’s outfit, and others claimed the gag order violated freedom of speech and freedom of the press. A more knowledgeable commentator believed Judge Perkins wanted to avoid a repeat of the media circus surrounding the O.J. Simpson trial. David could not find one article that took an in-depth examination of the case. The media only swallowed the details that he fed to them, and he had no issues with that.

Chapter 26

Monday, January 4, 2010

Before leaving his apartment, David checked the weather report and groaned. The high temperature would hover just below freezing, and a stiff breeze blew through the streets of Manhattan. As he had every other winter of his adult life, he kicked himself for not moving to a warmer climate. He would have preferred to stay in bed yet braved the elements to attend a sentencing hearing in federal district court.

After the hearing concluded, David went to the Morelli home in Bensonhurst. Once again, Paul greeted him at the front door and brought him to the awful kitchen table with the plastic flower-print cover, where Amanda and Lorraine were waiting. He took a seat and skipped any small talk.

"Just before going to court this morning, I received a phone call from Jacqueline Marshall, and she offered a deal. If Amanda pleads guilty to manslaughter, she will recommend a sentence of twelve and a half to twenty-five years in prison. It's not good, but it's better than twenty-five to life, which comes with a first-degree murder conviction."

Amanda bit her lower lip and turned her gaze to a wall.

"Do you know why the DA made the offer?" Paul asked.

"She didn't say. Early on, Marshall said she might drop the charge to murder two, and now she's offering manslaughter. Perhaps she believes the jury will see Simpson as the bad victim, which won't go down very well. Maybe her boss wants her to make the case go away, or maybe it's something else. Who knows? She doesn't have to show us all her cards."

Amanda continued to look away, and David tried to draw her attention by touching her hand. She glanced at him and then stared at the floor with a distressed expression.

David sighed. "I'm sorry. I know this isn't a fun conversation, but we must have it. We have some options, and it's ultimately your call, not mine. You can take the deal, or we can make a counteroffer of a plea to manslaughter in exchange for a recommended sentence of six to twelve years. If the DA's office really wants the case to go away, they might take it."

Tears welled up in her eyes. "Why are we talking about deals? Do you believe I killed Simpson?"

David shook his head. "No," he said in a soothing voice. "I don't, and I don't believe Marshall can convince a jury beyond a reasonable doubt you committed any crime. Unfortunately, there's always a risk of conviction, and that's why I suggested a counteroffer. However, I'm recommending no deal, and we go to trial. What do you think?"

Amanda grimaced as a tear slid down her cheek. "Uh, this is too much right now. I didn't do it, and I really don't want to go to prison for twenty-five years. Even six years sounds really awful. Mom, Dad, what do you think?"

Paul puffed out his chest. "Your mother and I know you didn't do it. The jury will agree. Don't take any deal. Right, honey?"

Lorraine nervously shook her head. "I– I don't know. Is there another way out of this?"

Paul patted her hand. "We already talked about this, remember? The DA won't drop the case. Amanda will win. You'll see."

Lorraine grabbed Paul's hand and nodded.

"Look," David said as he addressed Amanda, "we've gone through all the discovery and conducted our own investigation. While some things don't look good, the DA has no direct proof against you. I can't absolutely guarantee the jury will return a not guilty verdict because we don't live in a perfect world. However, I'm very confident we can win at trial. So, what do you want to do?"

"Can't I just click my heels three times and keep saying there's no place like home?" Amanda asked with a worried expression.

"I'm afraid not, and we need to give Marshall an answer this morning."

Amanda sighed. "Yeah, right. Okay, okay. Give me a minute."

She wiped away a tear and stared at the kitchen table. The Morelli home became silent, and seconds passed as if they were hours. Amanda then raised her head. "No deal. Let's go to trial."

David slapped the table. "Good. I'll let Marshall know."

Amanda grimaced again. "It felt good for a second, but now I feel sick to my stomach again."

"It'll pass, Pumpkin," Paul said. "Don't worry about it. David, anything else you need from us before the trial?"

"Not really. On Wednesday evening, I'll give a mock opening statement at my office, and all of you are welcome to attend. Even though I've given many openings, it's always good to practice and get some feedback."

"Maybe we can make it," Paul said. "Are you going to call any of us to testify?"

David shook his head. "It's never a good idea to put the defendant on the stand. As for you and Lorraine, the jury would probably dismiss your testimony as loving parents trying to protect your daughter. Sitting in the first row behind Amanda will convey the same message. Also, you can't confirm Amanda was in her apartment and in bed at the time of the murder."

David withheld additional reasons he did not want the Morelli family as witnesses. He genuinely believed that, in most circumstances, putting a defendant on the stand was a misguided and potentially damaging move. Amanda's case did not present an exception to the rule, and she did not need her past statements thrown in her face.

While David liked Amanda's father, he didn't trust him because he had lied to him twice. Paul could commit perjury on the witness stand, and no ethical attorney would risk it.

As for Lorraine, David suspected testifying in open court would be too stressful for her. The combination of her nerves and her tendency to be scatterbrained could cause her to forget certain facts or not present them in an organized fashion. He feared the jury could confuse her issues with evasiveness and deception, which could reflect negatively on Amanda, so the potential downside of Lorraine's testimony outweighed any upside.

On his way back to the office, David reviewed the DA's case and his defense in his mind. He knew he and Bev would make good points through the cross-examination of Marshall's witnesses, which would dictate the number of witnesses the defense would call. Fortunately, Valerie's testimony would make a significant difference, and David intended to call her last so the defense's presentation could end on a high note.

Chapter 27

Wednesday, January 6

The start of the Morelli trial was only five days away. David thought his long hours in the office had prepared him for virtually any contingency and had no doubt Bev would be more than ready. Nevertheless, he felt under more pressure than any other time in his legal career as both his client's freedom for decades and his law firm's reputation were on the line. In an effort to reduce his stress level, David avoided Irene as much as possible yet was not entirely successful.

While David was working in his office and deep in thought, he noticed a shadow fall upon his desk. He looked up and saw Irene standing two feet in front of it.

"When are you going to give me the filings for trial?" she demanded with her hands on her hips.

Although David didn't appreciate Irene's body language and attitude, he didn't let his disapproval show. "It's fine. We have plenty of time," he said instead. "You'll have the filings as soon as I'm finished, okay?"

"When will that be?" she asked in a condescending tone.

"Well, I don't know right now, and I'm fully aware of the court's deadlines. It's all under control. Don't stress over it."

Irene scoffed. "I need to know. I have a lot to do, and we have a deadline. I'm under a lot of pressure and–"

"*You're* under a lot of pressure?" A deep well of anger rose to the surface. "You're not trying a murder case, a case for all the world to see. My client's looking at twenty-five to life, and *you're* the one who's under pressure. Give me a break!"

Irene leaned forward and slammed her hands down on his desk. "I don't like your attitude! You don't have any respect for me!"

David jumped to his feet and was about to curse her out. Before he could speak another word, Bev and Marc rushed into his office and got between him and Irene. Bev escorted Irene to her desk, and Marc closed the door.

Marc then held up his hands. "Yeah, I know. I get it. She's a real pain, but now's not the time to deal with her. We still need her for trial preparation."

"No, we don't," David said, his anger boiling over. "I know how to file documents with the court. Get her out of my sight, now!"

Marc's eyes bugged out.

"You heard me!" David continued. "Send her home for the rest of the day and keep her away from me until the trial is over. I already have too many things to do without dealing with her crap." He waived his right arm. "It's not just Irene being a pain in the rear. Despite the gag order, reporters keep calling me and asking for off-the-record comments. I don't need them chewing up my time."

Marc nodded. "I know. They've been calling me too. One gossip columnist offered a sizeable reward for an exclusive story, and she wouldn't shut up. I had to threaten her with Judge Perkins to make her go away."

"At least she went away." David tilted his head. "You know what? Let's make Irene go away permanently." He took a step towards the door.

Marc gently placed his right hand on David's chest. "Wait a minute. I understand where you're coming from, but we still need her. You know how things can pop up, and if they do, Irene and I'll have to bust our tails while you and Bev are in court. Let's just get through the trial. Okay?"

David glanced at Marc and then stared at the floor. He needed a couple of moments to process what he had heard. Although he was still boiling, he could still engage in rational thought.

"All right, fine. She stays, for now." He glared at Marc. "You're a great friend and law partner, but I swear, really soon, either she goes, or I go. Got it?"

Marc sighed. "Yeah, I guess I do. I'll keep Irene away from you. Can we just table the status of her employment until after the trial?"

"Fine. Maybe you should keep her out of the office as much as possible until it starts. If we still pay her, I don't think she'll care. Just keep in mind, if she gets on my nerves before the trial's over, I'm going to fire her right on the spot."

* * *

That evening, David was ready to give his mock opening statement. Earlier in the week, David, Marc, and Bev had agreed that a few non-attorneys should listen to his opening so they could provide input from the prospective jurors' viewpoint. Thus, Marc had asked Stephanie to invite her fellow airline employees.

Shortly before eight, Amanda, David, Bev, and Marc were waiting in the conference room, when Steph and three of her co-workers arrived with pizza. Everyone enjoyed it, except for Bev, who had brought chicken salad.

After Steph finished eating, she guided David to his office and closed the door.

Steph tucked several strands of her long strawberry-blonde hair behind her ear. "So, now that I've finally met Amanda, I can see why you're attracted to her."

David attempted to wave her off.

"Oh, come on. You can't hide your feelings from me. I've known you too long and can spot all of your tells."

"It doesn't matter because I don't date clients."

"What about after the trial?"

David scoffed. "Yeah right. Do you really think she'll want to see me again? I'd remind her of the nightmare she went through."

Steph raised her eyebrows and held up her hands. "You never know. Stranger things have happened."

"I'll give it some thought," he said even though he had little intention of doing so.

David returned to the conference room, where he announced the mock opening statements would begin. Marc played Jacqueline Marshall's part and went first, so the audience had a better understanding of the case. David then presented his opening. He engaged with his audience, was professional and, perhaps most importantly, concise. Overall, Bev approved of the speech and had a couple of minor suggestions. All others in attendance praised his performance except for Steph.

"Your opening was impressive," she said, "but there was one little issue. May I?"

David waved his right hand toward her. "Please, go ahead."

"You used the term 'circumstantial evidence' and didn't explain its meaning. I know what it means, but a juror or two might not. If they don't, they could get lost and not pay attention to everything you have to say. Drop the term, and your position will still be clear. The DA's whole case contains nothing directly linking Amanda to the murder."

David noticed a thin smile on Bev's face, her version of high approval – a truly rare event. He also appreciated Steph's comments. "Thanks. I'll keep that in mind."

* * *

Once everyone else had departed for the evening, David and Marc asked Amanda to return to the conference room. Marc had told him that he wanted to ask Amanda some questions but had refused to provide any specifics.

"If you don't mind, I'd like to go over a statement you made to the police," Marc said.

"Okay," Amanda said. Her voice was full of apprehension.

"You told the police you went home early because you were feeling ill."

"That's right."

"How were you ill?" Marc asked.

"What do you mean?"

Amanda's evasiveness was a red flag.

"What symptoms were you showing?" Marc asked.

"Oh that. My stomach was really bothering me."

"Then why did you tell a detective you had a headache?"

David knew she had never said anything about a headache. Marc was testing her.

"Oh yeah, I forgot," Amanda said nervously. "I had a headache, and I felt nauseous another day."

"Actually," Marc said, "you told the police you were nauseous, and Valerie saw you holding your stomach when you left for the day."

"I guess it was both. I must have told one detective one part and another detective the other part."

Marc stared at her, which made her squirm in her chair and look away.

"Actually," Marc said, "you only told the police you had a stomachache. I made up the part about the headache. What was the real reason you left the office the afternoon before the murder?"

"I was sick!"

"Sorry," David said calmly, "I don't believe you either. What happened?"

Both Marc and David remained quiet, which seemed to unnerve Amanda even more. Eventually, she tossed her hands into the air.

"Okay, okay. I wasn't sick. I left the office because why not? I was tired of dealing with Simpson and didn't care about the firm because they didn't make me a junior partner. After Simpson arrived, other people were calling in sick or leaving early. I didn't see the big deal."

"Then why did you tell Valerie you were sick?" Marc asked.

"Just to make it look good, I guess."

"You never told her the truth?"

Amanda shook her head.

"Why didn't you tell the truth to the police?"

"I needed to stick to the same story so the partners wouldn't catch me."

Why didn't you tell the truth to us? David said to himself. To make matters worse, the firm and Amanda had repeated the story about being sick over and over to the media. Now potential jurors would expect to hear the same thing, and Valerie could not repeat the false story in court, even though she believed it was the truth. At least Amanda provided a reasonable explanation for why she lied to the police.

"Were you at home during the evening?" Marc asked.

Amanda exhaled and appeared despondent. "No, I was out on a date. I had met the guy a few days beforehand."

"Where did you first meet?"

"When I was shopping."

"Did you go shopping by yourself?" Marc asked.

"Yes."

"Which store?"

"Some clothing store. I don't remember which one."

"If you remember the name, do you think anyone working there would recall the two of you together?"

Amanda paused and stared at the glass-top table. "I don't think so. We only talked for a little bit inside and some more outside."

"What was his name?" David asked.

"Tom something. I don't remember his last name."

"Do you still have his phone number?" Marc asked. "We'd like to confirm you two were on a date."

Amanda grimaced and shook her head. "I never got his phone number, and I never gave him mine. I'd just met him, and he seemed okay, but I couldn't be sure if he was putting on an act and he was really a creep, so I only agreed to meet him at a restaurant for dinner."

"Where did you have dinner?"

She shrugged. "At some place he recommended."

"What was the name of the restaurant?"

"I don't know. I'd never been there before, and I haven't been since because the food wasn't very good."

"Did anything unusual happen during the date?" David asked. "Maybe something that would have caught the host's or the server's attention."

"No, not really. I only found out the guy was a total loser and unemployed. Right before the check came, he said he accidentally left his wallet at home. Yeah, sure. I had to pay for dinner."

"What credit card did you use?" Marc asked.

"None. Their machine was broken, and I paid in cash."

"Let me see if I got this right," Marc said. "You were on a date when the murder happened, and there is no way to confirm it, including speaking with Tom something."

Amanda sighed. "That's right."

David was disappointed Amanda had lied to him, and he felt worse because they could not establish a solid alibi, but he didn't want to dwell on her deception and moved onto other matters.

"Have you ever taken part in a trial?" he asked.

"No. I was occasionally present for a hearing and sat in the back."

"A trial is much different from a routine hearing, and we must consider the juror's perceptions. With that in mind, well… we need to address your appearance."

Amanda's nose and forehead wrinkled. "What? What's wrong with the way I look?"

"Well, uh, nothing," he sheepishly said. "It's just–"

Marc interrupted. "My learned colleague can't get to the point. There's nothing wrong with the way you look. You're attractive, really attractive."

Amanda briefly smiled. "Thanks. So, what's the issue?"

"Since you make a nice appearance, many potential jurors will have a favorable first impression of you, and let's keep it that way," Marc said. "Don't change your appearance during the trial. If you do, you might unintentionally create the impression you're trying to call attention to yourself, which won't go over well with some people." He paused and held up his right hand. "Come to think of it, many potential jurors have already seen you on TV or seen your picture in a newspaper or an internet article. Don't change your hair color or its length until the end of the trial. You also need to dress professionally. Wear only a modest amount of makeup and jewelry, and don't wear anything distracting."

Amanda nodded. "Okay. Can David and Beverly try to seat a jury full of single men who want to date me?"

David chuckled. "That'd be nice, but we can't discriminate based on gender. As for your clothing, your business suits are fine. Perhaps you should wear your hair up the first day, maybe in a French twist?"

"Sure. I can do that."

"Another important matter," Marc said. "You should assume at least one juror will be watching you at all times. Same goes for the media. Judge Perkins will tell the jurors to ignore the news, but some won't listen, and they'll blab to the other jurors. So, you must always make a good impression in court, and it's not as easy as it sounds. Trials can get dull and tiresome, and you can never look bored. If you have a tough time staying focused, take notes. Sometimes I take notes no matter what's happening to keep me alert and engaged with the case."

Amanda nodded. "Okay. Got it."

"You might've noticed Marc and I joke around a lot," David said, "but there's nothing funny about a murder trial. Don't whisper jokes in my ear, and don't pass me a note with a joke or sarcastic comment. Passing other kinds of notes is perfectly fine, and–"

"It's okay to laugh if someone says something funny," Marc said.

"Not in front of Judge Perkins," David said with a scolding expression. "We also need to be careful about what we say in front of others because they'll try to eavesdrop. You may think one ordinary person overhearing a comment isn't a big deal, but that same person could repeat it to a reporter or to someone else in a juror's presence, and both scenarios would be pretty bad."

Amanda sighed. "Okay, I added it to the list. It almost sounds like I'll be an animal on display at the zoo."

"No," Marc said. "It'll be *exactly* like that."

Amanda groaned. "That's just great."

David tapped his right index finger on the conference room table. "I almost forgot something. Last November, you wore a maroon outfit to court. Do you still have it?"

"The maroon one? Yeah. It's in my closet."

"Don't wear it on the first day of trial. Wear it another day, and I'll let you know when."

"Okay… What's the big deal?"

"It'll take a while to explain. For now, just trust me."

Chapter 28

Monday, January 11

David grumbled because another Monday came with below freezing temperatures. The frigid weather was the least of his concerns, however, as January 11, 2010, was the first day of trial. In the last few days, the media had re-focused its attention on "The Bensonhurst Babe." Many commentators speculated what would happen, and David surmised these talking heads were clueless. A local news channel had even mentioned someone was selling Free Amanda T-shirts. Anything for a buck.

David arrived at the Morelli residence around 7:30 a.m. and, as expected, Paul, Lorraine, and Amanda were dressed and waiting for him. Paul looked uncomfortable in a suit and tie, but his mood was still bright, while Lorraine seemed in a daze. Amanda appeared stressed, and the twitch in her left leg had returned. David requested they sit for a quick meeting at the horrible kitchen table.

"David, how do I look?" Amanda asked.

"You look good."

"Really? I don't think I slept much last night. I used more makeup than normal to cover the dark circles around my eyes."

David gave his honest opinion. "If you didn't tell me, I wouldn't have known. You look great. Lorraine, how are you doing?"

"Oh… I'm okay, I guess," she said nervously. "My doctor gave me a prescription for… for…"

"Xanax," Paul said.

Lorraine grabbed her husband's arm, apparently leaning on him for strength. "Yeah, that's it. I took a pill this morning."

David nodded. He knew the Morellis were under great strain. "I understand. In the days ahead, you'll get used to sitting in court and won't need the pills anymore. Not much will happen right away. Today, we'll begin jury selection, and Beverly will meet us at the courthouse. Both Marc and our private detective, Frederick Ferguson, are standing by to assist, if necessary."

Lorraine gave a weak smile. "Aren't you nervous?"

"Nope."

David lied as he didn't want to increase Lorraine's stress level. Besides, he would feel much better as soon as Judge Perkins took the bench. Once a trial started, a switch flipped in his head, which caused his anxiety to disappear and his drive and focus to assert themselves.

"Here's some last-minute advice," David said. "When we arrive at the courthouse, reporters and camera crews will be outside. Please don't smile or engage with them at all, which includes waving to anybody or shaking hands. Just walk past them. When we're out in public, both inside the courthouse and outside, please don't talk about the case. We can discuss anything in private during a break, during lunch, and after court adjourns for the day. Okay?"

No one raised an objection, and only Paul nodded in agreement.

"All right. Time to go, and I have a little surprise waiting for you."

David and the Morelli family stepped outside and saw a black limousine parked by the curb. The driver, dressed in black, stood next to the right front bumper.

David gave a wide smile. "So, I thought for the first day, why don't we ride in style? I'm not billing you for this. It's on me."

* * *

The drive to Lower Manhattan was typical for a weekday morning: a slog through heavy traffic. Even in the limousine's comfort, David was anxious. Every minute he spent in the limo gave him more time to worry about what could go wrong during the trial. Despite leaving the Morelli home extra early, he also worried about arriving at the courthouse on time.

Shortly before reaching their destination, David ordered the driver to drop them off around the corner from the front entrance. He feared if the media saw the limousine, they would assume the Morelli family was wealthy or pretentious, and many potential jurors would not appreciate such reporting. Besides, he assumed news vans would be parked in front, which would leave no place to pull over.

The frigid air made every moment outside an ordeal, but David heard no complaints during their short walk to the courthouse steps. When he turned the corner, he noticed a group of reporters huddled together, trying to stay warm. Others trained their cameras on the approaching group. As instructed, Paul, Lorraine, and Amanda walked past them without acknowledgement. David imagined Paul had to make an enormous mental effort to restrain himself.

* * *

Once David passed through the courtroom doors, he observed spectators throughout most of the gallery. He also heard a muted buzz, as no one spoke above a whisper due to the judge's ridiculous quiet rule. Bev arrived moments later, and they took their seats at the defense counsel's table; David in the middle, with Amanda to his left and Bev to his right. Paul and Lorraine took their places in the first row behind them and next to their son, Daniel, and his wife, Trudy. Pete, Debra, and other family friends sat in the second row.

Jacqueline Marshall arrived without a trial partner, which surprised David, because flying solo was extraordinary for a high-profile murder trial. Before taking her seat, Marshall coldly glanced toward the defense table, and pursuant to the judge's standing orders, she provided a copy of her witness list with the names in the order she would call them. David and Bev studied it for about a minute and then heard a familiar refrain.

"All rise! The Supreme Court of the State of New York is now in session! The Honorable Sherman Matthias Perkins presiding!"

While the judge never had a pleasant disposition, he appeared even more disappointed than normal and failed to greet others in attendance. David suspected he was having a rotten morning, had grown tired of jury trials, or was ready for retirement.

Judge Perkins cleared his throat. "Do the parties have any last-minute motions?" he asked in his raspy voice.

"No, Your Honor," Marshall said.

"None for the defendant," David answered. In fact, he knew "none" was the only reasonable response. The judge considered last-minute motions ambush tactics and did not look favorably upon attorneys who made them.

Judge Perkins ordered the bailiff to bring in the first portion of the jury pool. Early in his legal career, David had enjoyed jury selection. He had met people from all walks of life who had their own stories, some of which were vastly different from his own. After several trials, however, he started to find the process tedious, having heard every excuse as to why someone could not serve as a juror. Despite his boredom, he remained focused and knew besides his legal skills, Bev was the master of jury selection. By noon, Perkins had dismissed many potential jurors for several reasons, including being self-employed, caregiver for a family member, and for medical reasons.

Once court recessed for lunch, David announced to Bev and all five members of the Morelli family, "I know the perfect place to relax and eat in private. Shall we go?"

"Sorry, Trudy and I can't," Daniel said. "I need to take her to the train station. I'll be back for the afternoon session, and I'll try to attend the trial as much as possible."

After Daniel and Trudy departed, Amanda grabbed David's arm and whispered, "As I said before, Daniel and I are on much better terms, but Trudy's another matter. She's still a complete bitch to me. Daniel probably begged her to come to the city for one half-day."

David stepped in front of her to block the view of any spectators and made certain anyone remaining in the gallery only saw the back of his head. "Don't you remember what I told you about talking in public?" he whispered. "I meant any talking. Some people don't need to hear you since they can read lips. Please, don't screw up again."

Amanda's eyes widened. "Okay, okay. I'm sorry."

"Apology accepted," David said in a softer tone. "Hopefully, no one was paying close enough attention. Now, let's go to lunch."

* * *

David took Bev, Amanda, and her parents to the Red Chili House, the same Chinese restaurant where the Morellis had previously eaten with him. When they arrived, patrons filled all the tables, and various loud conversations overlapped each other.

Paul appeared bewildered, as if someone had asked him to teach a class on astrophysics. "We're going to talk and eat in private here?"

David gave a wry smile. "Just wait."

Less than one minute later, Mr. Chen, the diminutive owner with wire-rim glasses and a bad comb-over, approached David and shook his hand. "Follow me, please," he said.

Mr. Chen escorted the Morelli party past a score of tables and into the kitchen, where the staff worked at a frantic pace. Between shouting in Cantonese and the banging of pots, pans, and woks, the back of the house was noisier than the front. Once Mr. Chen reached the end, he opened a door, revealing a tastefully furnished private dining room, which included eight armchairs draped in red leather surrounding a round table covered with a white tablecloth. A gold double happiness Chinese character hung from a red wall. Mr. Chen swung out his arm, inviting them to enter. "Always available for special guests. Enjoy your lunch."

After a waiter took their orders, David turned his attention to the witness list. "Interesting. Marshall's calling Bill Saxer first."

Bev gave a subtle nod.

"Why's that interesting?" Paul asked.

David looked at Bev. "Would you like to answer, or shall I?"

She motioned for him to proceed while maintaining her usual stoic appearance.

"During most murder trials, the district attorney's office first lays out the crime scene for the jury. They parade photos of the deceased and present their scientific evidence, which can be very compelling."

"Okay," Paul said. "What's their strategy this time?"

"Marshall wants to begin by explaining why someone would want to kill Simpson and inoculate the jury as to his highly inappropriate behavior. Better to hear it from her witnesses than wait for us to engage in character assassination. Unfortunately for her, her trial strategy is flawed."

"Why is that?" Lorraine asked.

This time David motioned to Bev, who said, "We can litigate our theory of the case starting with the prosecution's first witness."

Chapter 29

Wednesday, January 13

Jury selection had continued Monday afternoon and throughout Tuesday. During this process, Paul Morelli had scribbled notes regarding who should be kept on the jury and who should be excluded. David had found his thoughts insightful and speculated he had read Jury Selection by Beverly Cohen a little too well. By the end of Tuesday, a twelve-member jury was in place, consisting of five women and seven men, plus four alternate jurors, two men and two women. All sixteen individuals came from various backgrounds, races, and religions, and none were young, single men who wanted to date Amanda, as she had jokingly hoped.

Prior to the start of the third day of the trial, David, Amanda, Paul, and Lorraine sat in a booth at a coffee shop two blocks from the courthouse. The scent of black coffee coming from the mugs in Paul and Lorraine's hands mixed with the aroma of the onions and bell peppers from a Denver omelet at the next table.

Paul took a sip of coffee. "So far so good."

David nodded. "Pretty much. We have a decent jury but not a great one. I'm a little concerned with Juror Number 7. His body language and the tone of his answers tell me he favors law enforcement. However, if we started over and picked the jury again, I don't think the result would be more favorable."

"Who's Juror Number 7?" Lorraine asked.

"The white guy with the big stomach and goatee. On another note, how are you feeling?"

Lorraine gave a weak smile. "Fine, I guess."

David looked at Amanda. "And you?"

"Nervous."

"That's understandable. And, Paul, I take it you're doing well?"

The big man smiled. "Hey, I'm doing great. When's that not the case?"

David chuckled. "Hard to argue with that."

* * *

Back at the courthouse, the morning session began with Jacqueline Marshall's opening statement. As expected, she told the jury she intended to prove Amanda had conspired with a mysterious, tall blonde woman who had led J. Robert Simpson to his death. She also alleged that during the evening in question, Amanda had communicated with the blonde woman by cell phone and had the motive, means, and opportunity to commit the murder.

Marshall's statement was long-winded, and David believed she did not adequately connect with the jury. About forty minutes into her opening, he noticed half the jurors looked bored, and she didn't appear close to being finished. David and Bev had a plan B if Marshall droned on and on. He would give a much shorter opening statement, even shorter than last week's mock opening. They had theorized the less he spoke, the more likely the jury would pay attention.

Once Marshall had finished, Judge Perkins turned his gaze to the defense table. "Mr. Lee?"

David stood and buttoned his suit jacket. With an air of confidence, he stepped into the well, the area between the attorney tables and the judge's bench.

"Ladies and gentlemen of the jury, the evidence will demonstrate much of what Ms. Marshall asserted this morning is absolutely true. The deceased was a sexual harasser on steroids, and my client, Amanda Morelli, hated him. So did everyone else who encountered him."

He paused for dramatic effect.

"Yes, it's true Ms. Morelli knew how to fire a gun, but how much training does someone need to fire one at point-blank range? It's true Ms. Morelli worked for years in the building where the murder occurred, which meant she was familiar with its security measures. Many others also worked there and had the same knowledge. So did frequent visitors."

David scanned the face of each juror and noticed a couple were already losing interest.

"However, there are serious flaws in the prosecution's case. They do not have the gun used to shoot J. Robert Simpson, and they cannot put it in Ms. Morelli's hand. They also cannot show she was in the building during the murder, and they cannot connect her to the tall blonde woman who led Mr. Simpson to his death. So, why did they charge my client?" He held out his hands and raised his eyebrows. "Well, they needed to pin the murder on someone."

David nodded to the jury and took a couple of steps towards the defense table. He stopped when he heard Judge Perkins clear his throat.

"That's it?" he asked.

"Yes, Your Honor," David said. "The lack of evidence will speak for itself."

The prosecution's first witness was Bill Saxer, who arrived in a brown sports coat and bland yellow tie, the same outfit he had worn when he first came to David's law firm. David wondered if Saxer always tried to dress as boring as possible.

At a slow and deliberate pace and between sips of water, Saxer testified about his prior law firm's history and its financial difficulties after the mortgage meltdown. He explained why his firm had brought in Simpson and why the senior partners had kept him on board despite his constant sexual harassment. Saxer acknowledged everyone had hated "Big Bobby," as Simpson had called himself. He also noted the women had referred to him as "Big Bastard."

Saxer also testified about Amanda and her work product. While he had liked her as a person, he and the other senior partners had denied her a junior partnership. He attempted to gloss over his reasons, but Marshall made him discuss them in detail. At that point, David glanced at Amanda, who appeared hurt, even though this testimony came as no surprise. He wrote her a note:

> *Sorry about that. By tomorrow, no one will remember this part.*

After a few more questions from Marshall, David began his cross-examination.

"Mr. Saxer, I believe you testified that about two weeks before the murder, Mr. Simpson left a meeting to chase after a tall, blonde, female messenger. Is that correct?"

"Yes," he said while staring straight ahead.

"Did you ever hear Ms. Morelli threaten to commit any acts of violence towards anyone?"

"No, never."

David took two steps closer to the witness. "Do you remember Donna Conway?"

Saxer cast his eyes toward the floor. "Yes, I do."

"Did she work as a paralegal at your old law firm?"

"Yes, she did," he said without raising his head.

David edged closer to the witness stand. "Was she working at the firm when the murder occurred?"

"No, she wasn't. She'd been let go."

"Did she ever make any inappropriate comments?"

Marshall jumped to her feet. "Objection, hearsay."

Perkins leant forward. "Sustained."

David glanced at Judge Perkins. "I'll rephrase, Your Honor." He returned his attention to Saxer. "Did you take part in the decision to fire Ms. Conway?"

"Yes, I did."

"What was the basis of the decision?"

"Objection, hearsay," Marshall said.

Perkins shifted his gaze toward David.

"Goes to the witness's state of mind, Your Honor," David said.

The judge nodded. "Overruled."

Out of the corner of his eye, David observed four jurors lean forward. "Why was Ms. Conway fired?" he asked.

Saxer swallowed and raised his head. "She had threatened to slit Simpson's throat."

David heard gasps throughout the courtroom, and at least three jurors appeared startled. He strolled to the defense table. "No further questions, Your Honor."

"Any redirect, Ms. Marshall?" asked the judge.

"No, Your Honor," she said.

Judge Perkins remained expressionless. He raised his right hand to the level of his head and swiveled in his chair a quarter turn to the right. After about ten seconds, he turned his head to the left to face the attorneys. "It's getting close to the lunch hour," he said in a rather hoarse voice. "We'll take a recess a little early."

Once the jurors had filed out of the courtroom, the judge's expression became more severe, and a vein in his neck bulged. "Counsels, in my chambers right now."

Marshall, Bev, and David followed him and barely made it through the door to his office when he slammed it.

"What the hell is going on? Are you wasting this Court's time, because the actual murderer isn't on trial?" he demanded as he waved his right arm.

"No, Your Honor," Marshall said in a matter-of-fact way.

"May I?" David asked while attempting to sound as deferential as possible.

Perkins stared at him. "Go ahead."

"Last June, Donna Conway was in Philadelphia recovering from back surgery."

"Are you certain?"

"For the most part, yes."

"Uh-huh. For the most part." Perkins again threw his right arm into the air. "That's not reassuring. Ms. Marshall?"

"Your Honor, NYPD investigated Conway's whereabouts, and we're certain she was out of town on the night in question. Through medical records, we confirmed she was recovering from surgery at a rehabilitation facility in Philadelphia."

The judge glared at her and then David, while the bulge in his neck continued to throb. "This Court won't allow the jury to be misled, intentionally or otherwise, for even a brief period. The parties shall immediately draft a factual stipulation concerning Ms. Conway's whereabouts at the time of the murder, and we *will* read it to the jury after lunch. Is that clear?"

"Crystal clear," David said.

Marshall nodded.

"Now get out!" Perkins ordered as his outstretched arm pointed towards the door.

* * *

Jacqueline Marshall's next witness was Kelly Holcomb, a thin woman in her early thirties with intense, mahogany-brown eyes. Holcomb testified she had organized many women at the firm against Simpson, and she discussed various accusations of sexual harassment. Shortly before the murder, Holcomb had decided that if the senior partners did not reign in Big Bobby in the immediate future, she would have sued on behalf of all the women who worked at their law firm. Bev asked no questions on cross-examination.

Leslie Van Martin, the EEOC employee, then took the stand. She was a heavyset woman whose eyes darted back and forth as she entered the courtroom, which caused David to suspect she was uncomfortable speaking in public. Nevertheless, she testified Amanda came to her office to file a complaint against Simpson.

About five minutes into her direct examination, Marshall asked, "After you explained the EEOC process, did the defendant react in any way?"

"Uh, yes. She seemed upset because it'd take too long."

"Did she appear to be angry?"

Van Martin twisted her mouth. "Maybe… yes, yes she did."

"Did the defendant make any comments about Mr. Simpson's physical condition?"

"Yes, she said he'd be better off dead."

"Were those her exact words?"

Van Martin nodded. "Yes."

Once again, the defense waived cross. David expected another witness would testify given one hour remained for the normal court hours. However, Judge Perkins announced they were finished for the afternoon and provided no explanation.

Chapter 30

Thursday, January 14

Pursuant to David's request, Amanda arrived wearing her maroon business suit with a knee-high skirt and matching two-inch heels, looking nothing less than stunning. David planned for the jury to get a closer view of her without her taking the stand.

The fourth day of trial commenced with Judge Perkins taking the bench in another irate mood and refusing to allow the bailiff to seat the jury. He instead ordered the attorneys and Amanda into his chambers. David didn't know who or what had lit the judge's fuse. He and Bev never crossed an ethical line, and Marshall was not foolish enough to get herself in trouble, so David suspected perhaps a juror had an agenda or had been caught conducting independent research. A juror could have inspected the O'Connell building, the site of the murder, and had blabbed to another juror, who in turn informed a bailiff.

Judge Perkins closed the door to his office. "Counsels and Ms. Morelli, remain standing."

David had been in court for several of the judge's less pleasant moments but had never seen him so upset. The bulging vein in his neck had returned, his facial muscles were tense, and his eyes almost popped out of their sockets. David glanced at Bev, who seemed unmoved and had her hands clasped in front of her. Her ability to keep her composure even in the most trying circumstances amazed him.

Perkins moved within inches of David, which made him uncomfortable and allowed him to smell the judge's bad breath.

"Mr. Lee, have you read this morning's edition of *The New York Times*?"

"No, Your Honor."

He took a step back, twisted his body, and reached for the newspaper on his desk. He twisted back and smacked the paper onto David's chest.

"Here's my copy of the front section, folded to the correct page," he said.

David grabbed it with his right hand.

"The article in the upper left-hand corner has several quotes from an unnamed source who discussed the defense's strategy in detail," Perkins said. "Did you speak to a reporter in violation of the gag order?"

David was taken aback and offended. Attacking his character was the third rail, and normally, he would give a swift and angry reply. This time, he held his fire to avoid a fine or a night in jail.

"Of course not, Your Honor," he said calmly.

"Uh-huh. Prior to the final pre-trial hearing, an unnamed source told reporters the defense was ready for trial. That was you, wasn't it?"

"Yes, it was, and at the time, there was no gag order."

Perkins glared at him. "And I'm supposed to believe you now?"

David no longer cared if he was speaking to a judge. He was about to bark back when he noticed Bev giving him a subtle look, encouraging him to contain himself. Bev also took the judge's copy of the paper from his hand.

"Your Honor," David said deferentially, "as opposed to many other attorneys, I don't lie to the Court. I'm also not stupid enough to violate the gag order and risk getting sanctioned."

While Perkins still appeared upset, his eyes returned to their normal positions, and his neck vein stopped throbbing. David noticed Bev reading the article in question.

"Your Honor," Bev said, "I know for a fact my colleague did not recently speak with a reporter from *The New York Times*."

Perkins scoffed. "Oh really! How do you know, magic?"

Bev made a slight frown. "No, I recognize my own words in the article."

"What!" he exclaimed as his eyes bugged out again.

"I gave an interview to a reporter three days before you imposed the gag order. The article was published the next day and included some of the same quotes in here," Bev said as she pointed at the paper in her left hand. "Someone recycled the piece and made it seem more current."

"Are you certain?" Judge Perkins asked.

"Absolutely. I recognize my own words."

Perkins crossed his arms and stepped toward his desk and then toward the attorneys. He stared at David for a couple of seconds before turning his attention to Bev.

After about five more seconds, he said, "Counsels, get out! Ms. Marshall, call your next witness."

As David and Bev left the judge's chambers, David gestured for Bev to follow him into a hallway outside the courtroom and away from the spectators in the gallery.

When he was certain no one was nearby, he whispered to Bev, "Do you think Judge Perkins will sanction us?"

"I sincerely doubt it."

"What if he does? I can handle a fine, but I don't want it going on my record."

"If it happens, I'll contact a friend on the judicial disciplinary committee. We'll request a hearing, and she'll haul in the judge. We'll show her a copy of today's article and the one printed last month." She raised the paper in her left hand. "Why do you think I kept his copy?"

David released a light chuckle.

"During the next break," Bev added, "I'll call Marc and ask him to order a copy of the December 12th edition, which has my quotes. Will that put your mind more at ease so you can focus on the trial?"

He nodded. "Yeah, it will. Thanks."

* * *

The prosecution's first witness of the day was Jonathan Ellrod, a nondescript, middle-aged attorney who had reviewed Thorton's emails. He had found the "Let's kill him" email, which Amanda had sent to Valerie three days before the murder. On cross-examination, Bev used this witness to admit into evidence five other emails containing negative comments about Simpson, although none suggested injuring or killing him.

Marshall's next witness was Evan Huang, the bartender from the restaurant near Amanda's former place of employment. With his goatee, spikey hair, and tattoos peeking out from the long sleeves of his white dress shirt, he stood out in the crowded courtroom. Huang testified that Amanda and her friend, Valerie Fernandez, sat near the bar the Monday before the murder. Both were drinking, but neither appeared intoxicated. Since the restaurant was not busy, he overheard them discuss how to kill someone called Big Bastard, and they settled upon shooting him twice in the head.

"Were Ms. Morelli and her friend whispering?" Bev asked on cross-examination.

"No. They were talking normally."

"Did they use any code words or euphemisms?"

"Uh… I don't think so," Huang said as he rubbed his left arm.

Bev walked into the well and toward the jury. "Based upon what you saw and heard, do you believe the two women tried to keep their conversation confidential?"

"No, I don't believe so."

Bev stopped in front of the witness stand. "Did they know you were listening?"

"Yeah. One of them, the defendant sitting over there," Huang said and pointed at Amanda. "She asked her friend if I was listening, and her friend said she didn't care."

"So, they were serious about plotting a murder and didn't care if you heard them, even though you could call the police or testify against them?"

"Objection, speculation," Marshall said.

"Sustained."

"Did my client, Ms. Morelli, and her friend appear to be so stupid or foolish that they would openly discuss a murder plot?"

"Objection, speculation," Marshall said.

"Sustained," Judge Perkins barked. "Move on, Ms. Cohen."

"Did the women ever smile or laugh?" Bev asked.

"Maybe."

Bev raised an eyebrow. "Maybe? You're not sure? Didn't you tell the police they were smiling and laughing?"

"I guess so."

"Do you think they were serious about killing someone?"

Huang shrugged. "Maybe, it's a tough town. I've heard people say a lot of things."

"Did you call the police?"

"No."

"No?" Bev removed her glasses. "Mr. Huang, if you thought Ms. Morelli and her friend were serious about killing someone, why didn't you call the police? Are you that callous?"

He shifted his gaze from Bev to his hands in his lap.

"Do you have an answer? Why didn't you call the police?"

"Uh… I don't know," he said while still looking away from Bev. "Maybe I didn't take them seriously. It's a nice place, and our clientele doesn't commit crimes."

Bev put on her glasses. "No further questions, Your Honor."

* * *

After the morning break, the prosecution summoned Jason Hill, the crime scene investigator, who had a pear-shaped body and a pock-marked face. Based upon Hill's manner of speech and quick responses to questions, David concluded he was very intelligent.

Through Hill's testimony, the photos of the deceased and his office were admitted into evidence. Hill testified he had found fingerprints on Simpson's desk, including Amanda's thumbprint. He also found smudged prints on the glass door to Simpson's office, which he could not identify. Hill further stated the office's door handles had been wiped, which erased any fingerprints.

Based upon the body's position and its entry and exit wounds, the two holes in the throw pillow, and the two holes in the wall, Hill reasoned the bullets traveled on a slightly downward trajectory, about five degrees from horizontal. He determined Simpson's and his killer's locations at the time of the first shot, and to assist the jury, he presented a detailed drawing. Two mannequins represented Simpson and the killer. One mannequin sat on the couch and, with both hands, held a pillow in front of its face. The second mannequin stood with its knees bent and held the handgun with both hands. The second mannequin's arms stretched out and the gun's muzzle contacted the pillow. Hill concluded the mannequin with the gun was the same height as the defendant.

Hill also testified that he had seen the white takeout box in Amanda's office. The box was seized and processed as evidence because a red spot had been present on its edge, and the spot's appearance was consistent with blood. He concluded his direct testimony by stating no one found any blood outside of Simpson's and Amanda's offices.

On cross-examination, David asked, "As part of the police's investigation, someone spoke with the maintenance crew, correct?"

"Correct."

"Isn't it true they made their rounds during the early morning hours the same day as the murder?"

"Correct. After the murder, I believe they reached the tenth floor around three in the morning, and that's when they found the body."

David cocked his head. "However, they were not certain as to the last time they had cleaned Mr. Simpson's desk."

"I believe so."

"So, isn't it true Ms. Morelli could have placed her thumbprint on the desk earlier the same day as the murder, the day beforehand, or earlier in the week?"

"Sure," Hill said in a blasé manner.

"All right. Did you conduct a thorough examination of the crime scene?"

"Yes, of course."

"And no shell casings were left at the scene?"

Hill nodded. "Correct."

"And there were no shoe prints on the carpet inside Mr. Simpson's office?"

"Correct again."

"Do you believe someone accidentally transferred blood from Mr. Simpson's office to Ms. Morelli's office?"

"Yes, that's correct. We found a smudge on the edge of the blood splatter, which means someone touched it. The mark on the takeout box was consistent with a small transfer from the wall to a person, and to the box."

"So, the blood on the takeout box belonged to the deceased?"

"Yes, DNA lab analysis came to that conclusion."

"Did you find a fingerprint within the smudge on the wall or on the takeout box?"

"No, and we believe the killer wore gloves."

"And you cannot state with any certainty Ms. Morelli was the one who transferred the blood simply because it ended up in her office."

"That's correct."

David was pleased, and he was about to use Hill's expertise to his advantage.

"Let's next address the height and position of the shooter," David said. "As part of your analysis, you assumed the killer took a proper shooting stance with their knees slightly bent and arms stretched out."

"Yes, I did."

"If a slightly shorter person, say someone five foot three, stood straight and fired, the bullets would have traveled on the same trajectory?"

Hill took a breath and stared into space. A moment later, he said, "That's a fair assumption."

"Suppose the shooter was a taller person, about five six or five seven, and their knees were bent a little more. Would the bullets have travelled along the same trajectory?"

"There's a problem with your theory. If the shooter crouched more, they would've lacked balance, and the shots would have been less accurate."

David feigned surprise. "Well, how accurate does someone need to be at point-blank range?"

He heard two jurors chuckle and noticed Judge Perkins was not amused.

"Mr. Hill, based upon my hypothetical, could a slightly taller person have fired the fatal shots?"

"I suppose so," the witness said with a half-frown.

* * *

After the lunch break, David watched the jurors as they re-entered the courtroom. Most appeared refreshed and ready for more testimony, except Juror 7, the Caucasian man with the large stomach and goatee. He plodded towards his seat with his hands in his pockets and cast a dirty look towards David.

* * *

Judge Perkins cleared his throat. "Ms. Marshall, please call your next witness."

"The People call Dr. Manfred Witherspoon."

David jumped to his feet. "The defense objects because his testimony will be cumulative and unnecessary."

"Why is that?" Perkins asked.

"Dr. Kaufman will testify that the DNA found on the takeout box matched the deceased's DNA. It was already established during cross-examination of the last witness."

Marshall looked flustered. "Your Honor, I believe the jury should hear further testimony about–"

"Mr. Lee," Perkins said, "does the defense stipulate that the blood on the takeout box belonged to the deceased?"

"Absolutely, Your Honor," David said.

"Then we don't need to hear from Dr. Witherspoon."

With that, the jury would hear less scientific evidence and could focus more on other matters, the ones David and Bev intended to emphasize.

Marshall next called the waiter from the restaurant where Simpson ate shortly before his death. During his brief testimony, he said he had seen Simpson having dinner with a tall blonde woman. The defense had no questions.

The next witness was Eric Walker, one of the O'Connell building's security guards. As he plodded toward the witness stand, David noticed his pale, round face displayed resignation, as if he were dragged to the principal's office due to his misbehavior in class. On top of that, instead of showing respect by wearing a suit and tie, he was dressed in a short-sleeved shirt with a collar.

"On the evening of June 18, 2009, did you see J. Robert Simpson?" Marshall asked.

"Yeah."

"Was he with anyone else?"

"Yeah. A tall woman."

"What was the color of her hair?"

Walker sighed and crossed his arms. "Blonde."

"Where did you see her and Mr. Simpson?"

"In the lobby."

David was unimpressed with Walker given his rotten attitude and his short, blunt answers. Two security guards had been on duty during the evening of the murder; could the other one have made an even worse witness?

"While in the lobby, did the tall blonde woman say anything?" Marshall asked.

"Yeah," Walker said. "She said she needed to make a phone call. She told Simpson to go upstairs, and she'd join him in a few."

"Did Mr. Simpson go upstairs?"

Walker snickered. "What do you think?"

Judge Perkins growled, "Answer the question."

"Yeah. He used the elevator."

"What did the blonde woman do?" Marshall asked.

"She stepped outside."

"Did she ever return?"

"No."

Marshall played the video from a security camera in the lobby, which depicted what Walker had described. "Is that what happened?" she asked.

"Yeah."

* * *

A cell phone company employee told the jury a woman named Bonnie Parker bought two cell phones sixteen days before the murder, and their numbers ended in 7881 and 7882. For two weeks, the 7881 phone communicated with Simpson's cell phone and no others. The 7882 phone only had activity during the evening of the murder. It received a brief call from the 7881 phone, and several minutes later, 7882 communicated with 7881 for several seconds. For both calls, the cell tower closest to the O'Connell building made the connection.

During her questions, Marshall suggested that the tall blonde woman and Bonnie Parker were one in the same, and the tall woman had called the shooter, who had made the return call. Normally, David would have objected to such leading questions, but he wanted the jury to reach the same conclusion. Once Marshall had finished with the witness, he asked no questions.

Judge Perkins reacted by opening his mouth and swiveling his chair to the right. David recognized this behavior as the judge unintentionally signaling that he did not understand what the defense was doing. If it dawned on him, he would spin back to face the attorneys. "I'll see the attorneys and Ms. Morelli in chambers," he ordered instead.

* * *

This time, the judge did not slam the door, but given the look on his face, David suspected his blood pressure rose without a good reason.

"Mr. Lee and Ms. Cohen, there was almost no pre-trial litigation, and you gave a very abbreviated opening statement. You've objected to none of the prosecution's questions, and you made no objections to almost all exhibits. For most witnesses, you asked no questions on cross. I don't want this case coming back to me based on ineffective assistance of counsel. Mr. Lee, do you know what you're doing?"

"Yes, Your Honor," he said confidently.

Perkins scoffed. "Really? Ms. Cohen, do you know what you're doing?"

"Absolutely," she said.

"And I'm supposed to believe it?" He waved his right arm in the air, stomped toward shelves filled with legal books, and stomped back. "Ms. Morelli, do you approve of your attorneys' performance?"

"Yes, Your Honor."

He scoffed again. "Unbelievable!"

Bev took one step forward and stared at the judge. "Permission to speak freely?"

"Go ahead."

"I've been a defense attorney for a long time, and you should know better," she said as she shook her right index finger. "When you were a prosecutor, you had an outstanding record filled with trial victories, except when you lost three times to me. In this case, the defense hasn't engaged in scorched earth litigation because it would have been unnecessary and pointless. We're putting on a defense, and don't forget, the trial's far from over. Just wait. Soon enough, you'll have a very different opinion about the defense."

Perkins raised his eyebrows, and his eyes bugged out. David tried to look away and waited for him to explode.

"Fine," he said instead, "but I'll be watching you. We're in recess for fifteen minutes."

As David and Bev returned to the courtroom, he whispered, "Perkins lost to you three times?"

"Yes," said Bev. "One defendant had two mistrials, and the judge dismissed the case after the second one. Another case was dismissed due the property room mishandling evidence. That's three wins in my book."

* * *

Following the afternoon break, Marshall called Derek Collins, a video and computer expert with NYPD. His pinstriped blue suit, white dress shirt, and red and blue striped silk tie covered his lanky frame. Collins' dark-brown hair was perfectly coifed, and David suspected he used a daily facial cleanser. His purposeful stride and raised chin reflected confidence to the point of arrogance.

Collins testified he had reviewed video footage from the O'Connell building's lobby, from the camera in front of the parking garage entrance, and from the camera down the street. Marshall played the relevant portions of the original and enhanced videos concerning the street view. While the enhanced version played, Collins pointed out a woman with a gray wig and a cane emerging from the O'Connell building's north side several minutes after Simpson had entered the lobby. Collins also explained why he believed the cane was only a prop.

As David stood to begin his cross-examination, he knew Judge Perkins would not appreciate his upcoming courtroom theatrics. But while he wanted to stay on the judge's good side, he was more concerned with making a substantial impression upon the jury, who would decide his client's fate.

"Mr. Collins, does the video footage confirm Ms. Morelli left the building mid-afternoon on the day of the murder?"

He leaned back in his chair and crossed his legs. "Yes, it does."

"Did she ever re-enter the building later the same day?"

"None of the cameras captured her image again."

"Did you see any footage of the woman in the gray wig entering the building?"

"No."

"And you believe the woman in the gray wig is the same height as my client, correct?"

"Yes, that's correct," Collins said with his chin thrust in the air.

"Well, the woman in the gray wig was hunched over. Doesn't that make it difficult to determine her exact height?"

Collins smirked. "No, I don't think so."

"Have you ever seen my client standing right in front of you?"

"No."

David turned to the bench. "With the Court's permission, I'd like Ms. Morelli to stand before the witness."

Judge Perkins flicked his right hand.

Amanda rose and walked until she was five feet in front of the witness stand. Not coincidentally, she stood closer to the jurors, most of whom stared at her.

Collins uncrossed his legs and sat upright.

David remained in the well and behind Amanda so the jurors could still see him. "Now, can you say Ms. Morelli is the same height as the woman in the video?"

"Your client's wearing high heels, and the woman in the video wore more practical shoes," Collins said in a condescending tone.

David smiled. "My apologies." He strode toward the defense table and reached into Amanda's purse. He retrieved a pair of tennis shoes and gave them to her. David then stood between his client and the judge.

Amanda took off her heels and put on the tennis shoes. David noticed four male jurors examining her legs as she did so, including Juror Number 7. David grabbed the heels and placed them on the defense table.

David knew Amanda changing her shoes to attract the male jurors' attention was a sexist move, but he didn't care. Her freedom was on the line, and he would exploit any advantage so long as he would not upset the state bar. Some female jurors could have been offended by the men staring at Amanda's legs, and if so, David assumed they would release their scorn on their male colleagues, not him.

David returned to his prior spot in the well. "Mr. Collins, is my client the same height as the woman with the gray wig?"

"Yes, she is."

Amanda clasped her hands behind her and knew what would happen next.

"Is it possible Ms. Morelli is slightly taller or shorter by an inch or less?"

"No," Collins said bluntly.

"Uh-huh." David cocked his head. "So, despite the woman in the video hunching over, you can determine her height to the smallest fraction of an inch and know it was exactly the same as my client?"

Collins looked away and shifted in his chair.

David glared at him. "You don't have to answer the last question. Aren't there many women in New York the same height as Ms. Morelli, an inch shorter, or an inch taller?"

"Of course."

"Aren't some *men* the same height?"

Collins smirked with his chin once again in the air. "Yes, but do they have the same build? I don't think so."

David again turned towards the bench. "Your Honor, I respectfully request another person stand next to my client."

Judge Perkins gave another permissive wave.

David turned his head toward the back of the courtroom. Marc opened the door, and a short, slender man entered, whose fair skin matched his blonde hair, which had a permanent windswept appearance. The slender man wore a dress shirt, tie, and slacks but no jacket or sports coat so the jurors could observe his build. The man walked into the well and stood between Amanda and the jury box.

David pointed at him. "Doesn't this man's height and build match my client?"

Collins' arrogant attitude disappeared, and he looked at the floor.

"Let the record reflect the witness didn't answer the question. I'll ask it again. Doesn't this man's height and build match Ms. Morelli's? Yes or no."

"Yes," Collins mumbled.

"If we walked around the courthouse, do you think we could find another man with the same height and build?"

"Uh, I don't know."

"I don't know, really? Take a guess," David said.

"Objection, badgering," Marshall said.

"Sustained," said the judge.

"What about if we went to the nearest racetrack and checked out the jockeys? What about them?" David said.

"Objection, badgering," Marshall said.

"Sustained," said Perkins.

"According to the Department of Motor Vehicles," David said, "how many men in Manhattan have the same height and weight as the man standing before you?"

"Your Honor!" Marshall said.

The vein in Judge Perkins' neck made another appearance. "Counsels, approach," he said.

David, Bev, and Marshall came within inches of the bench.

Perkins fumed and put his left hand on his microphone. "Mr. Lee, that's the last stunt you'll pull in this courtroom. Now stand back." Once the attorneys returned to their original positions, the judge commanded, "Ms. Morelli, go sit down." He then pointed the man next to her. "You, sir, leave my courtroom now."

The slender man acknowledged with a nod and made a swift exit.

"No more questions, Your Honor."

As David strolled to the defense table, he noticed Bev twice tap her right index finger on the table, indicating her approval. He also saw a wide smile on Paul's face.

"That was fun," Paul mouthed.

Yes it was, David thought to himself. Yes indeed.

Chapter 31

Friday, January 15

The prosecution's next witness was Nathan Flynn, the lead detective for the Morelli case. His cheap suit matched his unruly gray hair, and his deep facial wrinkles and bad skin reflected decades of drinking and smoking. In fact, as the detective passed by the prosecution and defense tables, David noticed the stale scent of cigarette smoke.

With a voice as refined as coarse sandpaper and between coughing spells, Detective Flynn testified about the investigation's various stages, beginning with the initial interviews of all those who worked for Thorton, Saxer & Caldwell at the time of the murder. He also described how his team eliminated individuals as suspects and then addressed the evidence against Amanda.

Marshall questioned her witness for an extended period without a script or notes. David believed if most attorneys tried it, they would stumble and bumble before the jury. However, her performance was an impressive feat, and she had not yet finished.

"Detective Flynn, did you ever speak with the defendant?"

"Yes. On the Monday after the murder."

"Did you ask the defendant her opinion of J. Robert Simpson?"

"Yes." Flynn coughed into his sleeve. "She said, 'He wasn't so bad.'"

"Based upon your investigation, did you ever come to any conclusion regarding this statement?"

"Yes. It was wildly inconsistent with the 'Let's kill him' email."

Marshall paused for a few seconds, presumably to let the last answer soak into the jurors. "Did you ask the defendant whether she ever owned or handled any firearms?"

"Yes, I did. She admitted–" The detective pulled out his handkerchief and twice coughed into it. "Excuse me. She admitted a family friend taught her how to fire a variety of weapons."

"Including a .38 handgun?"

"Yes."

Marshall paused again, and this time David knew it was intentional.

"Did the defendant own any guns?"

"She said she didn't."

"Did you ask her if her parents owned any firearms?"

"She said her parents used to own a .38 handgun, the same caliber as the murder weapon. I oversaw the search of their residence, and no firearms were located."

"No further questions, Your Honor."

Judge Perkins glanced at David, who moved toward the middle of the well.

"Detective Flynn," he said, "let's address the search of the Morelli home in Bensonhurst. You were looking for a gray wig, a cane, certain articles of clothing, a .38-caliber handgun, and two cell phones, correct?"

"That's right."

"And you found none of these items?"

"That's right."

"Okay. Let's focus on Ms. Morelli's interviews. Was she always cooperative with the police?"

The detective again coughed twice into his handkerchief and then said, "Yes, she was."

"Did she ever invoke her right to remain silent?"

"No."

"Did Ms. Morelli ever lead you to believe she was trying to hide something?"

"You could say that."

"Are you referring to her saying the deceased wasn't so bad?"

"Yes." Detective Flynn coughed again. "I later concluded she wanted to deflect attention from herself. She tried to create the appearance she didn't hate Simpson and didn't have a motive to kill him."

"Uh-huh," David said and cocked his head. "Well, isn't it possible she meant the deceased wasn't so bad that someone should have killed him?"

"No, I don't believe so."

"Isn't it true neither you nor anyone else ever asked any follow-up questions regarding my client's opinion of the deceased?"

"That's correct."

"Could you explain why?"

The witness coughed three times and stretched his arm towards the bailiff, who brought him a bottle of water. After drinking half of it, he seemed ready to continue.

"Detective Flynn, do you have an answer?"

"What was the question?"

"Why didn't you or anyone else ask follow-up questions to determine what Ms. Morelli actually meant?"

"There was no need."

David scoffed. "Oh really? So, you believe your investigation was very thorough?"

"That's right."

David smiled to himself because Flynn had stepped into a little trap. "Prior to my client being arrested, you and your team didn't talk to any of the law firm's former employees, more specifically, any former employee who hated the deceased. Is that right?"

The detective gave him an icy stare.

David cocked his head again. "Let's try it another way. Isn't it true Donna Conway used to work for the same law firm as Mr. Simpson?"

"Yes."

"Isn't it also true she was fired for threatening to slit his throat?"

"Yes, but so what?" Flynn said while flashing a glowering expression. "We investigated, and she was in Philadelphia when Simpson was shot."

"Uh-huh. Isn't it also true that the NYPD never knew Ms. Conway existed prior to my client's arrest and indictment?"

"Yes, but so what?"

"You first heard about Ms. Conway from the assistant district attorney, correct?"

"Yes."

"And the ADA heard about her from the defense?"

"Yes."

"Detective, perhaps you weren't so thorough. Anything else you forgot to investigate?"

"Objection, argumentative," Marshall said as she jumped to her feet.

"Sustained," said the judge.

"Detective, did you ever determine the identity of the tall, blonde, female messenger who came to the law firm sixteen days before the murder?" David asked.

"No," Flynn said, frowning. "We never had any good leads."

"Were you able to identify the tall, blonde woman with Mr. Simpson minutes before his murder?"

"No. The security guards on duty only gave a general description."

"Could they have been the same person?" David asked.

"It's possible."

"And you discovered that during the last two weeks before his death, Mr. Simpson was communicating with a woman who bought cell phones under the name Bonnie Parker?"

Flynn coughed again. "Yes. Someone bought cell phones using that name."

"Do you believe the name Bonnie Parker was an alias?"

"Yes. She provided the cell phone company with a driver's license number, address, and credit card number. All of them were bogus."

"Do you believe Bonnie Parker and the tall blonde woman were the same person?"

"It's possible."

David feigned surprise. "It's only possible? The security guards and a waiter saw the tall blonde woman with Mr. Simpson right before his death. The last two calls on the Bonnie Parker cell phones occurred within minutes of the murder, and they connected through the cell tower closest to the building where the murder took place. Yet, it's only *possible* the tall woman and Bonnie Parker are the same person?"

"That's right," Detective Flynn said.

"One last thing. Do you believe many people disliked and even hated J. Robert Simpson?"

"That's a reasonable conclusion."

"Are you certain you found all his enemies?"

Flynn stared ahead while his jaw muscles tightened.

David waved his right hand. "That's fine, Your Honor. The witness doesn't have to answer. No further questions."

Judge Perkins turned his gaze towards Marshall.

She rose and said, "No redirect, Your Honor."

As he stepped from the witness stand, Detective Flynn cast a sneer towards David, who imagined they had equally low levels of respect for each other.

The prosecution's next witness was Detective Katherine Brown, a thin, stern woman with a tight face and red hair coiled in an equally tight bun. Brown testified she had overseen the execution of the search warrant at Amanda's apartment, where no items listed in the warrant had been found, including a .38-caliber handgun. She instead located a .22-caliber pistol in the bedroom closet. Photographs of the closet, the gun case, and pistol were admitted into evidence. Detective Brown also noted she had found the pistol after Amanda said she did not own a firearm.

"Who was the pistol's registered owner?" David asked on cross-examination.

"Ms. Morelli's ex-husband," Brown said with all the emotion of a soulless robot.

"So, at some point, he gave her the gun?"

"That's a fair assumption."

"Detective Brown, you found the pistol in a back corner of the bedroom closet, correct?"

"Correct."

"On the top shelf?"

"Correct."

"And the pistol was inside a small black case?"

"Yes," she said without a hint of emotion.

David wondered if she possessed the ability to interact with others in a social setting. "Isn't it true no one could easily see the case containing the pistol? Someone had to remove a few items first?"

"That's right."

"Okay. Please, turn to the first photo depicting the gun case." David waited while she did so. "There's a layer of some gray substance on top. Isn't that dust?"

"I believe so."

"Which shows no one moved the case for a long time, correct?"

Brown scoffed. "Yes, of course."

"Had the gun ever been fired?"

"No, it looked brand new," she said.

"Detective Brown, you found two ammunition clips inside the case. Were there any bullets in either clip?"

"No."

"Was there a round in the gun?"

"No."

David nodded. "Did you find any ammunition in Ms. Morelli's apartment of any caliber?"

"No, we didn't."

"Detective Brown, isn't it true a .38 has a lot more firepower than a .22?"

"Yes, of course."

"Your service weapon is a 9 mm handgun, correct?"

"Objection, relevance," Marshall said.

Judge Perkins stared at David.

"Your Honor," he said, "if you'd allow the defense to ask a few more questions, the Court will see the connection momentarily."

Perkins did not react.

David interpreted his lack of response as permission to proceed. "Your service weapon is a 9 mm handgun, correct?"

"Correct."

"It's fairly comparable to a .38 in terms of firepower, isn't it?"

"That's right."

"Detective Brown, do you know of any police department issuing .22-caliber handguns as a standard service weapon?"

"I'm not aware of any."

"Because a .22 lacks sufficient firepower?"

"Most likely."

"All right. Please consider the following scenario."

Brown remained stone-faced and motionless.

David walked at a slow pace towards the jurors. "We know Ms. Morelli was familiar with firearms, and a .22 doesn't have much firepower. We also know the .22 in question was in the back of her closet." He stopped just before blocking the jury's view of Detective Brown. "Dust covered the case, no one had ever fired the gun, and my client didn't buy it." David held out his hands. "Ms. Morelli thought little of it, because in her mind, it wasn't a real gun. She just threw it in the closet," he said as he made an underhand tossing motion, "and forgot about it. Therefore, when asked about owning any firearms, she made an honest mistake by stating she didn't own a gun. Does this scenario sound plausible to you?"

Detective Brown scoffed. "No. How can someone forget about owning a lethal weapon?"

"Oh really? No more questions, Your Honor."

Marshall's next witness was Detective Joseph Blackwood, a white male in his late thirties with short brown hair and an athletic build. Blackwood had conducted a follow-up interview with Amanda after the police had found her fingerprint on Simpson's desk. According to Blackwood, Amanda had said she never went into Simpson's office.

Moments before Bev launched into her questions, David passed a note to Amanda:

Time for some more fun!

"Detective Blackwood," said Bev, "according to your testimony, Ms. Morelli told you, 'I never went into Simpson's office.' Are you sure those were her exact words?"

"Yes, I am," he said confidently.

"Isn't it possible she said she tried to stay out of his office as much as possible?"

"No."

"By the time you spoke with my client, did you consider her a suspect?"

"Yes, we did."

"Didn't your interview provide a partial basis for Ms. Morelli's arrest and indictment?"

"I don't know. Ask the DA."

Bev raised her eyebrow. "Are you serious? You don't know?"

"It wasn't my call."

"Detective Blackwood, have you ever committed perjury on the stand?"

"Never."

Bev took two steps closer to the witness and stared at him. "Are you certain?"

He paused and then said, "Of course."

"Isn't it true you've been with NYPD the past seven years?"

"Yes."

"Weren't you previously a police officer in Newark?"

Blackwood turned pale. "Yes, I was."

Bev continued to stare at him. "Isn't it true that while you were with the Newark Police Department, you worked on the Leon Washington case?"

"Uh, yes," he said. He shifted in his chair and glanced at Marshall, as if he were pleading with her to rescue him.

"The appellate court threw out Mr. Washington's conviction over your false police report and lying on the witness stand, correct?"

"No, I never lied!"

Bev walked to the defense table, grabbed a quarter-inch stack of papers, and held them high in the air. "Your Honor, this is the relevant decision from the New Jersey appellate court. I'd like it marked and admitted into evidence." She dropped the papers on the table. "I'm done with this witness."

On redirect examination, Marshall asked, "Do you remember earlier today you took an oath to tell the truth?"

"Yes."

"When you testified about your interview with the defendant, were you telling the truth?"

"Absolutely," Detective Blackwood said a little louder.

"Did you take notes when you interviewed the defendant?"

"Yes, of course. I always take copious notes."

"Were your notes an accurate reflection of what the defendant said?"

He nodded. "Yes."

"When did you incorporate those notes into your report?"

"I'm not certain as to the exact time, but I always type up my reports within twenty-four hours of an interview."

"Did the report accurately reflect the defendant's statements and what was in your notes?"

"Yes."

"No further questions."

As she sat, Marshall kept a stoic appearance, but David knew she was angry because no one had told her about Blackwood's termination for misconduct. David also surmised she was frustrated as he was the last witness for her case-in-chief and the last witness of the day, so his damaged testimony would stick with the jury over the weekend.

Chapter 32

Monday, January 18

About thirty minutes before the trial resumed, David isolated himself in a quiet corner of the courthouse and panicked. He called Marc on his cell phone.

"We've got a serious problem. Valerie's a no-show, and I can't reach her on her cell and home numbers."

"Ah, crap!"

"Where are you? I need you to find her ASAP."

"I'm at home and was about to leave for the office. Valerie lives close by. I'll get over there right now."

"Okay, please call me back." David ran his hand through his hair. Despite his present mood, he did his best to project a calm appearance. He turned the corner and found Bev and Amanda standing side by side, waiting for the bailiff to unlock the doors to the courtroom.

David smiled at Amanda. "Excuse me." He turned to Bev, and with his false expression still in place said, "Could I speak to you for a couple of moments?"

Bev nodded to Amanda, and David escorted her to the secluded location around the corner. He dropped the façade and felt his chest tighten.

"We've got a big problem," he said. "Valerie's not here, and I can't reach her by phone. Marc's trying to track her down."

Bev remained calm. "Let's not get carried away. She could be running a few minutes late, or she could be in the subway and can't get a signal."

David ran his hand through his hair again. "Yeah, I know, but…"

"Let's not assume the worst or jump to conclusions. She's also not our first witness, and we can buy some time." Bev raised her eyebrow. "However, it wouldn't hurt to run through our options."

"Good idea," David said while trying to control his anxiety. "If Valerie is a little late, we're… uh… In another trial, Perkins didn't allow a short continuance for a witness to appear. So, he probably won't this time, regardless of the reason." He exhaled. "Last weekend, we discussed calling no witnesses, and during closing we'd argue we didn't need any since the prosecution failed to prove its case. I think that scenario is still off the table."

"Agreed. Even if Valerie doesn't testify, we should call our first two witnesses. They'll make some good points."

David nodded and looked at the floor. "Yeah, but I'd rather not stop after them."

"We have other witnesses on our list, but I strongly suspect Perkins won't allow us to call a multitude to bash Simpson's character. He'd consider it cumulative testimony and a waste of time."

"Yeah, sure. Valerie is a character witness, and other people from her former employer don't know Amanda nearly as well. So, uh, I guess they're out."

"We only briefly mentioned Charles Thorton during our last meeting. Is he definitely not an option?"

David shook his head. "When I finally met with him, he was in bad shape, and I'm not sure what was wrong with him. He could barely communicate at all. He's definitely out."

"I see. That leaves only two other people on our witness list."

"Oh crap," David said while rolling his eyes. "We're down to Paul and Lorraine, and Paul is a non-starter for obvious reasons. Lorraine… well, the jury might not give her testimony any weight and view us as playing the sympathy card."

Bev took off her glasses and tapped her cheek with a temple tip. "Probably true, but do we think her testimony would hurt us?"

"Well… I don't think so if I keep it simple. On the first day of trial, she needed Xanax, but she's seemed okay the last few days. Obviously, we'll need to ask her if she's up for it."

"And if Fernandez shows, we don't have to worry about it."

"Right," David said. "Could you explain to Amanda what's happening without freaking her out?"

"Of course."

For the next twenty minutes, David paced and kept checking his phone, making certain he still had a signal.

Then Marc finally called. "Hey, Valerie's really sick," he said. "I think she's got the flu."

"Damn it, Marc! Stop messing with me!"

"Whoa! Hang on. I'm not messing with you. I'm at Valerie's place right now. She looks terrible. She couldn't answer the front door, and one of her kids let me in. There's no way she can take the stand. Her mother's coming over, and she'll take Valerie to the ER."

"Terrific," David said sarcastically. "Sorry about the outburst. Looks like Lorraine will be our last witness for the day."

"Uh, I guess so. That was a fast decision. Don't you want to run it past Bev first?"

"We already discussed our options. After Valerie's mom arrives, please come to the courtroom. I need another set of eyes to check out Lorraine's disposition before we ask her if she's willing to take the stand."

* * *

Once the trial resumed, Beverly Cohen questioned Theresa Quintero, a Latina in her mid-thirties. Except for her blonde hair showing its darker roots, Quintero had no distinguishing characteristics and could blend into any crowd. As she sat in the witness chair, she tugged at her purse strap.

"Ms. Quintero, where were you employed in early 2009?"

"I was a paralegal at the Law Offices of Thorton, Saxer & Caldwell."

"Where was your cubicle?"

"Close to Mr. Simpson's corner office."

"How did he treat you?"

"Not very well," Quintero said and tugged the strap again.

"Could you please elaborate?"

"Okay… He was a… horrible person and constantly harassed me. One time, he slapped me on the behind. A couple of times, he asked if I was a prostitute in Mexico. Excuse me." She took a tissue from her purse and wiped away a tear below her left eye.

"Did Mr. Simpson make other comments you found inappropriate?"

"Do I have to tell you all of them?"

"No, it's not necessary," Bev said. "How often did he make inappropriate comments?"

"Almost every day."

"Ms. Quintero, did you respond to the comments in any manner?"

"I… I don't know. A few times, I called in sick. Eventually, I spoke with Mr. Thorton, and he let me move to another cubicle away from Mr. Simpson's office."

"Did the move improve your situation?"

Quintero wiped her left eye again. "No, not really… He still bothered me from time to time. I started looking for another job, but I was still working there when he was killed."

"What was your reaction to Mr. Simpson's death?"

"I… I know it's not a nice thing to say, but a great weight had been lifted from me."

Bev gave the witness a couple of moments to collect herself before moving onto the next topic.

"While working at the Thorton firm, did you ever lose your key card during the last year prior to Mr. Simpson's death?"

"Yes. It happened two times."

"Did you get them replaced?"

"Yes. I went down to the security office and told them I lost my card. I showed my ID and got a new one. That was it."

"Did they ask you how or when you lost your key card?"

"No."

"No further questions."

Marshall began her cross-examination with one mundane question after another, and David didn't know where she was going with it. He glanced toward the jurors and saw three of them looking bewildered, while the others appeared disinterested. Juror Number 7, the man with the large stomach and goatee, crossed his arms and frowned.

Then Marshall asked, "Are you a violent person?"

Quintero gave a faint smile. "Oh, no."

"Was anyone else at the Thorton law firm a violent person?"

"I'm not sure. Give me a moment, please." Quintero closed her eyes. "I'm trying to remember…" She opened them, and her face brightened. "Oh yeah. Donna Conway threatened to slit Mr. Simpson's throat."

Marshall clenched her left hand behind her back, indicating she knew she had made a mistake.

Amanda showed David a quick note:

Oops?

David wrote back:

Yup! No clue how she knew

David called the next defense witness, Michael Dobson, a young African American. He was short in stature, and his suit barely contained his muscular frame.

"Mr. Dobson, where do you currently work?" David asked.

"I'm a manager at a warehouse in Queens."

"Where were you working in June 2009?"

"I was a security supervisor at the O'Connell building."

"Why did you change jobs?"

Dobson scowled. "They fired me, made me the scapegoat for the murder so that they could keep the building's contract."

"Please describe the building's security last June."

He scoffed. "It was a joke, man. The owners were too cheap to pay for real security."

"Could you please elaborate?" David took two steps into the well.

"Last June, there were no cameras in the elevators, outside the building, or on the upper floors, and the emergency exit doors had no alarms. Shoot, anyone on the inside could've opened one and allowed someone on the outside to enter the building without security knowing about it." Dobson shook his head. "Man, we were just window dressing."

"Did building security issue key cards?"

"Yeah. You needed a key card to use the regular elevators during the off hours and the freight elevators 24/7."

"How did the key cards work?"

"They were crap."

Judge Perkins turned toward the witness. "Watch your language, young man. Please, answer the question in a more professional manner."

Dobson swung his head toward the judge. "Sorry." He redirected his attention to David. "We programmed the cards by floor. The Thorton law firm was on the ninth and tenth floors, which meant during off hours, their cards only opened the elevator doors on those floors and the ground floor."

"Uh-huh. Did each card belong to a particular person?" David asked.

Dobson scoffed again. "No, it would've made too much sense. We didn't code the cards that way and didn't keep track of which ones were lost. Instead, we reprogrammed them every six months on a rotational basis, which deactivated lost cards."

"Prior to the murder last June, when was the last time security reprogrammed the cards for the ninth and tenth floors?"

"In April."

"During last June, did security guards patrol the upper floors?"

"No."

"Why was security so lax?"

Dobson shook his head. "Do I really need to spell it out? The owners were too damn cheap to pay for it."

"Thank you," David said. "No further questions."

On cross-examination, Marshall asked, "Aren't you bitter because the security company fired you?"

"Yeah, sure," he replied hostilely. "No one likes to be fired, especially when he didn't deserve it."

"Do you think your bitterness tainted your testimony?"

"Give me a break."

"Have you read the security company's personnel file on you?"

"No."

"Would you be surprised to learn your superiors claimed you were difficult?"

"That's the way they put it?" Dobson asked as he shook his head again. "I wanted to fire a couple of lazy guards, and the company wouldn't let me. Another time, I tried to explain to Mr. O'Connell why building security was inadequate. He didn't want to hear it, and he went behind my back to complain to corporate. If that makes me difficult, then yeah, I am."

"Nothing further, Your Honor."

Judge Perkins cleared his throat. "We're in recess for the morning break."

* * *

Marc was sitting in the gallery's first row and gave David and Bev a quick thumbs-up, indicating Lorraine was in a good mood.

David then whispered to Amanda, "Please follow us."

The three attorneys and Amanda stepped out of the courtroom and around the corner to an attorney conference room. Once everyone was inside and the door was closed, Bev calmly addressed Amanda.

"We might have one more witness, and afterward we'll ask for a continuance and hope Ms. Fernandez will be well enough tomorrow to testify."

"Do you think Perkins will grant the motion?" Amanda asked.

"Probably not. With or without Ms. Fernandez, we've presented a good case, but we'd like to finish on a positive note. This means we'd like to call one more witness to vouch for your character."

"You mean my dad?"

"No," David said. "Your mother. She might impress the jury a little more. How do you feel about it?"

"Yeah, I guess so, but I don't want to push her into it."

"Not a problem," David said. "Please, go get her right now. Beverly, we might need a few extra minutes. Could you stall in court, if necessary?"

* * *

Moments later, Amanda returned to the conference with Paul and Lorraine, who were in their usual good moods.

"Sorry, but we need to keep this brief," David said. "You probably know Valerie is sick and cannot come today. We want to call one more witness to vouch for Amanda's character. We would like to–"

"I'll do it," Paul interrupted. "Anything for my pumpkin."

Marc's eyes popped, and David knew he was thinking the same thing as him. Paul was too radioactive to put on the stand. Instead of stating so aloud, David delivered a statement he had rehearsed in his head.

"Thanks, Paul. I appreciate the gesture, but I believe Lorraine is the better choice. The prosecutor would less likely attack her on cross than you because the jury will find her more sympathetic. Sorry, it's a big man, petite woman kind of thing."

Paul raised both hands in a surrender position. "Sure, sure, I get it. No need to explain it anymore."

Amanda gently grabbed Lorraine's arm. "Mom, are you up to it? If this is too much for you, that's okay. Just let us know."

Lorraine let out a wide smile. "No, I'm okay. I can do it. What should I say?"

"Just follow my lead," David said. "We'll talk about Amanda and how she's a good person. We'll also go over how she handled some things in life. No tough questions."

* * *

Once everyone returned to the courtroom, Judge Perkins looked at David. "Please, call your next witness," he said.

"The defense calls Lorraine Morelli."

Lorraine rose from her spot in the gallery's first row. As she passed the jury, she smiled at them. Some returned the smile, while others seemed indifferent. After she was sworn in, David began his direct examination from the podium.

"How do you know Amanda?"

Lorraine gave another wide smile. "Oh, she's my daughter, my pride and joy. So is Daniel, her older brother, but he couldn't be here today."

"Could you briefly summarize Amanda's childhood?"

"Oh sure. She was a happy child and very smart, too. She had many friends. She got along with everyone in the neighborhood, even Mrs. Esposito, who didn't like anybody."

"Did she have any violent outbursts?"

"No… not really." Lorraine briefly looked down. When she focused again on David, she patted her lap. "Wait, there was one time she got really upset. Her brother broke one of her dolls on purpose. She punched him in the arm, gave him a big bruise. We told her she shouldn't act out like that, and she never did it again."

David glanced at the jurors from the corner of his right eye. At least a couple seemed amused. So far, so good. Keep it up, Lorraine, he said to himself.

"Prior to getting arrested for this case, did Amanda ever have any trouble with the law?"

"Oh, no. Nothing like that."

"What is her marital status?"

Lorraine's expression became more serious. "She's divorced. It was really sad. Paul, that's my husband, and me thought they made such a great couple, and it all fell apart."

David restrained himself from turning to Amanda to gauge her reaction.

"How did Amanda handle it? Any violent outbursts?"

"No, of course not. She didn't even make any comments like it. Naturally, she was upset, disappointed, and maybe a little depressed, but she hung in there. She got over it."

"How does Amanda feel about guns?"

"She hates them." Lorraine turned toward the jury. "She bugged her father and me for the longest time to get rid of our pistol. We only had it for protection. We finally got rid of it to please her. Even though Amanda didn't tell me, I found out about the little gun that her ex-husband gave her when she moved out. She never wanted it, and she only kept it in a closet to avoid another argument with him."

"How did you feel about Amanda becoming a lawyer?" David asked.

Lorraine beamed with pride. "We were so proud of her. We never had a lawyer in the family. She certainly did better than Paul and me. We never spent a day in college."

"How did Amanda feel about J. Robert Simpson?"

"Not too good," she said as she became more serious again. "She wanted to get away from him, and before he died, she was looking for another job."

"Did she provide details about what was happening at the law firm prior to last June?" David asked.

"No, not really. When I met her for lunch, we discussed lots of things, but not that."

"What did you discuss?"

"Mostly men," Lorraine said while her cheeks blushed.

David heard chuckling and laughter throughout the courtroom. Lorraine was still going strong. Just one more question, and she would be done.

"Do you think Amanda was capable of killing J. Robert Simpson?"

Lorraine straightened her back. "She's not, and I know she didn't do it… because I did."

David froze and heard a chorus of gasps. He imagined the news stunned Amanda but could not turn around to look at her or anyone else.

"Why did you kill Mr. Simpson?" he asked once he had regained his composure.

Lorraine shrugged. "I really didn't want to kill him. It just happened."

"Why?"

She sighed. "Amanda didn't tell me everything, but I knew he was treating all the women very badly. It nearly broke my heart. I figured something had to be done."

"What happened on that evening?"

"I took the chance he would be in his office, and he was. I tried to talk to him really nice and make him realize his behavior was really awful." Lorraine frowned. "He didn't care. He just laughed at me. So, I pulled the gun out of my purse and waived it in his face. He still didn't take me seriously. That made me really mad, and I shot him." She gave a sad shrug. "I really didn't want to kill him. It just happened."

"No further questions."

As David returned to his seat, he noticed Marshall twirling a pen in her left hand. From his past experiences, he knew she was confident and ready to attack. He dreaded what was about to occur.

"What kind of firearm did you use to shoot Mr. Simpson?" Marshall asked.

"I didn't remember what kind until they talked about it in court. It was a .38-caliber pistol."

"The same gun that you and your husband owned?"

Lorraine smirked. "Oh no, like I said, we got rid of it."

"Where did you get the gun that you used to shoot Mr. Simpson?"

"I bought it at a pawn shop."

"Which one?" Marshall said while staring intensely.

"I don't know."

"What happened to the gun?"

"Um… I think I threw it away."

"Where?"

Lorraine shrugged. "Somewhere. I don't remember where, sorry."

"Uh-huh," Marshall said. "So, you decided to visit the law firm late in the evening, hoping Mr. Simpson would be there?"

"Yes, that's right."

"Why didn't a security camera film you entering the building?"

Lorraine shrugged again. "Beats me. They must've missed me."

"How did that happen?"

"I don't know. It just did."

"Why did the security guards never see you that evening?"

"I… I don't know."

"That's what I thought. No further questions."

With her last answer, David knew Lorraine's last shred of credibility had disappeared.

"Mr. Lee," Judge Perkins asked, "any redirect?"

"No, Your Honor," he said as he rose. "May we have a brief sidebar?"

The judge motioned for the attorneys to come forward and placed his left hand over his microphone.

"Your Honor," David whispered, "the defense has one more witness, Valerie Fernandez. She's an important character witness and can also rebut some of the prosecution's evidence. Right now, she's suffering from the flu and had to go to the ER."

"Too bad, Counsel. Does this mean the defense rests?"

"Your Honor, I'm not asking for much, and–"

"Yes, you are," he growled. "If the defense rests, we'll proceed with the rebuttal case for the prosecution, if any. If there's none, the jury can hear closing arguments and begin deliberations."

"I understand, Your Honor," David said, "but may we still adjourn early and give Ms. Fernandez one more opportunity to appear? She's a critical witness."

Perkins appeared unimpressed. "Ms. Marshall?"

"The People take no position."

He paused for about ten seconds. "All right. We'll adjourn, and if Ms. Fernandez isn't present first thing in the morning, the defense rests."

* * *

A few minutes later, David and Marc conferred in an attorney conference room.

"Where's Bev?" David asked. He rubbed his forehead and leaned against a table.

"Talking to Amanda, or maybe consoling her would be the better term."

"Why the hell did Lorraine do that? I was too busy watching the car accident; did you get a look at the jury?"

"Yeah, I did. I think all of them knew she lied. The judge knew, Amanda knew. Everyone in the courtroom knew."

"During her closing argument, Marshall will hit us over the head with that testimony, won't she?"

"Oh yeah," Marc said. "If I were still a prosecutor, I certainly would. I'd argue the defense is desperate and maybe imply you instructed Lorraine to commit perjury."

"Terrific. At least Marshall didn't object to a continuance until tomorrow morning."

"I think you missed a couple of things," Marc said. "First, she didn't object to avoid causing an appealable issue – if Perkins denied your request anyway, oh well. Second, I think she wants Valerie to take the stand and tell more lies. We know she won't, but Marshall will go after her very hard. If she scores some more points, she will really hammer us during closing."

David lowered his hand and closed his eyes in resignation. "Great. Thanks for the pep talk."

"Sorry. I've got to call them like I see them. What are our chances with the jury?"

David exhaled and gazed at the ceiling. "If Valerie doesn't appear, and we have to rest our case tomorrow morning… Well, we made some good points, but thanks to Lorraine… I don't know." He looked at Marc. "Maybe we get lucky and have a hung jury. It's better than a conviction, but second trials usually favor the prosecution. What are the odds Valerie makes a speedy recovery and testifies tomorrow?"

"Not good at all."

"Damn! I was afraid of that."

Chapter 33

Tuesday, January 19

The media, the Morelli family, and their friends packed the courtroom as everyone anticipated closing arguments and a jury verdict. But first, Judge Perkins began the morning session outside of the jurors' presence.

"Does the defense rest?" he asked.

"Your Honor, Valerie Fernandez is still too ill to testify. Is there any possibility of continuing for one more day?" David asked, even though he knew it was futile.

"No," the judge said coldly. "The defense rests. Ms. Marshall, do the People have a rebuttal case?"

"No, Your Honor."

"Very well. We'll bring in the jury and hear closing arguments."

In the state of New York, the defense presented its closing first, which did not make sense to David. Since the prosecution had the burden of proof, it should argue first. Perhaps more importantly, by providing the first closing, the defense could not respond to comments in the prosecutor's argument. This forced a defense attorney to make an educated guess regarding the prosecution's pitch and give a proactive rebuttal before the assistant district attorney spoke. Despite this obstacle, David and Bev were well prepared, and since this was her last trial, David gave her the honor of making the final closing argument.

Bev rose and stood next to the defense table. "Ladies and gentlemen of the jury, in one way, this is a simple case. You only need to answer one question: do you believe beyond a reasonable doubt that Amanda Morelli murdered J. Robert Simpson? I submit to you the answer is no. In fact, you should have more than a reasonable doubt in your collective mind."

Bev walked into the well and toward the jurors. The courtroom was so quiet that David could hear her footsteps.

"Mr. Simpson was a loathsome individual, and the women at Thorton, Saxer & Caldwell despised him. He made their lives miserable, and others hated the deceased as well. Despite a wide variety of potential suspects, the district attorney's office settled on my client. Why? She could not stand Mr. Simpson, and nobody can confirm she was sick and in bed during the evening of June 18, 2009." Bev removed her glasses and shook them. "That's certainly not enough to prove she's guilty."

David noticed Bev had the attention of all twelve jurors and the four alternates, but Juror Number 7 had folded his arms on top of his large stomach, which he interpreted as a terrible sign.

"According to the DA, Ms. Morelli knew how to enter and exit the building without being detected because she was familiar with its security measures or the lack thereof. The DA also believes she's the same height as the shooter, whom she believes was the person in the gray wig. Belief alone isn't enough, not even close."

Bev donned her glasses and walked to the jurors' left side. "The police concluded the murder was an inside job, and the shooter worked at the law firm." She opened her arms. "Why? Only someone at Thorton would have known that no one else would've been working there in the evening. That same someone would've known how to enter and exit the building without detection." Bev held up her right index finger. "Not so fast. The law firm wasn't a secret government agency, and its work habits were a matter of public knowledge. Furthermore, building security was porous at best and easy to circumvent, which widens the possibilities as to who could've committed the murder."

All the jurors were paying close attention, except Juror Number 7, who continued, with his arms crossed, to scan the audience in the gallery.

Bev approached each juror member and made eye contact. "NYPD claims they conducted a thorough investigation. Do you think so? I don't. They never knew about Donna Conway until after they arrested my client. The police interviewed Ms. Morelli but asked no follow-up questions to clarify some of her comments. Why did they fail to do so? Because they had already concluded she was guilty. However, you must reach a verdict based upon the facts and the law, not mere assumptions."

David thought he saw a female juror nod in agreement.

As she spoke, Bev strolled in front of the jurors again. "Let's not forget one detective previously lied on the stand. Did he lie to you? How many other detectives had an agenda? How does this affect your analysis?"

Juror Number 7 was looking down and picking at his fingers.

"Let's not forget Donna Conway threatened to slit Mr. Simpson's throat, but the police never knew about her until we told the district attorney's office. What else did the police miss? They failed to recognize the murder was a professional hit. Somebody wanted J. Robert Simpson dead and paid a hit man to do it, and the evidence supports this conclusion."

Amanda scribbled to David:

She's really good.

"In early June 2009, someone sent the tall blonde woman to the law firm to attract Mr. Simpson's attention. Also in early June, the same woman bought two cell phones under the name Bonnie Parker. Using one phone, she communicated with Mr. Simpson and strung him along, and on the evening of the murder, they had dinner. The blonde woman told Mr. Simpson she wanted a drink and maybe more in his office. Of course, Big Bobby was more than willing to oblige. Who was this woman?"

Bev waited as if she expected someone to answer but knew otherwise.

"She was a skilled con artist. She was also aware of the security cameras in the building's lobby and made certain they did not record her face. This woman stepped outside and made a phone call to alert the killer that Mr. Simpson was heading upstairs. After shooting him, the killer called the blonde woman to confirm Big Bobby was dead." Bev removed her glasses again.

David observed a male juror check his watch, which he found disappointing.

"Please, note I'm referring to the murderer as a person, not a woman, because the evidence presented to you doesn't reveal the shooter's gender. The DA claims the person in the gray wig who appeared on the street shortly after the second call was the shooter. Perhaps, but even the enhanced video of the scene failed to reveal this person's sex or facial features."

Bev returned her glasses to their proper place and paused while a spectator in the gallery sneezed three times.

"The lack of evidence at the crime scene shows the killer was a professional. He didn't leave any shell casings and wiped off the handles to the office door. Those were the actions of a cold and methodical person. He didn't leave behind any DNA, which again is consistent with a professional contract killer. The prosecutor might tell you using a pillow as a silencer means an amateur committed the crime. Is that so? Nobody knows why the shots were fired through a pillow. If the shooter knew how to bypass security and was aware nobody else would be on the tenth floor, he probably was also aware of the throw pillows and used one to his advantage. Besides, since the killer and the deceased were the only persons on the floor, he didn't need a silencer because no one else would've heard the shots."

Bev took three steps back.

"It's clear a professional hit man was responsible for Mr. Simpson's murder, not my client, who cooperated with the police. Isn't her full cooperation consistent with an innocent person's behavior? Suppose you believe the defense's theory is a decent one, but you aren't convinced. That's fine and not the point. The defense doesn't need to prove its alternate theory of the crime. Instead, the prosecutor needs to prove her theory beyond a reasonable doubt, and she falls far short of the mark. Therefore, you have no choice but to find Amanda Morelli not guilty. In fact, it's your only reasonable choice."

Marshall then gave her closing argument, and David was unable to focus on her words, as he felt adrenaline rushing out his body. Although he had experienced the same effect at the end of other trials, it was more pronounced this time. He resorted to scribbling drawings on a legal pad to remain alert. After Marshall finished her argument, Judge Perkins provided instructions on the applicable law, which took far too long but were essential for the jury to hear. The judge then dismissed them to deliberate.

David told the Morelli family he would meet them at the coffee shop down the street.

* * *

Once David arrived, he noticed Daniel, Amanda's brother, had tucked himself away in a booth by himself and appeared to be in the middle of a business call. Pete sat in a corner with other men in their sixties. Lorraine and Debra shared a small booth. David was amazed Lorraine could maintain such a carefree attitude after the damage she had caused. Paul once again greeted others and worked the room.

Someone mentioned the trial to Paul, and he said, "Hey, I know my Amanda didn't do it. Don't worry about it."

David imagined "don't worry about it" was the big man's attitude about life in general, and he couldn't afford the luxury of embracing such a philosophy himself.

David flopped into a small booth and sat across from Amanda. He felt drained and famished.

"I don't need to see the menu, thank you," he said as soon as the server arrived. "I'll order a club sandwich, fries, and a Coke."

"Nothing for me, thanks," Amanda added. "I'm too nervous to eat," she said after the server left. "It feels as if my stomach is on the worst rollercoaster in the world."

David nodded. "I understand. Maybe you should distract yourself by thinking of something else. What's happening with the hockey season?"

Amanda's mood somewhat brightened, and she talked about the Rangers and the Islanders. Even after his food arrived, she continued to talk about hockey. While David had no interest in the sport, the topic helped pass the time and relaxed Amanda to some extent.

David guessed the jury would be out for the rest of the day and into the next, but at 1:30, he received a text message from the court clerk, stating the jury had reached a verdict. David was shocked because they had probably deliberated for less than an hour after lunch.

* * *

About fifteen minutes later, all parties and spectators were back in court. Tension filled the air as everyone held their breath, and the courtroom fell silent. When Judge Perkins entered, his footsteps sounded like thunder.

When the jury arrived, David's heart pounded. He could not keep his eyes off them as he reached for Amanda's hand. He thought a short deliberation meant a "not guilty" verdict, but no juror made eye contact with him, which indicated otherwise. Three jurors glanced in Marshall's direction, which increased his anxiety level. He feared he was about to hear the worst.

"Has the jury reached a verdict?" Perkins asked.

"We have, Your Honor," said Juror Number 7.

Oh no! David thought. They picked the worst possible foreperson!

Juror Number 7 handed the verdict form to the court clerk, who turned it over to the judge. David could not determine the verdict from the foreperson's body language and facial expression, and his heart pounded harder.

Perkins read the verdict form without any reaction. He then said, "On the sole count of the indictment, murder in the first degree, how do you find the defendant, Amanda Morelli?"

There was a long pause. David could not handle the suspense and almost screamed, "Say it, damn it! Say it!"

"We find the defendant not guilty."

A roar erupted from the defense side of the courtroom. David was elated, and the next several moments were a blur. Amanda could have hugged him, and maybe he received a slap or two on the back. Once he regained his focus, he turned to Bev.

"Thank you."

Bev nodded. "That was my job."

David wanted to hug her, but he knew she was not that kind of a person. He also wanted to thank her for being his mentor and so much more, except he could not get the words out of his mouth. "Ready for the press conference?" he said instead. "Should be a good one."

"No, thank you. As of right now, I'm officially retired again, and I'll leave through the back entrance. Go, enjoy the media circus." Bev grabbed her satchel.

David watched her leave the courtroom with her head held high. He then detected a tap on his shoulder and turned around.

"Remember me?" Amanda asked with a devilish grin.

"I think so," David said with a smile. He grabbed Amanda by the hand and guided her to a spot between the defense table and the judge's bench. He also turned his back to the remaining spectators.

Amanda looked puzzled. "What are you doing?"

"I don't want others to hear me or read my lips because I might make a fool out of myself."

"What?" she said with a nervous laugh.

"Will you go out to dinner with me?"

Amanda rolled her eyes. "The whole family's going out to celebrate, and you're obviously invited."

David cradled her hand and looked into her eyes. "That's not what I mean. I don't date clients, but the case is over, and you're no longer a client. Will you go on a date with me?"

Her eyes got wide. "Huh? I mean yes, but there's a problem. You made us both famous. How are we supposed to have a date in public?"

He chuckled. "We'll figure something out. Now, are you ready for the press conference? Let's take the high road. We're glad it's over, and the jury made the right decision."

"Got it. Let's go."

Chapter 34

February to early June 2010

Three weeks after the trial, David made a phone call to Jacqueline Marshall.

"Oh, it's you," she said with contempt in her voice. "Why'd you call? Rubbing it in?"

"No, not at all. I'm calling for a different reason, but I first need to mention something else. I hope you know I didn't tell Lorraine to falsely confess to the murder."

"I know. It was obvious by the look on your face."

"Which was?"

"A deer in the headlights. Should you be admitting that she lied?"

David chuckled. "Well, she wasn't my client, and I didn't need to spell it out for you. Besides, you probably won't prosecute her for perjury."

"No one is. The DA doesn't want the public to be reminded of what happened with Amanda Morelli."

David stood to stretch his legs. "Makes sense. Anyway, here's why I called. Our law firm is getting busier, and Marc and I are looking for a third partner. How about it? Want to go into private practice?"

There was a long pause before she replied. "Are you serious?"

"Of course. You're a brilliant attorney, and we need one more. We're starting to represent individuals charged with white-collar crimes, and not all attorneys can handle the complexities they can present, but you certainly can. If you join us, we'll change the firm's name to Marshall, D'Angelo, and Lee. Look, I know I'm making an offer right out of the blue. So, if you need some time to think about it, that's fine. Just get back to me when you can."

"Huh. I never expected this call," she said following another long pause. "I'm flattered by the offer, but I can't accept. To be perfectly candid, I already left the district attorney's office and joined Malik Watkins' firm."

David was stunned and put his left hand on his head. "*The* Malik Watkins, last year's African American Attorney of the Year?"

"That's him."

"Holy crap! I didn't even know a public servant ran in the same circles as him. How do you know him?"

"We've been married for the past three years."

David chuckled. "Really? I had no clue. That's great!"

"We didn't tell anyone because we wanted to keep our private lives private. Since we'll be working together, it's bound to come out, eventually. Please don't tell your reporter friends. We'd like to release the information when the time is right."

"Sure, not a problem. As long as you're sharing, I have a question. Why didn't you have a trial partner?"

"I guess it wouldn't hurt to tell you. Simpson had a friend at City Hall who pushed very hard for an indictment." Marshall scoffed. "Simpson having a friend in high places, now there's a nauseating thought. Anyway, even though we could present a decent case, there were some problems, which you exploited. I expressed my concerns in an email to the DA and recommended we wait on an arrest pending further investigation. The DA rejected my opinion and ordered me to proceed. I could take the political hit if we lost, but a trial partner might not be so fortunate. So, I convinced the DA I could handle it by myself. Even though I loved being a prosecutor, I hated politics, and I decided Morelli would be my last defendant, regardless of the outcome."

"Well, Jacqueline, I never heard about the DA blaming you."

"He didn't, and it would've been a very foolish idea. I sent a copy of the email with my comments about the case to Malik. If the DA had tried to throw me under the bus, Malik would've released the email and thrown him under a larger one, ran over him, put the bus in reverse, and ran him over again."

David chuckled. "That's awesome. Did the DA know Malik had a copy of the email?"

"Absolutely. I told him right after closing arguments and before the jury verdict."

He laughed hard. "Nice! Was he mad?"

"Of course, and I didn't care. Why should I?"

"Okay, thanks for the information, and good luck with your new career."

* * *

A few days later, David and Marc offered a partnership to Angela Williams, a law school classmate and an Assistant US Attorney in Brooklyn. In addition to her excellent legal skills, to David's amusement and Marc's chagrin, Angela routinely beat Marc at Nerf basketball.

* * *

In early June, David proudly stood before a full church as a groomsman for his sister's wedding. Escorted by their father, Courtney came down the aisle in an elegant, white mermaid-style dress with exposed shoulders. David glanced at his mother in the first row. Her frown showed she disapproved of Courtney wearing her hair down and not wearing the veil she had selected for her.

As the bride and groom took their respective places, David scanned for familiar faces in attendance. He spotted Bev and her husband, Stanley, whom he finally met earlier in the day. David thought the adage of long-married couples looking like each other could be true. Stanley appeared remarkably similar to Bev, except his hair was gray and curly, while hers was white, layered, and straight. Marc and Stephanie sat next to them. Even though Marc would have to wait a considerable period of time before his doctors would give him the all-clear, he had privately told David that he and Steph were trying for a baby.

Valerie and her new boyfriend sat in the same row. While David had thought she would make an excellent addition to the firm, she had been an even better fit than expected. Since she had a sharp and quick mind, David had recommended she apply to law school. After giving it some thought, she declined and stated she was happy in her present position.

David also noted Irene's absence. Marc had fired her, and to his surprise, his extended family had taken the news in stride. Marc had told him the worst comment he heard was, "So, she had to go, huh?"

David then directed his attention to the most amazing woman in the church: Amanda, his girlfriend of the past six months. She sat between his parents to the left and her parents to the right. David had introduced her during the rehearsal dinner last night, and his mother had been so impressed, she insisted Amanda sit next to her during the wedding. He had long since forgiven Lorraine for lying on the stand, and it had been easy to do so, given her testimony no longer mattered.

After Amanda's name had faded from the news, a commercial bank in Manhattan had hired her as part of their in-house counsel. She had accepted the position after confirming the bank had a zero-tolerance policy for sexual harassment, as the female CEO did not want the organization ran any other way.

* * *

During the wedding reception, David and Amanda snuck up to her hotel room and stood on the twentieth-floor balcony. Since it was a warm evening, David left his tuxedo jacket and bow tie on the king-size bed. With champagne glasses in their hands, the couple gazed at the city lights.

"This is just like a romantic movie," Amanda said. "A young and handsome couple fall in love. They get married in a beautiful church surrounded by family and friends, and the bride gets to wear an absolutely gorgeous gown. The last scene should be them standing here, not us."

Do it now, David urged himself and turned to face her. "Perhaps the movie has a different ending."

"Oh?" Amanda said as she smiled and faced him.

"How about this one? The boyfriend gets down on one knee." David knelt and took her right hand. "He tells his girlfriend she's the most beautiful woman in the world, both inside and out. He can't imagine living the rest of his life without her, and he asks her to marry him."

Amanda laughed and pulled back her hand.

David dropped his head, and his heart sank even further. He then heard a gasp.

"What? You're serious?"

He felt Amanda's hands cusp his cheeks. She lifted his head and bent over so they were face to face.

"You're serious?"

"Yeah."

Amanda gave David an intense, passionate kiss.

"So, what's your answer?" he said when she pulled away.

Amanda knelt and lightly slapped him on the chest. "Very funny. You know, your proposal would have gone better if you'd bought a ring."

David threw up his head. "Crap. It's in my jacket." He rushed to the bed with Amanda right behind him. He reached inside it and retrieved a black ring box out of the right pocket and opened it.

Amanda's eyes lit up as she saw a one-carat, center-cut diamond, and for several moments, she could not stop staring at it.

David gave a wide smile. "Let's go downstairs and show it off."

Amanda started to rise and then paused. She sat and closed the box. "No, it's Courtney's day, and I don't want to take the spotlight away from her. I'll tell my parents tonight and show them the ring." She gave a wry smile. "Perhaps emergency medical personnel should be standing by. Maybe you can quietly tell Courtney before brunch tomorrow, and we'll be more open about it on Monday." She gave a light chuckle. "By then, if you want to make a fool out of yourself and shout it from the rooftops, go right ahead."

Chapter 35

Friday, June 11

Late afternoon, David once again arrived at the Morelli home in Bensonhurst. This time, he noticed pale blue and yellow flowers blooming within the brick enclosure in the front yard. He rang the doorbell, and Amanda answered in bare feet, jeans, and a T-shirt.

"Get down here, ya big ape."

David grinned and bent at the waist.

Amanda gave him a kiss on the lips and smiled when she saw the champagne bottle in his right hand. "Dom Perignon, very nice. You think it'll tip off Mom and Dad that we're engaged?"

"So, you don't think the ring on your finger gave them a clue?"

Amanda admired it. "Hmm, maybe. You got good taste, excellent color and clarity. How much did this set you back, at least ten grand?"

"Nice try. I'll take the Fifth."

She uttered a fake sigh. "Fine. Come inside."

Amanda's parents had not seen David since he had proposed, and once he stepped into the living room, Paul was the first to greet him.

"Congratulations!" he said as he gave David a firm handshake and a slap on the back.

Lorraine hugged him. When she released, David noticed the prominent scars on her left wrist. If he had not known any better, the scars were consistent with her slashing her wrist, and she was the complete opposite of suicidal. In fact, David had known no one more upbeat and optimistic than her, except for Paul.

* * *

Since the evening was an engagement celebration, Lorraine insisted on serving dinner at the dining-room table instead of the horrible one next to the kitchen. As for the meal, she almost outdid herself by creating a rustic Italian feast and panna cotta for dessert. David ate so much that his stomach begged him to stop.

After they had finished, Lorraine beamed at her daughter and future son-in-law. "Oh, I'm so glad the two of you found each other. It's so wonderful. It's too bad Amanda had to get arrested and put on trial for it to happen."

"Me too, Mom. But spending my life with David almost makes it all worthwhile." Amanda leaned to her right and gave him another kiss.

Lorraine and Paul took a few dishes to the kitchen, and when they returned, Lorraine said, "We should've gone to the police and told them I did it. It would have gotten Amanda off the hook."

David groaned to himself because Lorraine still thought lying to the authorities was a good idea. Instead of scolding her, he said, "It wouldn't have made a difference. The police would've concluded you were only trying to protect your daughter. Remember, we had a similar conversation before the trial."

Lorraine smiled. "Oh yeah. I remember now." She turned toward Paul. "Honey, why don't you sit, and I'll finish cleaning up in here and in the kitchen."

"Are you sure?"

"Of course, and the kids can get the… you know."

Paul sat while Lorraine gathered four dishes and silverware.

The big man then addressed Amanda and David. "We have an early wedding present for you. It's in the trunk in the attic."

"What is it?" Amanda asked.

"Oh, you'll see," Lorraine said. "Just go upstairs." She stepped into the kitchen with the dirty dishes and silverware.

"Okay," David said, a bit bewildered.

As Amanda and David went upstairs to the second floor, he noticed a squeak halfway up.

"It's been like that for years," she said.

David wanted to get a quick look at Amanda's bedroom out of curiosity, but the door at the end of the hallway was closed. He instead saw another bedroom with two exercise bikes and a small bathroom next to it. He also caught a glimpse of the master bedroom.

While standing in the hallway, Amanda grabbed a short drawstring above her head and pulled on it, which revealed a folding ladder. She unfolded it and stepped up to the attic. Once at the top, she flicked a light switch. "Come on up," she said.

David expected to see a drafty and creepy room. However, he found himself in a room well-lit by three bare bulbs and the absence of spiderwebs and dust. The room was as clean as the rest of the home. He spotted two trunks about four feet behind three boxes marked "X-mas."

"Which one?" he asked.

Amanda shrugged. "Let's start with the one on the left."

Both knelt in front of it, and Amanda opened the lid. Inside were thick and worn blankets for the winter.

"This can't be the present," David said.

"Yeah, I don't think so. Maybe Dad's messing with us a little, and it's underneath." She removed the blankets and placed them on the wood floor until there was nothing in the trunk except air.

"Must be in the other one," David said as he snatched two blankets.

Amanda grabbed his arm. "Wait, this trunk has a false bottom."

He put the blankets on the floor. "Are you sure?"

"Yeah. When Daniel and I were growing up, Mom and Dad bought us magic kits, and we had a wooden box with a hidden compartment. Look at the bottom. It's stained the same color as everything else, but the grain is different. I think it's plywood, and the rest of the trunk is probably oak… and look over there." She pointed to the right edge. "There's a tiny notch. I'll get something to stick in there and pry it open."

"Should we be snooping? Your parents might catch us."

Amanda smirked. "Who cares? We're not ten. Besides, you can wait here and listen for the squeak. Then you'll know someone is coming up."

David remained near the attic's opening while Amanda quietly headed downstairs to the second floor and went out of sight. He was amused they were sneaking around and still feared they would be caught.

As Amanda returned into view, she held a metal nail file and whispered, "Got it."

She snuck up the stairs to the attic, and they both knelt beside the open trunk.

In another whisper and with a devious smile, she asked, "Do you think we'll find Jimmy Hoffa?"

"Very funny," David said quietly. "Just open it."

Amanda stuck the nail file in the notch and angled it towards her. The plywood's right side popped up. She guided the file between the plywood and the trunk's side and pried it further open. Next, she grabbed the plywood and pulled it away, revealing a handgun with a short barrel.

David was stunned as he stared at the firearm. Even though he didn't know much about guns, he knew he was looking at a snub-nose .38 Smith & Wesson, the same type of weapon that had been used to kill Simpson. He shuttered over the thought this was the Morelli family's way of letting him know Amanda had committed the murder. He shifted his eyes to the left and noticed Amanda looked horrified.

"Is this…"

Amanda gave a slight nod while fixating on the gun. "Dad's… Yeah."

David tried to imagine an innocent explanation. "Maybe, maybe he bought another one."

Amanda grimaced and shook her head. "See the little nick in the butt? It's the same one." She slowly moved her right hand into the trunk and grabbed the gun. She opened the six-round cylinder, which was loaded except for two missing bullets. "Damn it," she said as she closed the cylinder and her eyes. Her right hand and the gun fell into her lap. "Damn it, he did it."

David could only stare at the gun.

"And where did the money come from?" she asked.

What money? David thought. The gun had mesmerized him so much he hadn't noticed anything else. He peeked into the trunk and was stunned again. Next to where the gun had been, he saw several small stacks of $100 bills wrapped in cellophane.

Assuming all the bills in the trunk were hundreds, David estimated he was looking at about $200,000, and they looked strange. Benjamin Franklin's head and the numbers were smaller, and the bills lacked any modern security features. He retrieved one stack for a closer examination. To the right of Franklin and near the bottom, he noticed "SERIES 1990," but the bill looked brand new. He leaned over and saw other hundreds from the 1980s and in the same condition.

Amanda ran both hands through her hair while the gun rested on her lap. "I can't believe this, the gun, the money. Where the hell did the cash come from?" She stared at the floor with her hands still on her head.

David also had difficulty processing everything he had just seen. His eyes darted from the gun to the money. He recalled Paul and Lorraine had paid him in cash, but except for a quick glance on one occasion, he had never examined the money. Irene never mentioned older bills. Perhaps she didn't notice or simply didn't bother to tell him.

Amanda grabbed the gun with her right hand and put it in her waistband behind her back.

"Should you be doing that?" David asked.

"It's fine. The safety's on." She reached into the trunk and grabbed a stack of bills. She also tucked the money in the waistband behind her. "Time to get some answers."

David followed Amanda down the stairs to the second floor and then to the first.

Right after the squeak, Paul called out, "Did you find it?"

"We found some old blankets," Amanda said coldly as she reached the bottom step. She turned the corner and headed to the dining room.

David was behind her and noticed Paul setting down a cup of coffee. He heard water running and dishes clanking in the kitchen.

Without looking at them, Paul chuckled. "That's not it. It's in the other trunk."

"We found this," Amanda said. She grabbed the stack of hundreds and dropped it on the table. "There's plenty more in the attic, and all of it was under the false bottom."

Paul shrugged and held out his hands. "What's the big deal? We keep some emergency cash in the house."

"Oh sure," Amanda said as she waved her right arm in the air. "What about this?" She retrieved the handgun and gently placed it on the table. "It's yours."

Paul gave another shrug. "Okay, I lied about getting rid of the gun. Your mother and me didn't want you to worry about it anymore."

"The police could have found it when they searched the house," David said.

"Yeah, but the cops were too stupid. So, it's not a big deal."

"Oh really, Dad!" Amanda said as she slapped her hand onto the table. "You did it! You killed Big Bastard, didn't you?"

Paul held out his hands again. "I swear I had nothing to do with it, honest!"

"Oh sure!" Amanda said as she threw back her head. "He was shot twice in the head with a .38, and your gun was fired twice. I know because you forgot to load two more rounds."

"I swear it wasn't me, Pumpkin," Paul said louder.

"Yeah, right! You've always had a fascination with the mafia, and you decided to carry out your own hit. Stop lying! You did it, didn't you?"

Lorraine came out of the kitchen, and her eyes fixated on the gun and the money on the table.

Amanda glared at her mother. "What?"

"Please leave him alone. He didn't do it," Lorraine calmly said.

Amanda held up her hands and rolled her eyes. "Oh sure! It was the Sugar Plum Fairy. No wait, it was Mickey Mouse. No, wait… It… was… Dad!"

"I swear," Paul insisted. "I had nothing to do with it."

Amanda scoffed. "Of course, then it was Mom," she said sarcastically.

David turned his attention to Lorraine, who had a half-smile and looked embarrassed. The wheels in his head began to spin rapidly. Could Lorraine have murdered

Simpson? She was short enough to have been the shooter and knew how to properly use firearms after the family outings at the cabin in the woods. Amanda had probably mentioned to her the routines of her old law firm, including no one working in the office late in the evening. Lorraine had been aware of Simpson's proclivity for sexual harassment, but she was scatterbrained, and the murder required a certain level of planning and sophistication.

Amanda was apparently too upset to notice her mother's odd expression. "Come on, Dad, out with it!"

"Please leave your father alone," Lorraine said. "I did it. I know no one believed me in court, but I'm telling the truth. I did it."

"What!" Amanda said. "It can't be you!"

"Yes, it was. It's not like it was the first time I killed someone."

"Honey," Paul said as he turned toward her. "You didn't kill the other guy."

"Yes, I did. I was involved."

David glanced at Amanda, whose mouth had fallen open. He shifted his gaze to Paul.

The big man briefly held out his hands. "Hey, what can I say?"

"What the hell is going on?!" David demanded.

Paul gave a dismissive wave of his right hand. "You already know too much. Don't worry about the rest."

"Really? No, not this time!" Amanda said as she slammed her right hand on the table. "Out with it!"

Paul sighed. "Honey, Amanda, David, please have a seat. Maybe we'd better explain everything."

Lorraine sat. "Okay," she asked, "where should we start?"

"1972," Paul said.

Chapter 36

The same evening

Lorraine stared into space, as if her mind traveled back in time. "It all started about two years before you were born, Amanda. One day, I was at the beauty parlor, gabbing with Debra and the other girls. I said I was happy. I had a great husband and a wonderful little boy. Even so, I wanted a little bit of excitement. It was… a little remark. I didn't give it another thought, but Debra did. When she got home, she talked to Pete, and back in the day, he was a wise guy."

Both Amanda and David were startled.

"Wait a minute, Mom. Pete was a mobster?"

Lorraine giggled. "That's right."

"Dad, did you know?"

"Oh sure. Everyone knew. Let your mother tell the story. Go ahead, honey," he said as he patted her arm.

"Pete got himself in trouble and needed to make up for it really quick. He never killed anyone, but Frankie ordered him to whack this guy named Bernie something. Maybe Bobby something, I can't remember. Paul?"

Paul shrugged. "Beats me. Bernie sounds about right."

"Okay, and he was on vacation in Miami."

Miami. The city's name grabbed David's attention so much it nearly shook him.

"Frankie thought it'd look better if Pete went with Debra, you know, a married couple would draw less suspicion. There was just one tiny, little problem. Pete had to get there really fast, and Debra was afraid to fly." Lorraine gave a light chuckle. "Imagine that. Debra worked for me at the travel agency, and she can't fly. That's okay, because–"

"Honey, please get back to the story," Paul said. "This is where you come in."

Lorraine smiled. "Right. Pete and Debra told me what was going on, and they asked me to pose as Pete's wife. I'd just fly down, have some fun, and not get involved with the whacking."

Amanda groaned. "Do you have to say 'whacking'?"

Her mother's eyebrows raised. "That's what they called it. I've been around and heard things. I've also seen *Goodfellas*. Anyway, Paul and I talked it over, and thought it was okay. I got a free trip, and he flew down on the next flight."

"How come?" David asked.

"Just in case," Paul said nonchalantly. "You know, if Lorraine needed me for anything."

"Oh sure," she said and giggled again. "We stayed in the same hotel as Bernie. Pete went to see Tony-something to get the gun. On the way, Pete got in a car accident and ended up in traction at the hospital. I called Frankie, and he was really mad. He wanted Bernie gone before he got back to New York." Lorraine cast her eyes toward a window. "All of a sudden, Frankie stopped yelling, and started thinking…" She re-directed her attention to David and Amanda.

David was fully engrossed in the story and hung on her every word.

"Frankie asked me to take care of it, and I said no." Lorraine smirked. "I mean, I'd never even hurt anybody, but Frankie told me some awful stories about Bernie, and I finally gave in. He said Bernie was a womanizer, chased anything in a skirt, including married women. Frankie said I could use that to get close and alone with him."

"So, then you shot Bernie?" David asked.

"Just wait," Lorraine said with a little smile. "It wasn't so simple. I first got the gun from Tony, and I bought a new tight and sexy dress. Back then I had a great figure."

"Great, Mom, just great," Amanda mumbled as she rubbed her forehead with her elbows on the table.

"I found Bernie at the hotel bar and chatted him up. I wanted him really drunk, so he couldn't put up a fight. After getting a few cocktails in him, we got a bottle of wine and went to his hotel room." Lorraine's eyes flashed. "That reminds me. Does anyone want another glass of wine?"

"Seriously?" Amanda said. "Just tell the story."

"Okay. I got more drinks into him and hoped he'd pass out. Then I could shoot him if I got up the nerve. Would you believe he never did? Bernie stepped onto the balcony and saw some girls by the pool. He yelled and waved at them, and I heard the girls yelling back, 'Come on down.'"

David leaned forward. "What happened next?"

"Now I see an opportunity," Lorraine said as she stared into space. "Bernie's room was on the seventh floor. I thought he could jump off the balcony and land in the pool. Since he was really drunk, he probably would've drowned, and I didn't think the girls could've saved him.

"The girls yelled to Bernie again, and he gives me a look, like he wanted to join them. He started toward the door, when I said, 'Take the easy way down. Jump off the balcony.' He laughs and says, 'Ya think so?' I told him, 'Sure, why not?' So, he went out to the balcony. He climbed over the railing and jumped. Then I heard the most horrible sound." Lorraine grimaced and shook her head.

"I ran to the balcony and looked down. Bernie's head slammed onto the cement next the pool, and blood was pouring out of him." She quivered. "It was really awful, and the girls were screaming and crying."

Lorraine's eyes opened wide. "I panicked for a second and then came up with a plan. I hid the gun and went downstairs as fast as I could. I got there before the police and the ambulance. It was really bad. They didn't bother to rush him to the hospital."

"Did you talk to the police?" David asked.

She smiled. "Oh sure. I gave them a fake name and said I was Bernie's wife. I told them we'd been drinking, and I was in the bathroom when he jumped. I was really nervous, and I guess that's why the police didn't believe me." She patted her hands on her lap. "So, I told them another story. Same fake name, but this time, I said I was married to Pete. I said he had cheated on me, and I was getting back at him. That's why I hooked up with Bernie. I asked the police to keep it quiet, and this time, they bought it."

"Paul, is this when the police interviewed you?" David asked.

"Yeah. I was keeping an eye on Lorraine when she was in the bar, and I stayed there until Bernie jumped."

"That's right," Lorraine said, "and when I got back to New York, the wise guys were really happy because I made it look like an accident. Nothing could be traced back to them. Frankie was so happy that he paid me a lot more than he had promised, and I used the money to buy the travel agency."

"Mom, are you sure this all happened the way you say it did?" Amanda asked.

Lorraine smiled. "Sure, I'm sure."

"Wait a minute," Paul said as he held up his right index finger. "I remembered we saved the newspaper from the next day."

He hurried off to another room on the first floor. David heard a drawer open and close, followed by the big man returning to the dining-room table. In his left hand, he held a copy of the *Miami Herald*, folded in half and wrapped in cellophane.

With his right hand, Paul pointed to date. "Check it out, March 4, 1972." He flipped the paper over. "See, right there at the bottom." He pointed again and chuckled. "How about that? We got the name wrong. The dead guy was Carmine, not Bernie. Carmine Cicero."

Lorraine smirked. "Oh, yeah. How about that!"

David and Amanda read the article, which discussed drunk Carmine jumping off the balcony and landing next to the swimming pool. It also stated Carmine had been staying at the hotel with an unnamed woman. Lorraine's story was accurate yet still difficult to accept.

Amanda appeared horrified. "So, it's true. My mom was a hit man for the Gambinos."

Lorraine waved her left hand. "I was never a hit man, and I told them I couldn't do it again. By the way, it wasn't the Gambinos. Pete was a Genovese."

David was flabbergasted, and his future in-laws' blasé attitude made the evening more surreal. Although he believed he would regret hearing any more details about their lives, curiosity got the better of him.

"Lorraine, did you say you bought the travel agency with mob money?"

"Uh-huh, and I was their travel agent. The wise guys mostly sent their wives and girlfriends to book the trips. It was fine, and it was all legitimate. We had plenty of regular people as clients too, even a couple of cops."

"Hey, David," Paul said, "that's probably why the police thought I had mob connections. The guys sometimes came to the house on the weekends to book their trips with Lorraine. The police or the FBI probably tailed one or two of them to here."

Lorraine smiled. "Oh sure. I was home after school and on the weekends. Sometimes, they came here. You remember, don't you?"

Amanda picked up her head. "Do I really need to do this? No, I don't. Whenever someone came over, you shooed away Daniel and me to do our homework, watch TV, or play in the backyard."

"Did you really kill Simpson?" David asked.

Lorraine looked into his eyes. "Oh yes."

Amanda flashed a pained expression. "Geez, Mom! You destroyed the firm!"

Lorraine smirked and slightly shook her head. "Oh, no. The firm was dying anyway, and people found new jobs. It all worked out. Right, dear?"

Paul nodded.

Amanda's eyes widened. "You've got to be kidding me! And do you have any idea what you did to Old Man Thorton?"

Lorraine gave a dismissive wave. "Oh, he's fine."

"I don't think so! Dad, did you know about this?"

"Not until after it happened. That night, I thought she was out with Debra. When your mother came home, she told me what she did. She showed me her disguise and handed me my .38."

"Mom, why'd you do it?" Amanda cried out.

"Because he was a really bad person. I knew you'd been telling your father about him. After all, you were always Daddy's little girl. Your father told me some, and I figured out the rest. I needed to do something to help you."

David held up his right hand. "Hold on a second. You're saying you planned Simpson's murder? Look, I hope you don't take it the wrong way, but–"

"I know what you're thinking, and I'm not that scatterbrained."

Paul patted Lorraine on the hand. "Honey, that's not exactly what happened." He turned toward Amanda and David. "Your mother had plenty of help. After she got home, I needed to get rid of the disguise, and I guessed Debra had been part of it. I called Pete and Debra, and they came over. It took some cajoling, but the girls explained how it all went down. Right?"

"Oh sure. It was confession time."

"The girls always talked about anything and everything, including Amanda's work. One day, Lorraine joked they should kill Simpson, and…"

"History repeated itself," David said.

"Right. The girls got serious, and Debra called Lenny."

"Who's Lenny?" Amanda asked.

"Don't worry about it," the big man said with a dismissive wave. "All you need to know is that Lenny arranged for Lorraine and Debra to meet... out-of-state talent."

"You mean the tall blonde woman?" David asked.

Paul pointed at him. "Bingo, and I'm pretty sure her name isn't Bonnie Parker."

Lorraine giggled. "Of course it isn't, and she wouldn't tell me her real name. She was really sharp. Debra and I met her at a little café where no one knew us. She told us what to do, laid out the whole thing really well. I listened carefully, and Debra took really good notes."

Amanda put her head back in her hands.

Lorraine seemed oblivious to Amanda's body language and continued. "First, I started having lunches with Amanda more often. Sometimes I brought Debra so that we could, uh..."

"I know," David said enthusiastically. "So, you could case the building and determine how to get in and out without being seen."

Lorraine nodded. "Yeah. Bonnie told us to do it."

Amanda groaned without picking up her head. "That's just great, Mom."

"Look, honey," Paul said, "you wanted to know. A little while later, your mother, Debra, and Bonnie had another meeting, and Bonnie told them the next steps. While Lorraine and Debra continued to case the building, Bonnie posed as a messenger to get Simpson's attention. She told him she'd be out of town for a couple of modeling assignments, and when she got back, they could get together. Bonnie also called and texted Simpson to string him along."

"Just before the murder, Bonnie stepped out to call Lorraine," David said. "How'd you get in and out of the building without anyone noticing?"

Lorraine smiled. "That was easy. Bonnie told me to swipe a key card from one of Amanda's co-workers. Then that day, she drove into the parking garage, and I was hiding in the trunk."

"Wait a minute," David said. "How'd you know about the security guard and the camera at the parking garage entrance? You don't drive."

Amanda raised her head and held up her left index finger. "I've got this one. Debra drives, and that's how they scoped out the parking garage. I probably don't want to hear the rest, but go ahead."

David remembered the camera at the parking garage entrance had not captured an image of a tall blonde woman driving into the garage before the murder. It instead had recorded a tall brunette with sunglasses and no passengers, so Bonnie had been wearing a wig.

Lorraine exhaled. "Okay. After we parked, I climbed out of the trunk, and I was wearing the old lady outfit. Bonnie told me to disguise myself because people had seen me in the building. I got up to the sixth floor or maybe the fifth." She shrugged. "I don't know. Bonnie took off, and I hid in a bathroom until I got the call to go upstairs."

"You did what?!" Amanda said.

"I hid in a bathroom. I brought a sandwich and a couple of magazines. It was fine."

"Not really," Amanda mumbled under her breath.

"After Bonnie called you, you went upstairs and shot Simpson," David said. "Why'd you use the pillow?"

Lorraine's face went blank. "What pillow?"

"The dark-blue pillow," David said. "It was in front of Simpson's face when you shot him."

"I don't know. Does it matter?"

"Maybe not," David said. "How did Simpson's blood get into Amanda's office?"

Lorraine shrugged. "I'm not sure. I was being very careful."

Amanda scoffed.

"Let's try this another way," David said. "Why did you go into Amanda's office that night?"

"Oh that!" Lorraine said. She gave a dismissive wave. "That was nothing. I put the old lady bag in Amanda's office, and then I pulled the gun out of it. I left the bag there because it was too much to carry it and hold the gun at the same time."

"After you shot Simpson, why did you try to remove the slugs from the wall?"

Lorraine rolled her eyes. "To leave less evidence, of course. Bonnie didn't tell me to do it. I just thought it on the spot. I had a file in the bag because I also did my nails while waiting in the bathroom."

"Why did you stop trying to remove the slugs?"

"Because it was too hard. Years ago, when we went shooting in the woods, I saw Bruce... What was his name?"

"Bruce Detweiler," Paul said.

"Yeah, that him," Lorraine said. "I saw him remove slugs from wooden targets all the time with a knife. However, it wasn't so easy, and I had to stop because Bonnie told me to get in and out fast."

"Then you went back to Amanda's office, where you called Bonnie on one of her cell phones," David said.

"Yeah, that's right."

"At some point, your right finger accidentally grazed the takeout box and left the blood."

"Yeah, I guess so."

"Do you know how that happened?"

"Mmm, not really."

"When you tried to remove the slugs from the wall, how did you avoid getting blood on your clothes?" David asked.

Lorraine giggled. "I didn't. I got a small spot on the back of the old lady skirt."

Paul chuckled and looked at his wife. "Yeah, I saw it. I'm surprised no one said something before you got home."

"Great, just great," Amanda mumbled.

"How'd you get out of the building?" David asked.

"With the key card," Lorraine said. "I used the service elevator and went out the back way."

"So that was you in the video!" Amanda said.

"Oh yeah." Lorraine laughed a little. "I guess so. I walked a block or two and then Bonnie picked me up and took me home."

"My turn," Paul said gently. "Your mother didn't know how to dispose of her disguise. Maybe Bonnie didn't tell her. After Pete and Debra came over, I told Pete to get rid of the stuff, and I reminded him he still owed Lorraine a big favor for knocking off that guy in Miami."

David took a deep breath. "What happened to the outfit, thrown into the East River with everything else incriminating?"

"Good guess, but no. Pete has a boat, and he dumped everything offshore."

"Why didn't you get rid of the gun?" David asked.

Paul chuckled. "Because it was my gun. No big deal. The cops were too stupid to find it."

Amanda mumbled to herself. Then in a louder voice, she said, "This is so unbelievable! Mom, you shouldn't have done it! I could've gone to prison for the rest of my life!"

Paul scoffed. "Not a chance. We had it all figured out."

"How?" David asked.

"First, we wanted to see if the case would go to trial. David, you're a very good attorney, and we hoped you would've convinced the DA that Amanda didn't do it. When that didn't pan out, we decided on something else."

"What was your plan?" Amanda asked. "Roll the dice, and pray I wouldn't get convicted… or better yet, did you bribe the jury?"

Weak smiles appeared on Paul and Lorraine's faces.

Amanda's eyes popped. "What the hell? You bribed the jury!"

Paul put up his right hand. "No, not quite. We thought about bribing a couple of jurors, but it wasn't necessary."

"How come?" David asked.

"A good buddy has a cousin who works at the courthouse. Before the trial, I asked this cousin to help us out and get us access to the jury."

"I imagine he didn't do this out of the goodness of his heart," David said.

Paul let out a chuckle. "Not really. He did it for twenty grand in cash."

"And how much were you going to pay the jurors?"

"We only needed two or three to make sure there wasn't a guilty verdict. You know, in case one of them got cold feet. We thought about paying them, oh, fifty grand a piece."

David tried not to physically react, but Paul's willingness to throw around so much money after paying his legal bills surprised him.

"Why didn't you bribe anyone?" he asked.

The big man let out an equally big smile. "We didn't have to. You know how judges tell juries not to talk about the case before they start deliberations?"

David nodded. "Yeah, and many jurors ignore the instruction."

"That's right. My buddy's cousin told me from the very beginning, three jurors couldn't keep their big traps shut. They didn't care if Amanda shot Simpson or not because they thought he had it coming." Paul chuckled. "Gotta love New Yorkers, right? Remember how you worried about Juror Number 7? He was one of the three. I was surprised the rest elected him to be the jury foreman. I guess they wanted to get out of there in a hurry."

Amanda turned sideways in her chair and looked away.

David pressed on. "Paul, how early did you know what was happening with the jury?"

"We knew about the three loudmouths after the first day of testimony. Before the verdict, we pretty much knew where each juror stood. Seven thought he had it coming, and the other five had no idea who killed Simpson. So, there you go."

"Lorraine, if you knew Amanda wouldn't get convicted," David said, "why did you take the stand?"

She scoffed. "Of course, I had to do it. Could you imagine what my little girl would've thought of me if I didn't?"

"Yeah, thanks, Mom. Great job," Amanda said with a thumbs up. "You nearly gave me a heart attack when I thought you tanked the case."

"About that," David said. "Why did you confess on the stand?"

Lorraine exhaled through her nose and patted her lap. "Well, I didn't mean to do that. It just came to me while I was up there."

"Why did you hold back some of the facts about the shooting, including you were the person with the gray wig?" David asked.

Lorraine's eyes got wide. "Oh, that would've been really bad. I could've gotten Debra and Bonnie in trouble, maybe Paul too because I used his gun."

Amanda mumbled and turned toward the table. "Yeah, it was all so great, and everything turned out so wonderful! And where was all this money coming from? There's a huge bundle in the attic. You were prepared to spend 150,000 on bribing jurors, and you paid the court officer 20,000. You also paid David's legal bills, which had to be…" Her eyes glanced toward the ceiling. "A lot. You covered my living expenses after I was fired, and there was the money for bail. How much did you pay the bail bondsman? Ten percent, which would have been 100,000?"

"No, we got a big discount," Paul said. "We only paid forty grand."

"Oh, what a bargain," Amanda said sarcastically. "Mom, how much did Bonnie Parker cost?"

She shrugged. "I don't know. Fifty or sixty thousand, something like that. I got the money from one of the safe-deposit boxes."

"Wait a minute," David interjected. "When you reported your cash assets for bail, you listed about $163,000 in a joint bank account. Did you burn through it?"

Paul gave a sly grin. "No. It's still there."

David rubbed the right side of his forehead. "Okay. Lorraine mentioned safe-deposit boxes, as in plural, not just one. How many do you have?"

"Six or seven," Paul said. "Some are larger than others."

"All of them filled with cash?" David asked.

"Of course."

"Mom, Dad, where was all this money coming from?" Amanda asked.

Neither parent answered.

Amanda slapped the table. "Out with it! Don't stop now!"

Lorraine glanced at Paul and then returned her attention to Amanda. "Fine, fine. I had a little side business. The travel agency also laundered money for the mob."

Amanda was shocked. "What the hell? Does Daniel know about the money?"

Lorraine smiled. "Oh no, and please don't tell your brother."

"Were you ever planning on telling Daniel and me about all of this?"

"No, not really."

Paul chuckled. "What should we have told you? After we died, you and Daniel would get a big surprise. You'd find all the money, wonder where it came from, and enjoy it."

"Lorraine, I'm not trying to be mean or anything," David said, "but it seems hard to believe you cooked the books at the travel agency all those years."

She giggled. "I didn't. Morty took care of it."

Amanda shook her head. "Sure, why not? Our family's accountant was involved."

"Of course he was," Paul said. "How else do you think he could afford his second home in Palm Beach County? Next time we visit him in Florida, come with us and take a look. It's got a great front yard, a nice indoor pool, and–"

"We got it," David said. "Getting back to the money. How much is in the safe-deposit boxes?"

"The funny thing is we never counted it," Paul said.

"Take a guess," Amanda said sternly.

Paul scratched his head and was lost in thought for a couple of moments. "I don't know, maybe 2.6 or 2.7 million."

David looked at Amanda, who again appeared stunned. She grabbed a half-full bottle of wine and turned to leave the table.

"Don't you want a glass?" Lorraine asked.

"No, I'm good," Amanda said as she traipsed around the corner. The squeak told them she had gone upstairs.

David was so overwhelmed he could only stare at a wall and hoped Paul and Lorraine had no more startling revelations. Despite something inside telling him to leave the house, he instead moved his field of vision from the wall to Amanda's parents.

"Hey, David," Paul said with arms spread out and a wide smile, "welcome to the family!"

Acknowledgements

Have you ever read the acknowledgements in a novel and wondered why the author had thanked so many people? The story originated from that person's mind, and there was no way so many other people could have made contributions. Sometimes I had these thoughts but not anymore, not after working on my first published work of fiction. Many people made contributions, and they should be recognized.

Every writer needs a stellar support system, and the bedrock of mine can be found in my publisher, The Book Folks. I must thank Erik Empson, Polly Phipps-Holland, Tarek Salhany and Arianna Bove for their editorial skills, creative insights, and suggestions for improving the storyline. Perhaps their most important quality is patience.

Before The Book Folks accepted my work, I hired William Greenleaf, a now retired editor and author. Bill reviewed two earlier versions of my manuscript and provided many helpful insights and advice. He was essentially my private tutor for an advanced writing class.

I'd also like to thank Stephen King. Yes, that Stephen King. I've never met him or communicated with him in any manner, although either one would be a great experience. Many websites recommend his book *On Writing: A Memoir of the Craft* for anyone who wants to break into his line of work, and I must concur. *On Writing* also discusses the early days of King's writing career and his horrific accident in 1999. If you want to gain a better understanding of one of the greatest authors of our time, both aspects of his life and his views on the writing process, you should read this book.

Jerry Rishe, Kay Bruce, and Ronald Phillips read earlier versions of the manuscript and gave their comments, criticisms, and suggestions. Even though Phillips is the Senior Vice Chancellor of Pepperdine University, I still refer to him as Dean Phillips, as he was the dean of the law school when I attended. In addition to providing a great legal education, Dean Phillips and the rest of the faculty cared about the students, which I still appreciate. Some names in the novel are direct or indirect references to Pepperdine.

I must also mention the following individuals. Peter Lee gave frequent words of encouragement, and I'm glad he finally found a better job. Dee Ann Deaton gave editorial tips, and author Brad Chisholm gave advice on the writing process and valuable suggestions for creating dialogue.

My daughter, Caitlyn, was a sounding board for several ideas and plot points. In fact, we spent too much time discussing the wedding dress mentioned later in the novel. Caitlyn, her two brothers, Michael and Andrew, and my wife, Carolyn, also gave their input as to the character names and personas. I also thank my family for allowing me to spend many uninterrupted hours on what they probably perceived as a quixotic endeavor.

Finally, I must acknowledge Claire Kim, good friend, attorney, and author, who provided many words of encouragement and conveyed her experiences with the writing process. Claire also deserves the biggest thank you of all because she inspired me to create this novel.

If you enjoyed this book, please let others know by leaving a quick review on Amazon. Also, if you spot anything untoward in the paperback, get in touch. We strive for the best quality and appreciate reader feedback.

editor@thebookfolks.com

www.thebookfolks.com

More fiction by the author

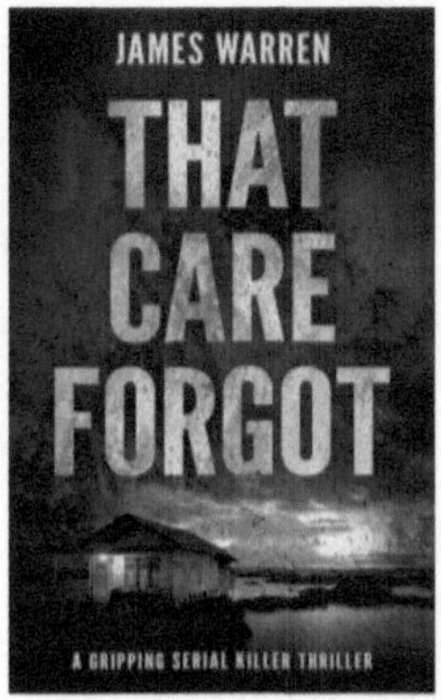

THAT CARE FORGOT

Junior attorney Rebecca Holt isn't too happy when given the pro bono case of a convicted murderer. Yet Nick Malone isn't really interested in his parole hearing, rather he is obsessed with a serial killer who terrorized New Orleans in the 1990s. When Malone reveals his secrets, Rebecca is faced with a life-changing decision.

FREE with Kindle Unlimited and available in paperback!

Other titles of interest

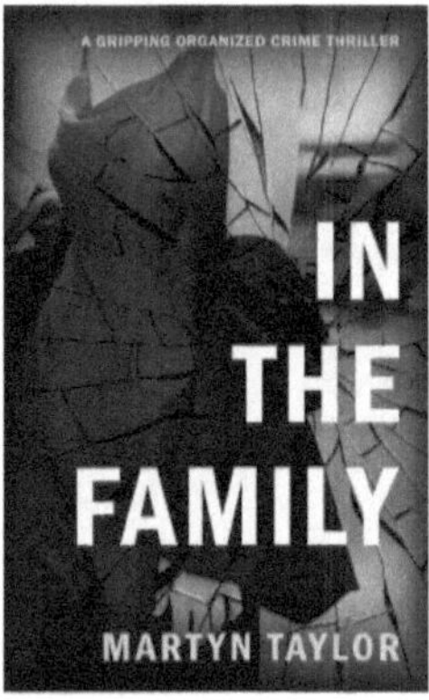

IN THE FAMILY
by Martyn Taylor

When a former gangland boss is found shot dead in his home, DI Penelope Darling knows that the investigation will take her into the nether regions of her city's criminal world. But finding the killer among the likely suspects will require keeping her eyes open to the unexpected. She'll need to have her wits about her to stop a ruthless individual from getting away with murder.

FREE with Kindle Unlimited and available in paperback!

CATFISH
by Sadie Norman

It is not without some malice that rookie detective Anna McArthur is called "crazy" by her colleagues. She certainly tends to act first and think later. But when Anna discovers the body of a murdered woman who has "catfish" carved into her chest, she feels a personal duty to do everything she can to up her game and find the killer.

FREE *with Kindle Unlimited and available in paperback!*

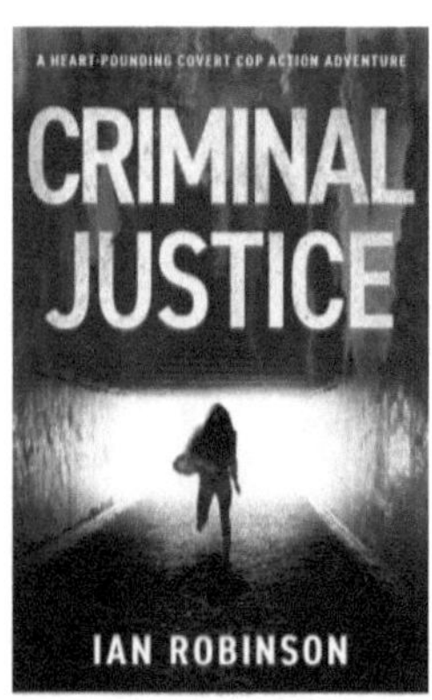
A HEART-POUNDING COVERT COP ACTION ADVENTURE
CRIMINAL
JUSTICE
IAN ROBINSON

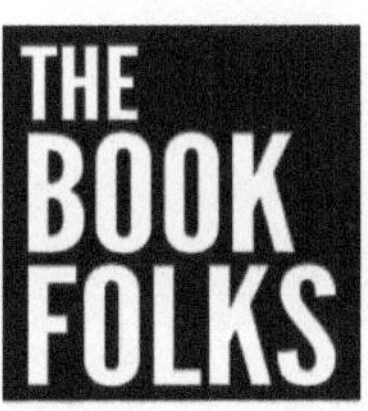
THE
BOOK
FOLKS

www.ingramcontent.com/pod-product-compliance
Lightning Source LLC
Chambersburg PA
CBHW031938210726
48290CB00006BA/1910

* 9 7 8 1 8 0 4 6 2 2 7 3 5 *